Le

CW00685410

S J Richards

LETHAL ODDS

Published worldwide by Apple Loft Press

This edition published in 2024

Copyright © 2024 by S J Richards

S J Richards has asserted his right to be identified as the author of this work in accordance with the Copyright, Design and Patents Act 1988.

All rights reserved. This book or any portion thereof may not be reproduced or used in any manner whatsoever without the express written permission of the author, except for quotes or short extracts for the purpose of reviews.

www.sjrichardsauthor.com

For Connie, Tracey, Mandy, Danella, Karen and all the staff at Springfield House in Bath who have been so wonderful in their care for my mum.

The Luke Sackville Crime Thriller Series

Taken to the Hills

Black Money

Fog of Silence

The Corruption Code

Lethal Odds

Sow the Wind

Chapter 1

Kim Shepherd gripped the bannister at the top of the stairs and tried to pull herself together.

She squeezed her eyes closed.

How had it come to this?

It was hard to believe that only twelve hours earlier she hadn't a care in the world. She had a loving husband, gained immense pleasure from her two-year-old son, enjoyed her job and had a wide circle of friends. Everything had been on the up. Brian had caught the eye of the England manager and seemed set to be selected for the Six Nations squad.

The last thing Kim felt like doing was going to work. She would rather spend time trying to find a way out of the mess they were in.

To have let their financial situation get out of hand was reckless, but she knew it wasn't fair to put all the blame on Brian. He was the one who was supposed to keep an eye on their financial situation, but they'd both been over-spending. They'd been like ostriches, their heads buried so deep in the sand that they'd failed to spot the gradually accumulating credit card balance, only paying the minimum each month while the interest accumulated.

And now it had hit £12,000.

How on earth had it got to that state? And more to the point, how were they going to bring the balance down? Paying the minimum each month was a stretch as it was. They were maxed out on the mortgage, already had a personal loan, hadn't been granted an overdraft the last time they asked…

She found it hard to see a way through the mess.

"Mummy!" Max called from the hall.

"I'm coming, darling." she said.

She walked down the stairs, her head spinning, and bent down to click Max's belt closed.

"Wait in the buggy, Max," she said. "Mummy needs a quick word with Daddy and then we'll leave."

"Baby Barn?"

"Yes, that's right." She bent to peck him on the chin. "You'll be able to play with Theo."

Max smiled in delight. "I like Theo. He's my bestest friend."

Kim walked into the kitchen where Brian was putting his mug in the dishwasher.

"What are we going to do?" she asked.

He stood up and turned to face her. "I told you," he said. "I'll sort everything out."

"How? You can't make money appear out of nowhere."

"Please, Kim. You have to trust me. I'm going to speak to the boss."

She raised an eyebrow. "Are you going to ask for an advance?"

"Something like that." He smiled and held his arms out. "Here, come in for a hug."

She returned his smile and walked to him, loving the feeling when his massive arms encircled her body. It made her feel safe and secure.

"Are you okay to pick Max up?" she asked.

"Should be. What time will you be back?"

"Probably around five-thirty. I've got a viewing at nine, then I'll be in the office for the rest of the day." She looked over his shoulder at the kitchen clock. "I'll have to get a move on."

Brian put his mouth to her ear and squeezed harder. "I don't want to let you go," he said, a tone to his voice that suggested he'd like to do a lot more than hug her.

"Mummy!" came a voice from the hall.

Kim laughed. "Come on Brian, let me go."

He released her and she stood on tiptoe to kiss him on the lips. "I'll see you later," she said as she pulled away. "Good luck with Phil."

She returned to the hall and pressed her finger lightly against the end of her son's nose. "Come on, little guy," she said. "Let's be on our way." She pulled his bobble hat down so that it covered his ears, donned her coat and scarf and wheeled the buggy out of the front door.

It was only a five-minute walk to Baby Barn, but as soon as she emerged onto the drive she realised she had been right to wrap up. It was supposed to be Autumn but the day had a wintry feel to it, the light drizzle feeling like it might change to sleet at any time.

As she turned towards Shakespeare Avenue, Kim's thoughts returned to the previous evening. It had come as an almighty shock when Brian had told her the amount they owed on the credit card.

She'd asked him how it had happened, and he'd shrugged and said it was purely down to living beyond their means. They'd agreed on ways of cutting back, but that still left the debt to clear off.

She sighed and mentally crossed her fingers in the hope he'd be able to secure an advance on his salary. He earned a reasonable amount; not as much as people assumed given his profile, but a decent figure nonetheless. With their new cost-cutting regime they would be fine, assuming of course that repayment of the advance could be spread out over a year or more.

She arrived at Baby Barn to see Jade, Theo's mum, emerging having just dropped her son off.

"Hi, Kim," she said. "Are you up for hot yoga this evening?"

"I can't Jade. Sorry, ah…" She paused, not wanting to share details of their financial difficulties. "I've got something else on."

"No problem. Another time then?"

Kim smiled. "Sure."

She dropped Max off, walked home and put the stroller into the boot of her Honda Jazz.

The car had been an impulse purchase, but she loved it. It was small enough to be easy to drive and park, but big enough to fit them all inside in comfort, no easy task given Brian's bulk. The thought of having to return it saddened her, but she was prepared to do it if she had to. She made a mental note to check whether a PCP contract could be ended early, and to do it as soon as she got into the office.

Once in the car, she headed south out of Bath on the A36 before turning towards Winsley and then left onto Blackberry Lane just before the village itself.

She'd only been to the house once, to provide her valuation to the owner, a partner at Goldman Sachs, and had high hopes for this first viewing. The prospective buyer had sounded very enthusiastic on the phone, and had insisted that she show him around as soon as possible.

Half a mile down Blackberry Lane, Kim entered the approach to Kingholm Manor through black iron gates which glided seamlessly open as she approached. Some people have all the money, she thought. The property was one of the most prestigious properties on their books, a mock castle in three acres which was on the market at £2.5m, and yet was the current owner's second home.

To her surprise, a vehicle was already parked outside the house, but it was an ancient-looking Peugeot van, a long way from the kind of vehicle she anticipated Mr Tennant driving. Assuming it belonged to a cleaner or gardener, she parked behind it and walked to the driver's window. There was no one inside which presumably meant that he or she was working inside the house or around the back.

Shrugging, she decided to let herself in and run through her preparation routine. She looked at her watch and saw that she had a few minutes before her viewer was due, hopefully enough time to ensure every picture was straight, cushions plumped and so on.

She took the keys out of her bag, put them in the lock and was about to open the door when she heard footsteps behind her. She plastered a smile on her face and readied herself to meet Mr Tennant, who in her head was a suave and elegant businessman in his early forties. Why she thought this she didn't know, but he'd certainly sounded well-educated on the phone.

Her smile vanished when she turned to see a man dressed entirely in black standing no more than two yards away. His face was covered with a black balaclava mask, with two holes cut for his eyes.

"What the…" she started to say, at the same time fumbling with her bag, trying to reach inside for her rape alarm, or for something she could hit him with.

The man was on her in an instant. He shoved her hard in the chest, causing her to fall back against the door. Winded, she dropped to her knees, scraping her hands in the process.

"What do you want?" she managed to gasp.

He ignored her question and handed her a black bag. "Put this over your head," he said. He had a strong accent.

"I'm an estate agent. My client will be here at any moment."

"I told you to put it on."

"I…" She tried to climb to her feet but he kicked her hard in the ribs causing her to yelp in pain and fall back to the floor, this time onto her side.

"Put the bag on," he said for the third time. There was no emotion in his voice.

She put the bag over her head.

Chapter 2

Brian was rinsing the shampoo off his hair when the team's fly-half popped his head around the corner of the shower block.

"Brian," he said. "Your phone's ringing."

"Thanks, Ricky. Can you see who it is?"

A few seconds later Ricky shouted, "It's Kim."

"Okay. Let it ring off. I'll call her back in a minute."

Brian turned the shower off, reached for his towel and started drying himself as he walked back to the changing room. Odd she should ring, he thought, and then it dawned on him that she was most likely calling to wish him luck for his meeting with the boss.

He decided he'd wait and ring her back once he was dressed. The morning workout had been pretty tough, and while the shower had helped he needed a few more minutes to relax his muscles.

No sooner had he thought this than his phone rang again. He picked up immediately, suddenly concerned.

"Kim," he said. "Is everything okay?"

He was taken aback when a man's voice answered. "No, Brian," he said in what Brian thought might be a Polish accent. "Everything is not okay."

Brian felt a surge of panic. "What's happened? Has she been in an accident?"

There was no response.

Ricky had heard Brian and looked across from the other side of the room. "What's happened?" he asked.

Brian shrugged and mouthed, "I don't know," then returned his attention to the phone. "Is Kim hurt?"

"Superficial bruising. A few scratches."

"Thank goodness. What…"

The man interrupted him before he could complete the question. "Her injuries may become a lot worse," he said.

"I don't understand." The man's tone was making Brian feel uneasy. "Who are you?"

"I am a messenger."

"A what?"

"Mr Smith sent me."

"No!" The exclamation was out before he could stop himself.

"All okay?" Ricky called.

Brian swallowed. "Yes, fine," he said, looking across at his teammate and forcing a smile. "False alarm."

"That's a relief." Ricky picked up his bag and put it over his shoulder. "I'll see you this afternoon."

Brian nodded. "See you later," he said, trying to maintain his smile. He waited until Ricky had left the changing room before asking, "Where's Kim?"

"Mr Smith is not a happy man."

Brian could feel his heart pumping. "Where is she?" he repeated.

"She is with me but she cannot talk." The man gave a bitter laugh. "She is tied up at the moment."

"What have you done to her?"

"Nothing." There seemed to be almost delight in his voice as he added, "Not yet."

"Please let her go. She hasn't done anything."

"Neither have you, Brian. That is the problem. Mr Smith is upset about Saturday. And believe me, you do not want to be with Mr Smith when he is upset."

"I couldn't do it. You have to understand."

"No. It is you who has to understand. You had an agreement, and you let him down. Mr Smith wants you to realise the error of your ways. That actions have consequences."

"But not Kim. Don't hurt her. She doesn't even know."

"What do you weigh, Brian?"

"What's that got to do with anything?"

"Answer the question."

"Just under 19 stone."

Another dry laugh. "It strikes me as funny, you being so heavy and yet you are punching way above your weight."

"What do you mean?"

"Your wife is attractive, that is what I mean. I have to deliver Mr Smith's message and I might as well enjoy myself."

"No!"

"As I said, actions have consequences." The man let this sink in before continuing. "There is an alternative."

"What? Anything." Brian gulped. "I'll do anything. Just let her go."

"I understand that you are playing again this weekend."

"You want me to do the same?"

"Not quite. Mr Smith says ten minutes this time."

"I can't. That's not long enough. Twenty was a stretch and ten's nowhere near enough time."

"If you are not prepared…"

"Stop! I'll do it but please, release Kim." Brian paused. "I don't want the money."

"It is not a case of wanting the money, Brian, it is a case of needing it. Mr Smith is a fair man. He knows the difficulties you have and insists on you having the £10,000. He said it will be transferred into your account straight after the match, and that if you do a good job there might be even more next time."

"No. This has to be a one-off."

"It is a case of carrot and stick, Brian. Mr Smith is offering you tasty carrots. They are good for you, but you have to eat them all. If you do not then those nasty sticks will come along to beat you. Your wife is one of those sticks, but there are others."

"What do you mean?"

"Max is two, isn't he?"

Brian couldn't believe what the other man was implying. "You can't be serious!" he exclaimed. "You wouldn't!"

"As I keep saying, I am only the messenger."

"Okay, okay. I'll do whatever it takes. Just leave my family alone."

"That is good, Brian. You have finally seen sense. One more thing before I go. Do not think of telling the police or anyone else about our conversation, and make sure Kimberley is clear on that as well. I know where you work and where she works. I even know about Baby Barn and believe me the security there is not good."

Brian gulped. "I won't tell anyone. What happens now?"

"Your wife had a 9 am appointment to show a Mr Tennant around a property. He will not be turning up but you will find her there."

The line went dead.

Chapter 3

The spreadsheet was refusing to play ball and Luke Sackville, ex-DCI and now Head of Ethics at Filchers, a business outsourcing company, was frustrated.

He was attempting to pull together the forecast annual spend for his team, something his nepotistically-appointed boss Edward Filcher had requested, but Microsoft Excel and its macros seemed to be against him at every turn. He had thought the admin regime was tough when he was in Avon and Somerset Police but Filchers took the biscuit.

At least he only had four people in his team. If he had dozens like other departments he would have been there all day.

He clicked on the 'human resources' tab where Sam Chambers was the first on the list. He smiled as he reflected on how valuable a member of the team she was. Her interpersonal skills were second to none, and she was someone he would trust with his life. More than that, they had developed a close working relationship.

Next on the list was Majid Osman, Maj for short, who had joined the team from security but had proven himself a whizz at technology. Third was Helen Hogg, a paralegal with decades of experience, and last, but not least, Josh Ogden, a recent graduate who was madly enthusiastic, full of ideas, and occasionally, well if he was honest frequently, irritating.

Luke's challenge was working out how to link the salaries in the 'human resources ' tab to the 'totals' tab. It ought to be easy but it had him totally bamboozled. He decided to spend a few more minutes and then ask Sam for her help. A qualified accountant, she was a whiz with numbers.

He was pleased to be interrupted by Maj who called over, his hand covering the speaker of his smartphone.

"Luke," he said, his strong Bristol accent belying his Somalian upbringing, "I've got an ex-colleague on the line. His name's Martin Ribble and he wants your advice."

"What's it about?"

"He won't say."

"Give him my number."

Maj passed the message on and Luke's phone rang a few seconds later.

"Luke Sackville."

"Hi, Luke. This is Martin, Martin Ribble. Thanks for saying you'll speak to me."

"No problem. How can I help?"

"It's kind of sensitive. Could we speak face-to-face, say in the canteen?"

"Of course. Do you mean now?"

"If you don't mind. There's something I have to get off my chest."

"Okay. I'm in the middle of doing something but I'll come down as soon as I've finished. Say about ten minutes?"

"Great. Thanks."

Luke wasn't in the middle of anything, or at least anything that mattered, but he wanted some background. He picked up his notebook and pen and walked over to Maj who looked up as he approached.

"I'm meeting Martin in the canteen," Luke said. "What can you tell me about him?"

Maj considered this briefly. "Martin moved out of Security into one of the account teams a few months back. I think it was in the retail sector. He fell out with Mr Steroid." He smiled. "That's one of the things we've got in common."

Luke smiled at the nickname for Glen Baxter, the Head of Security. It was undeniably appropriate given the man's enthusiasm for bodybuilding and his Schwarzenegger-esque build.

"What else?" he asked.

Maj's smile broadened. "Martin's a massive Bristol City fan. Follows rugby too, but I can forgive him that."

Luke decided not to rise to this last comment. "Have you ever been aware of difficulties he's had at work?"

"Aside from the challenges of working with Glen, no."

"What about at home?"

Maj shook his head. "Happily married as far as I'm aware. Two children. They're twins and I think they're ten or eleven. Something like that."

"Okay. Thanks."

Luke made his way to the canteen, which was already starting to fill up with staff looking to beat the lunchtime rush. He was wondering how to locate Martin when a man stood up from a table in the far corner and beckoned him over. He was about his own age, perhaps slightly younger, and of average height. Slimly built, he was probably handsome, though Luke found that very hard to judge in other men, with matt black hair, round-rimmed glasses and a tidy beard. The combination gave him a slightly geeky look.

Luke walked over and Martin shook his hand.

"Thanks for seeing me," he said as he sat back down. He smiled up at Luke. "I knew it had to be you. People your height are hardly two a penny."

Luke returned the smile, took the seat opposite and placed his notebook and pen on the table. "Do you mind if I take notes?"

"No. Not at all."

"Great. Now, how can I help, Martin?"

"I'm a Data Analyst on the Fortune Group account. Are you aware of it?"

"I'm aware of the account, although I haven't the foggiest what a Data Analyst does. I guess it's not relevant though."

"Oh, but it is. As you probably know, the Fortune Group comprises several retail brands. There are ten, although the three big ones are High End, Tom Crowther and Gambet."

Luke wrote these down. He was familiar with the first two names, both of which were fashion chains that his daughter was fond of. He hadn't heard of the third though.

"Gambet?" he prompted.

"Retail and online gambling. The retail outlets are branded Mudges. They're much like Ladbrokes but there are fewer of them. Most of Gambet's revenue and profit comes from the online side of the business."

Luke nodded. "Right. And you said you're a Data Analyst. That's a bit of a leap from working in security, isn't it?"

Martin smiled. "My job as a security officer was only meant to be a stop-gap, although in the end I worked for Glen for over a year." He gave a dour smile. "Not the most pleasant of experiences, I have to admit."

"You didn't get on then?"

"No, but that's a whole other story. Anyway, when I saw on the intranet that the Fortune Group's Futures Team was looking for a Data Analyst, I applied and was lucky enough to be offered the job. I've been there three months now."

"The Futures Team?"

"Yes. There are only four of us. We work across all the brands, pulling together trends and forecasts, both in the industry and in the businesses themselves."

"I take it you've found something you think is unethical?"

"It could be. I'm not sure. It's certainly odd though." Martin leaned forward over the table, aware of others sitting nearby, and Luke followed his lead.

"There were several incidences of data surges and I was worried about overfitting," Martin said in a whisper. "The algorithm uses unsupervised machine learning and fuzzy logic often brings inconsistencies, so at first I thought that was the problem. I tried data wrangling but that didn't get me anywhere, so I…"

Luke sat back and held his hand up. "Whoa," he said. "You lost me at 'data surges'. Can you say that again, but in English this time?"

"Sorry. I thought I was being clear." Martin took a deep breath. "I found anomalies in the data. Spikes that didn't follow the accepted pattern."

"Spikes in what?"

"Numbers."

"Of?"

Martin smiled. "Sorry. I tend to think in numbers rather than what they represent. The spikes were in Gambet's income. Not high in the scheme of things, but outliers nonetheless."

Luke was wishing the man would get to the point. He didn't want to spend the rest of the day listening to him spout about spikes and outliers.

"Naturally, I look at the macro picture," Martin went on.

"Naturally," Luke said, though he still didn't know what the other man was talking about. "But?" he added, hoping this might accelerate the story.

"But," Martin said with another smile, "I felt I had to look at the detail and I found something very odd."

About time, Luke thought, but said, "Which was?"

"All of the spikes were tied to Gambet's operation in Singapore, and there was a direct correlation between outs and ins." He paused, saw Luke's blank face and continued. "Sorry, by outs and ins, I mean revenue and outgoings or to be more precise, given we're talking about Gambet, bets and wins."

"So the wins are tied to bets. What of it?"

"Don't you see?"

Luke shook his head. "No, I don't. Surely all wins are linked to a bet."

"Yes, but every one of these bets resulted in a win."

"So you suspect there's fiddling going on?"

"Or money laundering."

"How many of these did you identify, and how much money are we talking about?"

"Seven, and the amount staked varied between 20,000 and 80,000 Singapore dollars. That's roughly £12,000 to £48,000. The average winnings were about four times that amount."

"I see. That's a lot of money." Luke paused. "One thing I don't understand is why you brought this to me and not to your boss."

"It's simple really. I focused down through the big data and used regression techniques to correlate…"

Luke held his hand up again.

"Sorry," Martin went on, his cheeks having the decency to turn a pale salmon colour this time. He took a deep breath and spoke in a whisper. "I found Adrian Critchley linked to one of the bets."

"And?"

Martin kept his voice low. "He's Director of Strategy for the Fortune Group."

"I still don't understand why you can't take it to your line manager."

"My boss is Yvonne Critchley. She's married to Adrian."

"I see." Luke closed his notebook. "Leave this with me, Martin. I'll get back to you when I've decided on the best approach to take."

Chapter 4

Luke returned to the Ethics Room and called the team together. It wasn't often that all of them were there at the same time, and he wanted their input after his meeting with Martin Ribble.

"Okay," he said, once they were all seated around the table in the centre of the room. "Sorry to tear you away from whatever you were doing."

"You can tear me away as much as you like, guv," Josh said. "Maj and I are wading through the information IT sent us."

"Is that for…" Luke shook his head and gave a wry smile before completing the question. "…Perfume?"

"Yes, guv," Josh said with a grin, pleased that Luke was using the name he'd come up with.

Project Perfume was an investigation into suspected misconduct by a middle manager in the Home Office team who was accused of falsifying environmental compliance certifications. Josh had said that his girlfriend Leanne wore an eau de toilette called 'Misconduct'.

"How's it going?" Luke asked.

It was Maj who answered. "Slowly, Luke," he said. "Very slowly. Even with both of us on it, I think it'll be a couple of days before we get to the bottom of it."

Luke turned to Sam and Helen. "How are you two faring?"

"I'm busy but doing fine," Helen said in her soft Scottish accent. She combined legal expertise with a dry sense of humour, and delighted in teasing Josh who at twenty-two was thirty-five years her junior. "Still drafting social responsibility clauses for the new BT contract," she went on. "After that, I'll be reviewing the documentation for the wee Shell extension."

"Sam?"

"I'm working on those two harassment cases," Sam said. "I'm going to make a start on the Woods accusation today."

Luke nodded. "And the other one? Was it Armstrong?"

"That's right. Jonathan Armstrong."

"Tiger and Lunar," Josh said.

The others all turned to look at him.

"I take it," Luke said, having become used to Josh's interruptions, "that those are your suggestions for project names?"

Josh nodded, his grin back. "Yes, because Neil Armstrong…"

"Aye, we get it," Helen said. "And Tiger Woods is a golfer."

Josh fired a finger gun at her. "Exactimo."

Luke sighed. "We don't need project names for everything we're doing, Josh." He turned back to Sam. "So how is the Armstrong investigation going?"

Josh started to correct him but stopped when Luke leaned over, put his hand on Josh's arm, shook his head and said in a firm voice, "Don't."

"I believe the man who's accused him is telling the truth," Sam said, "but I'll need a hand from Maj to track through CCTV footage."

"That's fine," Maj said quickly.

"Hey!" Josh exclaimed. "No! Don't leave me with those IT reports."

"Sorry," Maj said, his smile betraying the fact that he was anything but sorry.

"The main reason I wanted to speak to you all," Luke said, "is to ask for your ideas. I've just met with Martin Ribble, an ex-colleague of Maj's, who works as a Data Analyst in the Fortune Group team."

"Is that the group that owns High End and Tom

Crowther?" Sam asked.

"That's what they're best known for, but the most profitable part of the business is Gambet, their gambling arm, and that's where he's found something suspicious."

He explained about the link between a winning bet and the Fortune Group's Director of Strategy, Adrian Critchley.

"The problem we've got," he went on, "is that Adrian Critchley is married to Martin's boss." He addressed his next comment to Josh, who was now a subtle shade of beetroot following his earlier dressing down. "I hate to say this, but we're dealing with sensitive information and we're going to need a project name so that we can discuss it outside this room."

"Wowza!" Josh exclaimed, suddenly bright-eyed and bushy-tailed again. "Really?"

"Really."

"Barney." The suggestion came without a pause. "You know, as in the Flintstones."

"His name was Barney Rubble," Maj said, "not Ribble."

"Barney will do," Luke said, much to Josh's delight. "As I was saying, the issue is the fact that the Futures Team Manager is married to the Director of Strategy. I was thinking of finding a pretext for putting someone into Martin's team who can help him dig deeper. I have to admit he lost me when he explained how he'd found Critchley's name, so it would have to be someone good with data."

All heads swivelled to look at Sam.

Luke smiled. "I'd come to the same conclusion, but have you guys got any other ideas on the best approach?"

There was silence for a minute or so.

"I could research him on the internet and social media," Josh said. "His wife too. See if there's any other connections between him and gambling."

"Good idea."

"I could prioritise it, guv. Make it my main activity and shelve anything else for the time being. Put, uh…" He glanced over at the stack of IT reports on his desk. "... other work on the back burner and treat..."

Luke laughed and raised his hand to stop him. "I know what you're getting at, Josh," he said. "Okay, you research the Critchleys while Maj is helping Sam with the CCTV footage. When he's finished you can both shift your focus back to the IT reports."

Josh sat back, evidently pleased with himself.

"Any other ideas?" Luke asked, looking around the team. They all shook their heads. "We're agreed then. Sam, can I have a word?"

Helen, Maj and Josh returned to their desks.

Sam looked across at Luke and smiled. "What is it?"

"Do you want a coffee?" he asked.

She bent her head to the side and raised one eyebrow. Luke didn't say anything but stood up and led the way out of the room.

She caught up with him in the corridor. "Have I done something wrong?" she asked.

"No. Not at all. Quite the opposite. I'll explain in the canteen."

Once they got the drinks he led the way to a table by the window.

"Well?" she said, once they were seated.

Luke took a sip of his espresso, looked into her eyes for a second and then turned to the window. It wasn't a scintillating view, a few trees and distant office buildings, but he wanted to savour the moment when she took in what he was about to say.

"What is it?" she prompted.

He turned back to face her and watched as she took a sip of her diet coke.

"Sam," he began. "I've been thinking about our relationship."

She spluttered and almost dropped her glass. "About our relationship?" she managed to say.

"Yes. Are you okay?"

"Fine."

"Are you sure? It's just that you…" He gestured to her drink.

"No. Honestly." She wiped her mouth with a tissue and put the glass on the table. "I'm okay. You were saying."

"I'm very conscious, Sam, that you and I get on very well."

She nodded and smiled. "I've been thinking the same," she said.

"And I was thinking that perhaps…"

He hesitated and she put her hand out and placed it on top of his.

He smiled.

Here goes.

"I'm thinking of putting you up for promotion."

She withdrew her hand and stared at him. "This is about promotion?"

"Yes. You and I have such an excellent working relationship, and you're so good at working with the others, I'm thinking of making you my deputy."

"I, ah…"

"You don't seem very pleased."

She tried to smile but it was a weak attempt. "Of course I'm pleased," she said after a few seconds. "Heavens, who wouldn't be?" She sniffed and then looked at her watch. "Sorry, Luke. I've got to… I've got a meeting. About Douglas Woods."

She stood up abruptly and swallowed. "I'll let you know about the promotion idea," she said, then turned and walked away before he could say anything else.

Chapter 5

Luke was confused by his conversation with Sam.

She didn't look up when he walked past her to his desk, her eyes fixed on the screen of her laptop though he noticed she wasn't using the keyboard.

He'd thought she'd be pleased by the prospect of promotion, but if anything she'd seemed disappointed and he hated to see her upset. It was true what he'd said. She was fantastic to work with and would make an excellent deputy.

There was more to their relationship than that, though. He'd grown fond of Sam. Heck, a few months earlier he'd come close to asking her on a date but chickened out at the last moment. She'd have said no, though, he was sure of it. He'd struck lucky with Jess but that had been a one-off. What were the chances of a second stunning blonde falling for a scar-faced giant like him? No, he'd have to accept that she was out of his league.

Luke's phone rang and when he saw Filcher's secretary's name on the screen he immediately knew what to expect.

"Don't tell me," he said when he answered. "He wants to see me and he wants to see me now."

Gloria laughed. "You got it."

Filcher was pacing up and down outside his office when Luke got to the Executive Floor.

"About time," Filcher said, even though it had only been two or three minutes since Luke had been summoned. He held his hand out and Gloria passed him a piece of paper. "Here it is. You're lucky, Luke."

"Lucky?"

"You used to play rugger, didn't you?"

Luke hadn't heard anyone call it rugger since he was a

child. He caught Gloria winking from behind his boss, but managed to keep a straight face. "I used to play rugby union," he said.

"Professional?"

"Briefly, before I was injured. I played for Bath Rugby."

"Thought so. Here." He passed the piece of paper over and pointed at the words in large bold text at the top. "Bath are playing Gloucester." He moved his finger to the date. "This Saturday."

"And?"

"You're going."

Luke saw that the remainder of the sheet contained two columns of names. On the left were five Filchers' staff including Edward Filcher and Fred Tanner, the Head of Marketing, while next to them were fifteen names he didn't know.

He looked up at his boss, then down again as he realised that he did in fact know one of the names in the right-hand column.

"What is this?" he asked.

"Greet sheet."

"Greet sheet?"

Filcher harrumphed as if the question was too stupid to even consider. "Can't go," he said. "You need to stand in. Clash. Gloria, explain." He turned and walked into his office, closing the door behind him with a resounding thunk.

Luke turned to Gloria and waved the sheet of paper in the air. "What's a 'greet sheet'?"

She smiled. "It's created for every event where we have corporate hospitality. It lists the Filchers staff who are attending and who they have to look after."

"Look after?"

She nodded. "In this case, every Filchers attendee has been assigned three guests and it's their job to make sure they enjoy themselves."

"And he wants me to stand in for him?"

"Yes. Mr Filcher loves anything free, but he's got a freemasonry event on Saturday." She chuckled. "Not that I'm supposed to know it's a masons' do, but he's not very good at keeping secrets."

"I think I might take him up on the offer."

"I'm surprised. You've declined every hospitality event in the past. Is it because it's rugby?"

Luke smiled. "No. There's one of the guests I'd like to meet."

He left Gloria and made his way to the Marketing department where Fred Tanner's distinctive Yorkshire accent led him to the cubicle of one of his staff.

"Hi, Fred," he said. "Sorry, if I'm interrupting."

"No problem. We were just finishing." He turned to the consultant, a woman in her late twenties. "Send me the mock-up when it's done, Lizzie, and I'll let you know what I think."

"Will do," she said.

"Nah then," Fred said, turning to Luke. "How can I help?"

"Filcher's asked me to cover for him at the rugby on Saturday."

"Don't tell me you've said yes?"

"I have, but I was wondering if the guests I've been assigned could be changed." He held up the greet sheet. "I'd like Adrian Critchley to be one of my three rather than him being with the Fortune Group Client Director."

"Do you know him, like?"

"No, but he's been mentioned in one of our projects. I'd like the opportunity to find out more about him."

Fred raised one eyebrow. "Aye, that's all you're going to let me know, in't it? Tell you what, I'll have a word with Cora and see if she'll swap. Do you mind which of the three you lose?"

Luke shook his head. "Not in the slightest. I don't

know any of them. Thanks, Fred. Are you still up for squash on Thursday evening?"

"Too right. See you at the Leisure Centre."

Chapter 6

Sam tried to bury herself in her work but couldn't shake the conversation with Luke out of her mind. Aside from anything else, she was embarrassed by what she'd done. He must think she was nuts, putting her hand on his when all he was doing was talking to her as her line manager.

She ought to be pleased to be offered recognition. Promotion would mean a pay rise, more responsibility and it meant he valued her contribution to the team.

Contribution to the team!

Pah!

It was clear that he didn't see her as anything more than a hard worker who would be a good deputy. But then why would he? It wasn't much more than a year since his wife had died, and he probably wasn't ready for a relationship. Even if he was, what would he see in her?

She'd have to try Hinge again.

Online dating hadn't worked for her in the past. Most of the men she'd been linked with had been oddballs in one way or another. However, she needed to give it another go. Perhaps she'd be lucky this time.

It was pointless holding out for Luke when he didn't find her attractive.

She needed to stop stewing and concentrate on work.

She picked up the file on Douglas Woods, and re-read the contents to refresh her memory.

Woods was thirty-eight, married and worked in Filchers' IT department. There was a photo clipped to the HR printout, and while reasonably attractive there was something about his face that she found unsettling. He wasn't smiling, but that wasn't the issue. She peered at the photo and decided it was his eyebrows. They were thick and close to his eyes making him look very intense, but not in an altogether nice way.

He was a consultant, very technical by the look of his qualifications and experience, and had been with Filchers for two years having transferred from a software house. Unusually for a harassment case, Woods wasn't a manager and the accusation wasn't sexual. Indeed it was closer to bullying than harassment in many ways.

Sam pulled out the information sheet that HR had provided for Teresa McNee. She was also a consultant and worked alongside Woods. Although the same grade, she was only twenty-nine, so almost a decade younger.

She logged into her laptop and retrieved Teresa's email.

To:	*Sam Chambers*
From:	*Teresa McNee*
Subject:	*Private and Confidential*

Hi Sam.

I hope you don't mind me emailing you. I'm having problems with one of my co-workers, Douglas Woods, and HR suggested you might be able to help.

We've been working together for three months. It was okay at first, but in recent weeks he has been continually sniping at me, picking up on the slightest error I make, or even what I'm wearing. It's reached the stage where I'm having trouble sleeping at night.

I know this sounds trivial but it's affecting my mental health. I tried raising it with my boss but he told me to 'grow up and ignore him'. I don't know if you can help but could we at least talk?

Thanks
Teresa.

Sam had come across this kind of problem once before in the time she'd been working in the Ethics Team. In the end she'd had to advise the accuser, in that case a man, to move to a different account within Filchers. Human Resources had helped and it had been relatively easy because the two had been call centre agents.

A move would be much more difficult for Teresa because she and Douglas Woods had such specialised skills.

She picked up the phone and dialled Teresa's number.

"Hello. This is Teresa."

"Hi, Teresa. Sam here, from the Ethics Team. Can you talk?"

"Just a minute." After a few seconds, she came back on the line. "Thanks for calling, Sam. Sorry to bother you with this."

"Don't be silly. That's what I'm here for. Are you still having problems with Douglas?"

"I certainly am." There was a slight tremble to her voice. "It's awful. I don't know what to do to make things better."

"Has he always been like this?"

"No. He was fine for the first couple of months after I joined. We got on well. Then about four weeks ago he seemed to change. I made a mistake and he leapt on me for it, and since then he's been having a go at me several times a day."

"Have you tried talking to him?"

"I've told him to stop, but all that seems to do is make him worse."

Sam thought about this for a few seconds. "I'm going to have a word with him, and see if I can get him to agree to the three of us meeting."

"Thanks, Sam."

Sam ended the call and picked up the photo of Douglas Woods. Teresa had said he'd changed overnight. Had something happened in his personal life, something bad enough that he was still affected by it a month later?

She decided she needed to meet with Douglas Woods on his own before a three-way meeting and try to get him to open up. If she was right, and there was a reason for his sudden change of attitude towards Teresa, she needed to know what that reason was.

However, what she didn't want to do was introduce herself to Woods as someone from the Ethics Team because people tended to assume it meant they were in serious trouble.

Although she didn't want to, she realised that she needed to ask Luke for his advice.

As she was thinking this he came into the room.

"Luke," she said. "Have you got a moment?"

He smiled and walked over. "Of course. Have you come to a decision about being my deputy?"

"No," she said, more abruptly than she intended. She picked up the folder on her desk and waved it in the air. "It's about Douglas Woods. I need to speak to him and see if I can persuade him to meet with me and Teresa, the woman he's been upsetting, to thrash things out."

"And?"

"Give me a chance! I'm getting to it." She took a deep breath. "I don't want to tell him I'm from the Ethics Team. Should I say I'm from Human Resources?"

"Mmm. That might worry him just as much. Plus, it wouldn't be good to start with a lie."

"I appreciate that, for goodness sake. It was only a suggestion."

Luke raised an eyebrow at this. "Are you okay, Sam?"

"I'm fine." She gave a dry laugh. "You've talked about promoting me. Why wouldn't I be fine?"

"You seem a bit… I don't know."

"I've said I'm okay, haven't I? So, what do you suggest I say?"

Luke thought about this for a few seconds. "Why don't

you tell Woods you're from Internal Affairs and that you want his input on something? Then when you're alone with him you can broach the subject of his relationship with... What was her name?"

She sighed. "Teresa. I told you a minute ago." She looked up at him. "I'll do that. Thanks."

"Any time."

Luke walked to his desk and Sam wondered why he had been so rude. Telling her not to start her conversation with Douglas Woods with a lie was so patronising it was untrue.

It had to be down to that ridiculous incident in the canteen. He was probably regretting the idea of putting her forward for promotion. Heck, he might even be thinking he ought to get rid of her altogether, that she had ideas above her station.

She picked up her phone and sent a WhatsApp.

'Come to mine one evening this week? I need to Hinge.'

Her friend Hannah's reply was almost instantaneous.

'Defo. Thursday's good. Scarface problems?'

Sam chose to ignore the question and sent,

'I'll cook. See you Thursday.'

That done, she called Douglas Woods.

"Douglas here."

"Hi, Douglas. My name's Sam Chambers. I'm in Internal Affairs and I could do with your input on something. Would you mind sparing me a few minutes?"

"Sure. Tomorrow would be best for me. Is this something to do with the department's database?"

"Not quite. I'll explain when we meet. Is 3 pm okay?"

"That's fine."

"Great. I'll book a room and email you the details.

Chapter 7

Leanne was standing beside Josh's Renault when he emerged from Filchers' Head Office.

"Sorry I'm late," he said.

He clicked the remote and they both climbed in.

"Been busy then?" she asked as she clipped her seat belt on.

"You betcha." He put the car into gear and made his way towards the exit.

He wanted to tell her about his latest investigation but knew he should ask about her day first. He'd progressed a long way in his understanding of how to deal with her in the nearly three months they'd been living together.

"How was your day?" he asked.

"I booked people in and took their visitor badges when they left. Occasionally had the thrill of escorting someone somewhere. It was mentally challenging."

He saw a gap in the traffic and headed out onto the Lower Bristol Road.

"Excellento, excellento," he said, once he'd accelerated enough to get the Clio back into fourth gear.

"Are you listening, Joshy?"

"What? Uh, yes. Of course. You were saying that you had an exciting day."

"I said it was mentally challenging."

"Yes, uh…" He changed down into third as he approached Queen Square. "It must be, with all that… Out of the way!" He shook his head as a van driver pulled out in front of him. "Some drivers, eh?"

"I'm pregnant with triplets."

"Gucci. That's…" With a shock he realised what she'd said, looked over at her face and then down at her stomach.

"Buggery-boo!"

"Eyes front," she said.

He flicked his eyes back to the front. "But…"

"Don't worry, I'm not pregnant."

"Phew. Then why…"

"To get your attention."

He swallowed. "Sorry."

"It's okay for you, Joshy. You love your work and find it challenging. I'm bored to death."

This was the time to tell her.

"Leanne," he began, "there's something I want to run past you. I think you'll be pleased but I'll explain when we get home."

It was an idea he'd had for a while. He'd done some research, and thrown numbers around, and was reasonably confident they could make it work. It wouldn't be easy, and they might have to make the odd sacrifice here and there, but it was a long-term investment. More importantly, he was pretty sure it would make Leanne happy.

Once they got back to the flat he made them each a cup of tea and told her to sit on the sofa.

"Go on then," she said as she took her mug from him. "What's your big idea?"

He sat down on the edge of the settee and turned to face her. "University," he said and smiled.

"What about it?"

"You should do a degree." His smile morphed into a sheepish grin. "I've looked into it."

"You have?"

He nodded. "Yup. Bath University is an option. You've got high enough grades at A-level, and you're already doing that online Russian course. You'd sail in."

"Don't be silly. How could we afford it?"

"A student loan. We could put some money aside too."

"Joshy, you are sweet, but really?"

"Have a look online this evening and see what you

think. I'll prepare the meal."

She leaned towards him, smiled and then kissed him on the lips.

"Right," he said. "I've got some work I need to complete. Eat at 7:30?"

"That'd be great." She stood up, fetched her laptop and returned to the sofa.

Josh watched, pleased to see her so excited, then sat at their small dining table, opened his notepad and looked back at what he'd found out so far concerning Adrian and Yvonne Critchley.

They both had LinkedIn profiles, which gave him information about their careers but little else. Facebook hadn't been much better, Adrian's friends being limited to his wife and brother and his only interest appearing to be rugby. He knew they'd been married for twenty years and had no children, but aside from that, nada.

He decided to come at it from another angle, looked up the Fortune Group and downloaded their latest annual report. It was a long shot, but he wondered if it contained any clues as to how and why Adrian Critchley, a very senior member of staff, might be personally involved in gambling.

The beginning of the document used a lot of words like 'vision', 'mission' and 'strategic goals' without, it seemed to Josh, actually saying anything. It went on to talk about the visibility of their fashion brands, and their ambitions for the gambling arm, but he found it difficult to break down the figures to understand where they made most of their money. After struggling for a few minutes, he decided he'd ask Sam to have a look the next morning.

He moved on to the governance section which listed the nine members of the Group's Main Board. There was a Chairman plus three Executive Directors, including Adrian Critchley, and five Non-Executive Directors.

After a spot of googling, he learned that Executive Directors were full-time company employees, while the

Chairman and Non-Executive Directors were part-timers, typically senior staff from similar organisations who offered advice on planning and policy.

One name intrigued him.

Spencer Howell was a Non-Executive Director and he recognised him as a retired sports commentator, primarily known for rugby union which was interesting given Adrian Critchley appeared to be keen on the sport. A search returned lots of results, a few of Howell at events where he had been an after-dinner speaker, while the majority were articles referencing his most famous pieces of commentary.

After looking through over a hundred search items, Josh was about to concede nothing useful was going to come up when he spotted an entry headed 'Transformational Acquisition Continues Gambling Industry Consolidation'. The words were gobbledygook, but there had to be a reason why Google had flagged it. He clicked on the heading so that he could see the full article.

Transformational Acquisition Continues as Gambling Industry Consolidates

Market consolidation and strategic acquisitions are continuing to play an important part in concentrating the gambling industry.

In July 2022, we had the largest deal in the UK after 888 Holdings PLC acquired William Hill International for $2.35 billion.

Later the same year, the Fortune Group acquired SCHBet, a Singapore-based betting specialist, for S$400m, appointing its owners Spencer Howell and Maurice Brown to the Board.

In 2023, Entain CEE, one of the world's largest sports betting, gaming and interactive entertainment groups, announced the purchase of STS Holdings, a Polish sportsbook operator, for £750m.

He made a note, looked at his watch, and realised 7.30 was already out of the question.

He stood up and looked over at Leanne who was still heavily focused on her computer.

"Is it okay if we eat around 8?" he asked, and this time it was his girlfriend who seemed to be miles away.

She was nodding at the screen and smiling to herself.

"Are you okay with pickled tabby cat and minced mice for dinner?" he went on.

"Sure," she said without looking up. "Whatever."

"I take it you're getting somewhere."

She looked at him then. "I think this might work," she said, the enthusiasm evident in her voice. "As you say, I could get a student loan, and if I went to Bath Uni there wouldn't be any accommodation fees." She gestured to the screen. "I've been chatting online to a student who's in her second year. From what she told me their Modern Languages syllabus looks fantastic. I could do French with Russian." She paused, cocked her head to one side and raised an eyebrow. "What did you say we're having to eat?"

Josh smiled. "Spag Bol. Is that okay?'

"Lovely," she said, her attention already back on her laptop.

Chapter 8

Helen sat forward on the armchair in the small lounge of Ronnie and Becky's flat. Her son and his girlfriend were still talking in the bedroom and their voices weren't raised any more which boded well.

She hoped he would come to the right decision. If he didn't obtain help quickly a downward spiral into addiction seemed inevitable.

With a sigh, she stood up, walked to the window and watched idly as cars made their way along Newbridge Road, their windscreen wipers fighting hard to keep the rain at bay.

It was a miserable evening in more ways than one.

There was a noise behind her and she turned to see her Ronnie and Becky reappear. It was clear that she had been crying.

"Have you made your choice?" Helen asked, looking at her son.

"I'm sorry I said those things, Mum," Ronnie said, and she saw that the rims of his eyes were also red. "I was upset at the thought that you'd talked about me behind my back."

"Ach, come here," she said, opening her arms wide.

He walked over and they embraced. After a few seconds, he stepped back and grabbed Becky's hand, looked into his girlfriend's eyes and then back at his mother.

"I'm going to do it," he said.

Helen breathed a sigh of relief. "Thank goodness," she said.

"Come on," Becky said, leading Ronnie to the sofa. "Let's talk through the details."

Helen returned to the armchair. "You won't be able to contact them until Monday," she said. "They're open from nine in the morning."

"I'll go in my lunch break," Ronnie said. "I don't want to say anything to Simon."

Although Ronnie hadn't returned to the Jehovah's Witnesses, he still worked for Simon Abrahams, one of the church elders.

Helen passed him the leaflet. "Are you ready to look at it now?"

He took it from her. "I'm sorry," he said again. "I knew you were both right but I didn't want to admit it, to myself as much as anything."

Helen smiled sympathetically at Becky as her son started to read the pamphlet.

The poor wee girl had been so stressed when she'd rung her earlier in the week, worried that she was betraying Ronnie by speaking behind his back. She'd become concerned about his behaviour, saying he was increasingly self-absorbed and unwilling to engage in conversation. When he did talk, he was very negative about himself, saying that he was a failure and a disappointment to her and his mother. Becky had tried to reassure him but got nowhere.

When Helen heard this it immediately set off warning bells. If action wasn't taken, and taken quickly, she feared he was in danger of a relapse.

She still felt guilty for not having seen the signs of his drug addiction nearly a decade earlier. When she had finally realised what was happening it was too late. He had dropped out of university and she was unable to locate him.

She had blamed herself and feared the worst.

Being reunited after eight years had been wonderful but he was fragile and she'd known it wouldn't be easy for him to make a full recovery.

She only hoped the charity she had found could help. Called 'Help your Family', they offered a variety of services including structured support groups, 1:1 advice and counselling sessions.

She smiled at her son. "You have to stop apologising," she said. "This isn't your fault and all Becky and I want is for you to get well." She paused. "Do you want me to come with you on Monday?"

"Won't you be working?"

Helen laughed. "I get lunch breaks too, you know," she said. "And in any case, Luke wouldn't have a problem with me taking time off. He's aware of your problems, remember, and he's always been supportive."

"It would be great if you could," Becky said. "I'm visiting clients, otherwise I'd go."

Ronnie wiped a tear from his eye. "You're both fantastic," he said, looking first at his mother and then at his girlfriend. "I don't know what I'd do without you."

"Ach, get away with you," Helen said, trying to keep her emotions in check. "I'm going to leave you two in peace now."

She kissed Becky on the cheek and held her hands out for another hug with her son before reaching for her coat.

"Shall we meet outside their office around 1 pm?" she said as she opened the apartment door.

"I'll see you there," Ronnie said. "Thanks, Mum."

Helen left quickly and retrieved a tissue from her bag to wipe her eyes as she headed for the bus stop.

Chapter 9

Brian tucked Max in, kissed him on the forehead and returned downstairs.

Kim was sitting on the sofa, in the same pose as she'd been when he'd taken their son up for his bedtime routine. Her eyes were rimmed with red and she was staring out of the window.

She heard him and turned. "I can't believe you put us in this position," she said.

He hated seeing his wife upset and stepped towards her. "I'm sorry, Kim," he said. "Truly I am. I didn't dream he'd do something like this." He reached for her hands but she jerked them out of his reach.

"What on earth were you thinking?" she snapped.

"I don't know. I guess I thought it was easy money." He swallowed. "We owe a lot and when Mr Smith offered me £10,000 it seemed like manna from heaven."

"Is that even his real name?"

He sighed. "Probably not, I suppose."

"Do you know why he came to you?"

"No idea. He contacted me out of the blue, told me he knew about our financial problems and that he could help."

"So if you liked the sound of the money why didn't you do what he asked?"

"When it came to it, I couldn't go through with it. It wouldn't have affected the result, but it's still cheating." He swallowed. "I didn't think for one moment he'd react like this. He sounded so nice on the phone."

Kim shook her head. "It's pretty clear now that this Mr Smith is a long way from being Mr Nice Guy. That man he sent today was so scary. His voice was cold, and the things he said." She shuddered. "The man even threatened to hurt

Max, for goodness sake."

"I'll have to do what Mr Smith asks this Saturday."

"But he's now demanding you do it inside ten minutes. Is that even possible?"

"It'll have to be."

Kim turned back to face the window. "I think we should go to the police and ask for protection."

Brian shook his head. "That's too dangerous. If he finds out…"

He jumped as his phone started ringing and pulled it from his back pocket to see 'Number withheld' on the screen. He held his hand up to stop Kim from saying anything and accepted the call.

"Hello," he said.

"Hello, Brian."

Brian pointed to the phone and mouthed 'It's Smith' to Kim before replying.

"What do you want?" he asked.

"How is your wife?" The voice on the other end of the phone was flat and emotionless.

"Very shaken up."

"I'm not surprised. My associate can be somewhat rough. However, you're the one to blame, Brian. We had an agreement and you let me down."

"Yes, but you didn't have to do that."

"I suggest we draw a line under it. After all, what's done is done and the important thing is that you don't make the same mistake again. One mistake I can tolerate, but a second one could be very dangerous. Look what happened to poor Darren Jackson."

"The golfer Darren Jackson? Didn't he commit suicide?"

Mr Smith gave a bitter laugh. "I'm glad you think so." He paused to let this sink in. "The reason I'm ringing is to assure you that £10,000 will be in your account directly after the game."

"Ten minutes will be very difficult."

"Ten minutes is non-negotiable."

"I'll do my best, but…"

"Non-negotiable," Mr Smith repeated. "You need to be very clear on that. Am I making myself understood?"

Brian swallowed. "Yes, I understand."

"Good, good. Oh, and one more thing. Don't even think about telling the police or indeed anyone about our agreement."

"I won't."

"Because if you do," he went on, "or if you let me down again this weekend, I will be forced to let my associate off his leash again, and this time he'll be unmuzzled. I'd hate to have to do that, but I cannot afford anyone to be out of line."

The phone went dead and Brian stared at the screen, unable to believe what he'd just heard. The implication had been clear.

Darren Jackson hadn't committed suicide.

He'd been murdered.

"What was that about Darren Jackson?" Kim asked.

Brian had to make a split-second decision, and his wife was already scared enough. Telling her wouldn't help.

"Mr Smith told me that Darren was working for him, but killed himself because he felt he'd let his family down. He warned me not to think like that."

"Brian!"

"Don't worry, I'm not wired that way. I'll do what he asks."

"But he'll keep asking, won't he?"

He walked over and she let him wrap his arms around her.

He bent down to her ear. "I can manage this," he whispered. "I'll find a way."

Chapter 10

There was a knock at the door of the library.

"Enter," he said, without looking up from his book.

As expected it was Dolores.

"I bring coffee, Mr Smith," she said, delivering the words slowly and almost painfully, pronouncing 'coffee' as 'cobbee' in her strong Filipino accent.

She had been with him for only three weeks, but he was already pleased he'd taken her on as his housekeeper. Dolores was a hard worker but, more importantly, her limited English made it easier for him to talk freely on the phone when she was around.

"Put it there," he said, gesturing to the coffee table by the side of his armchair.

"Yes, sir," she said. She put the tray down as quietly as she could and then backed out of the room.

Once she had shut the door he closed his book, picked up the mug and stirred in two teaspoons of sugar.

He took a sip and sat back.

There was a lot to think about.

In particular, was he spreading himself too thinly with five syndicates on the go? They were all paying well but the operation took a lot of organising, even though he only recruited UK-based gamblers.

Selection, secrecy and manipulation were what put the greatest demands on his time.

Selection because it took a lot of effort to bring people on board. He had to ensure they had wealth and were innately immoral, or at the very least amoral, and that required a lot of research.

This was where Harvey Robinson's reports paid dividends. Robinson was a Bath-based private investigator who was able to dig deep into potential syndicate members' backgrounds. His reports revealed what motivated them, how far they were prepared to go for money, and whether they had skeletons in their closets that could be used against them.

They also helped him assess whether targets were better suited to the other arm of his organisation.

Secrecy was as important as selection. It was a core principle of his that no one, whether they were in a syndicate, fixing matches, or otherwise part of his operation, should know they were dealing with him. This was hard at times but essential.

Manipulation was in many ways the easiest, but it still took time and energy to choose the events, and then to ensure his fixers did exactly what was asked of them.

Brian Shepherd was a case in point.

He was unhappy with himself for mismanaging the situation.

There were lessons to be learned from what had happened. He had chosen Shepherd when he had got wind of his financial difficulties, but engagement should have been stronger, enticing the man in with money but being clearer about what might happen if he failed to deliver.

The stupid man understood now, that was for certain. Artem Petrov, the man he had referred to in the phone call as his associate, had put the fear of god into Shepherd's wife, and his own reference to the deceased golfer had sealed the deal.

As he'd said on the phone, he didn't give second chances. If Shepherd failed to deliver for two games running he would have to pay.

He'd also said that he'd hate it if he had to send his associate in again, this time unmuzzled and off the leash.

That had been a lie.

The fact was, he didn't care. As long as it was done carefully, and couldn't be traced back to him, he wasn't bothered in the least about what might happen to Brian Shepherd and his family.

This wasn't personal, this was business.

Chapter 11

Luke was first in the office.

Helen followed a few minutes later and had only just settled down when a very excited Josh bounced in.

"You seem a wee bit buoyant for first thing on a Wednesday," she said with a smile.

Josh beamed over at her as he hung his coat up and walked to his desk. "Leanne and I had a brilliant evening," he said as he put down his notebook and laptop.

"I don't want the details, thanks."

"Not like that. Well, not until, ah…" His cheeks moved quickly to pink and it took a few seconds before he recovered his composure. "She told me she was pregnant," he went on, "and she agreed to go to Bath University."

Helen raised an eyebrow. "I didn't even know they had a hospital, let alone an obstetrics department."

"Eh?" Josh paused. "No, you don't understand. She's not pregnant."

"But you said…"

"She said it because I wasn't listening in the car."

"Aye, right." Helen turned to Luke. "Do you know what the wee boy's jabbering on about?"

Luke held his hand up and kept his eyes down. "I'm staying out of this."

"I found out about Howell, guv," Josh said, now looking at Luke.

Luke looked up at this. "Howell?"

"Spencer Howell."

"The rugby commentator?"

"That's the one."

"Hang on a minute." Luke leafed through the papers on his desk and retrieved the greet sheet Filcher had handed him the previous day. "I'm going to be meeting him on Saturday." He held the sheet in the air. "These are the attendees for Bath versus Gloucester and he's on the list."

"I didn't think you went in for corporate hospitality," Helen said.

"I don't, but Adrian Critchley's going to be there and it would be good to meet him."

"That's a second connection," Josh said, "and you don't believe in coincidences do you, guv?"

He explained about Spencer Howell being on the board of the Fortune Group after they bought his company.

"I hate to disappoint you," Luke said when he'd finished, "but that's not a coincidence."

"What! But you saw him on that piece of paper," Josh waved his hand at the greet sheet, "and I found him over there." He turned to face his desk and gestured to his laptop and notebook.

Luke shook his head. "Same reason though, isn't it, Josh? They're both on the Board of the Fortune Group and that's why they've been invited to the game." He paused. "Good work though. I wonder if there are others from the Fortune Group going on Saturday."

Josh held out his hand. "Can I have a look?" Luke passed the greet sheet over and Josh looked through the names. "I recognise one of these," he said. "Give me a mo'."

He returned to his desk and turned on his laptop. A few seconds later he called over. "I thought so. Maurice Brown was co-owner of SCHBet alongside Spencer Howell and he's also now a Non-Executive Director."

Luke nodded. "That's interesting. Can you do some background digging on him as well please?"

"On it."

At that moment Maj and Sam came into the room.

Maj looked over. "Good morning, Luke," he said with a smile.

Luke smiled back. "Morning, Maj. Morning, Sam."

Sam nodded but didn't return his smile and walked straight to her desk. Luke wondered if she'd decided she didn't want a promotion and couldn't face giving him the news. Probably best to let her tell him in her own time.

Right now, he owed it to Martin Ribble to call him and give him an update.

"Hi, Martin," he said when the phone was answered. "Not a lot to tell you yet, I'm afraid, but I might have something after the weekend. Filchers are hosting clients at a Rugby match and Adrian Critchley is one of our guests."

"I was about to ring you," Martin said. "The oddest thing's happened. I was extrapolating figures, and checked the data points for the…"

"Martin!"

"Yes."

"Please remember who you're talking to."

Martin laughed. "Sorry." He paused. "Critchley's name is gone."

"What do you mean, gone?"

"He's no longer linked to one of the bets. The name there now is Ray Thomas."

"Are you sure you didn't make a mistake and look in the wrong place?"

"Definitely not. There have been DML changes and the custom tracking method we use means there should be an indication of the modifications in triggers or timestamps. However, there's no trace of the amendment on the database logs or the audit records."

"Which means?"

"Someone's made the change at the raw level. In layman's terms, they've used machine code to avoid detection."

Luke smiled to himself. Layman's terms these most definitely were not.

"Who could have made that change?" he asked.

"Not many people. I can think of only four, including me. Fiona, who works in my team, would be capable. Also Andrew Clarke. He's in audit but used to work for SAP and has a deep understanding of database interrogation techniques. The final one would be Douglas in IT."

"That wouldn't be Douglas Woods, would it?"

"Yes, that's him. Do you know him?"

"I know of him. Thanks, Martin. You've been very helpful."

Luke hung up.

Now this *was* a coincidence.

He called over to Sam. "Sam, could you spare me a moment please?"

Her shoulders seemed to sag slightly but she turned, stood up and walked over.

"If this is about my promotion…" she started to say.

"No, it's not about that." He tried smiling but again it wasn't returned. "When are you seeing Douglas Woods?"

"At three. Why?"

"There are some questions I'd like you to ask."

"Questions I wouldn't have thought of?"

"No. They're extra questions because…"

She interrupted before he could finish, but kept her voice low so she couldn't be overheard. "If you don't trust me, Luke, why don't you talk to him yourself? I've got plenty of other things I could be getting on with."

"Of course I trust you." He hesitated and then looked her in the eyes. "Sam, I can see you're upset about something. If there's any way I can help…"

This seemed to bring her to her senses. "Sorry," she said and swallowed. "I had a bad night and I shouldn't have said that." She tried to smile but it was a pathetic attempt. "What questions do you want me to ask?"

He explained about the removal of Adrian Critchley's name from the database, and how Douglas Woods was one of only four people who could have made the change.

"I see," she said when he'd finished. "So you're thinking his change in manner towards Teresa McNee could be connected to this?"

"Exactly. He could have made the changes for personal reasons, but I doubt it. More likely he's being put under pressure by someone, hence the change in mood. If you can, please ask him about his personal circumstances, and about the technical nature of his job, just to see if he lets anything slip."

Sam nodded. "Okay, Luke. I'll do that." She smiled again and this time it was genuine. "I'm sorry about earlier."

"No need, Sam. We all have rough days."

Chapter 12

Sam arrived at the Empire room five minutes early. She'd booked coffee and biscuits in the hope it would help Douglas Woods relax, although from what Teresa had said he was permanently wired and on edge.

When it got to ten past three she was beginning to think he'd forgotten all about their meeting, and was just about to give him a call when there was a short tap on the door and he walked in.

Somehow he wasn't what Sam had anticipated even though she'd seen a photo. It was his height, she decided. He had to be well over six foot, almost Luke's height, but with a slim almost streaky build. His edginess was clear as he shook her hand and sat opposite, struggling to get himself comfortable as he slid backwards and forwards on his chair.

"Thanks for seeing me, Douglas," she said. She picked up the jug. "Coffee?"

"Thanks. White please."

She made them both a coffee and offered him the plate of biscuits but he declined.

"Are you sure?" she asked with a smile. "They've treated us. It's not often we get jammie dodgers."

He half-smiled in return. "No thanks. What's this about?"

This was the tricky bit. Finding a way of making him relax was difficult when the reason she was seeing him was because he'd been harassing a co-worker.

She smiled again. "There's no need to be concerned. "I'm new to Internal Affairs and my boss has asked me to talk to a few people to help me understand how they feel about Filchers and how best we can support them."

"Why me?"

"No reason, really," she lied. "You've been here long enough to know your way around the company, but other than that your name came up more or less at random."

He relaxed as she said this.

"So tell me," she went on, "How do you find Filchers as a place to work?"

She led him through several questions designed to make him feel increasingly at ease.

"How do you find working here fits in with your personal life?" she asked, once she felt he'd settled down even more.

"It's fine. The hours aren't too bad, although there's the occasional weekend working when we have to do database maintenance."

"Are you married?" He nodded, but she sensed he was already uncomfortable with this line of questioning and decided to probe further. "What does your wife think of you having to work weekends?"

He stared at Sam for a few seconds before replying. "She didn't mind too much."

"Didn't?"

Douglas looked down at his hands and then back up at Sam. "We've separated."

"I'm sorry to hear that. Nothing to do with work I hope?"

"Not really."

"Financial problems?"

His eyes widened. "What makes you say that?"

"No reason other than that it's often the cause of marital break-ups."

"I'd rather not talk about our separation if that's okay."

"Of course. That's fine. What about your interests and hobbies? How does working at Filchers fit in with them?"

"I don't have many hobbies. I'm an online gamer and that's about it."

"That's interesting. What kind of games?"

"Casino games mainly."

"And that fits around work okay?"

"Yes."

Sam sensed resistance and decided to switch tack.

"What about the technical challenges at work, Douglas? Do you feel there are enough, or conversely are there too many making you feel pressurised?"

"They're fine."

"And your colleagues. Do you get on with them okay?"

He nodded and looked very deliberately at his watch. "Is that all? I ought to be getting back."

She smiled. "Yes, that's excellent. Thanks for sparing me the time."

He stood up, looked at Sam briefly and then turned and left the room.

She was left wondering what she had got out of the meeting. Looking at her notes, very little, and she hadn't even come close to asking him about Teresa. A second meeting was needed but she'd have to be more up-front about the reason this time.

Once she was back in the Ethics Room, Sam composed an email to Douglas Woods, thanking him for his time and asking if they could meet again to talk about technical training and development. This, she felt, was a safe subject.

She had just sent the email when Luke wandered over.

"How did it go?" he asked.

"I think Woods' difficulties with Teresa might stem from the break up of his marriage," she said. "However, I've asked if I can see him again next week and I'll try to find out more."

"Anything else of interest?"

"There was one thing. His main hobby outside of work is playing online casino games. I know it's a tenuous link, but given what you said about Adrian Critchley's name being against a bet of some kind…"

"Mmm. I don't think it's tenuous at all."

Chapter 13

Sam decided she'd make a stir-fry for dinner and stopped at Sainsbury's after leaving work to buy veg, noodles, sirloin steak and, on impulse, a bottle of red wine.

Once home she changed into casual clothes and set about preparing the vegetables, wondering as she did so how she would fare with online dating this time around.

The problem was assessing what was fact and what was fiction. Inevitably men would say they were successful at work, enjoyed sports and had an excellent sense of humour. All this would be accompanied by photos of them that for all she knew were over a decade old.

She smiled as she recalled one particularly torrid first date. His name, Elmo, should have given the game away. What kind of parents named their children after a character from Sesame Street? Perhaps they'd been hoping he would inherit a sense of humour from the irrepressibly cheerful furry red puppet.

He most certainly hadn't.

Elmo had been as dreary as they come, insisting on telling her long and rambling anecdotes about his work as a hospital janitor, seeming to forget that his Hinge entry had described him as 'having a high-pressured job in medical care'.

Needless to say, she hadn't seen Elmo a second time.

Shaking her head at the memory, Sam cut the steak into strips, then put the chopped veg and the meat into the fridge. As she did so the doorbell went.

"No luck with Scarface I take it?" Hannah asked when she answered the door.

"This evening isn't about him," Sam said.

Hannah raised an eyebrow. "It isn't?"

"No. This is about getting me out there. Glass of red?"

"I'd love one."

Sam went to the kitchen and returned with two glasses of Merlot, passed one over and sat on the armchair opposite her friend.

"What about you?" she asked. "How's your love life?"

Hannah smiled sheepishly. "So so."

A grin spread across Sam's face and she nodded knowingly. "What's his name?"

"Bertie." Hannah held her hand up. "I know it sounds kind of old-fashioned."

"Posh rather than old-fashioned." Sam took a sip of her wine. "What does he do?"

"He's a fitness coach."

"Wow. And is he?"

"Is he what?"

"Fit?"

Hannah laughed. "Well, I like him."

"That's obvious. How long have you been going out?"

"We had our fourth date at the weekend and I'm seeing him again on Saturday. We met on Hinge, talking of which we ought to update your profile."

"We'll do it after we eat."

"No. We'll do it now." Hannah tapped the sofa. "Come over here."

"Okay, okay," Sam said. She sat next to Hannah and opened the Hinge app on her phone.

"The photos you've got are fine," Hannah said, looking down at the screen, "but you should answer a few more prompts. Pass it here."

Hannah flicked through the app for a minute or so, pressed a few buttons and then handed the phone back.

"These three," she said.

Sam read the first prompt: *How my mother would describe me*. "That's a one-word answer," she said with a smile. "Single."

"Enter it then. It shows a sense of humour."

Sam entered 'Single' and moved on to the second prompt: *Believe it or not I…*

It was Hannah's turn to smile. "Put 'Believe it or not, I'm a karate black belt, third Dan'."

"Won't that put men off?"

"I guess it might." She pointed at the screen. "What about that one: *Two truths and a lie*? You could include the black belt."

"Okay. What other truth should I put?"

Hannah was about to say something when Sam stopped her. "Don't suggest anything about Luke."

Hannah thought for a moment. "What about 'I was locked in a pig sty by a serial killer'."

Sam laughed. "Okay. I need a lie as well. I know." She typed a few words and passed the phone over. "What do you think?"

Hannah read the words on the screen: *I've always wanted a boyfriend named after a Sesame Street character.*

"I hope you're referring to that Elmo guy you dated once."

"Of course. Who else would I mean?" Sam put her hand to her mouth. "Oh sorry, I forgot. There's a Bert on Sesame Street, isn't there?"

"As if you didn't know."

"I forgot, honestly." She stood up. "Right, let's finish after dinner."

"Do you need any help?"

"No thanks. I've prepared everything and it'll only take a few minutes."

Hannah held her hand out. "Give me your phone. I'll update your filters while you're cooking."

Sam passed her phone over and they went into the kitchen. Hannah perched at the breakfast bar while Sam pulled out a wok and the veg, meat and noodles.

"So," Hannah said, finger poised over the phone, "shall

I filter on ex-rugby players who are 6ft 6 or over with a scar on the left side of their face?"

Sam gave her friend a withering look and started to fry the spices before adding the veg and meat.

"Definitely tall," she said after a few seconds.

"I'll put 6ft or over. What about age?"

"Thirty to forty-five. I don't think I could go out with someone a lot younger than me."

"What else? Do you want me to filter on religion or politics?"

"No, although I'd prefer not to date a neo-nazi or a terrorist."

"Again," Hannah added.

Sam smiled ruefully. "Chris wasn't a terrorist," she said. "I just thought he was." She added the noodles and oyster sauce to the pan, fried everything for a few more minutes then divided it between two plates.

"Done," Hannah said as she tapped a button on the screen, put the phone down and took her plate from Sam. "After we've eaten, we'll have a look at what's on offer."

Once they'd finished their meals they returned to the lounge and Sam began looking through Hinge's suggestions. "Too many," she said and adjusted the location filter so that it only searched within 15 miles of Bath.

After an hour or so five men had 'liked' her profile and, after much to-ing and fro-ing with Hannah, she decided to match with two of them, Ollie and Joe, which meant they could start texting each other. Ollie said his job was 'sports-related' while Joe was a store manager.

Almost immediately Ollie sent her a message asking why she'd chosen him. Sam zoomed in on his photo. He was certainly attractive and she couldn't help comparing him to Luke; he was almost as tall at six foot three and shared her boss's broad shoulders and strong features.

"He looks like Luke," Hannah said.

"Right," Sam said, standing up from the sofa. "It's time

you went home. The rest of this I can manage on my own."

Hannah smiled. "You mean the smutty talk?"

"Hannah!"

Hannah retrieved her coat and went to the door. "Let me know how you get on, won't you?"

"Don't worry. I will."

Sam closed the door and returned to the sofa. She liked the look of Ollie and couldn't wait to start chatting to him.

Half her reply to his question was typed when a message from Joe popped up: '*Hi, Sam. Ready to chat?*'

She flicked over to his photo.

Joe had well-defined cheekbones, peppered stubble and vivid blue eyes. Hannah had described him as 'dishy', and Sam had to admit he was good-looking. He was about the same height as Ollie, or at least he said he was.

Decisions, decisions.

Chapter 14

"In your bed," Luke said, pleased he had put a towel down before taking Wilkins into the fields at the back of the house. The cocker spaniel, who was dripping muddy water onto the floor, obediently walked into his dog crate, turned in a circle twice and then flopped down.

Luke closed and latched the door and passed a dog biscuit through the gaps in the metal grid. "I'll be back in a few hours," he said, causing Wilkins to look up at him and tilt his head to one side as if to say, '*I know that, stupid*'.

Luke smiled, looked at his watch, realised he needed to get a move on if he was going to be at Springdale House by eleven, and darted upstairs to change out of his walking-the-dog clothes into something more presentable.

Within five minutes he was back in the car, only stopping to pass Wilkins another treat as he said goodbye.

It was great having the dog for company, but even so the house felt very lonely. The twins were back at University for their second year, Chloe at Portsmouth and Ben at Reading, and it was incredibly quiet without them.

At least he'd be seeing them soon, whereas his wife was gone forever.

As he started the car, Luke reflected on the fact that it was now over a year since she had been killed. It was a tragic waste of a life and he'd found it hard to cope, especially for the first six months. It was slowly becoming easier but there were memories everywhere, not least in the twins themselves. At nineteen, Chloe was the spitting image of Jess when she'd been that age.

His mind turned to his own mother. He tried to visit every couple of weeks if he could, though it was awful seeing her slowly deteriorate. She hadn't been a loving parent, but dementia was an illness you wouldn't wish on your worst enemy.

All in all, he had a full day ahead. There was time for an hour or so at the care home, but he'd have to be away from Springdale by twelve or so if he was going to get to the Recreation Ground on time.

The drive from Norton St Philip took fifty minutes and it was eleven on the dot when he parked the BMW. Mark and Hugo were standing by the entrance, his father dressed as if visiting his gentlemen's club in regimental tweeds and his Old Harrovian school tie.

"Hi, Mark. Hi, Father," Luke said as he walked up to join them.

He pressed the bell and the receptionist buzzed them in. "They're playing bingo with Tracey in the lounge," she said as they signed the visitors' book.

Mark entered the code to let them through the next door. Once inside, they saw seven people seated around a large table. Tracey, one of the carers, was at the far end pulling numbers from an envelope, while six residents, four women and two men, were seated around the table with bingo cards and pens in front of them. One of the men appeared to be asleep.

"Good morning," Tracey said with a smile when she saw them. "Are you taking the lovely Duchess away from me?"

Daphne appeared not to have spotted her husband and sons and took the opportunity to snatch up the bingo card in front of the woman next to her. She waved it in the air. "Elizabeth's cheating," she said, glaring at Tracey.

Elizabeth held her hand out for the card to be given back but didn't say anything.

"Elizabeth's not cheating," Tracey said.

"Elizabeth's cheating," Daphne repeated.

"Give the card back please, Daphne. You've got visitors."

Daphne turned to look at the three men at the end of the table and focused her attention on her husband.

"Elizabeth's cheating, Hugo," she said. She waved her hands at Luke and Mark. "Are you the police? You need to arrest her." She paused for a second and then scowled, a hint of recognition in her eyes. "Who are you?"

"Lucas and Marcus," Hugo said. "Your sons."

She grunted and Elizabeth took the opportunity to snatch her bingo card back out of her hand.

"Come on, Mother," Luke said. "Let's have a cup of tea in your room. I've got some photos of your great-niece Marion to show you."

"When am I going home?"

"You are home. This is your home."

Daphne looked around as if seeing the place for the first time.

Hugo held his hand out but his wife pushed it away, glared at him for a second and then pushed her chair back and stood up.

Another of the carers, Connie, who was preparing medicines for each of the residents, called over. "I'll bring you some drinks," she said. "Is tea okay?"

They all nodded. "That would be lovely," Luke said. "Thanks."

They led their mother to her room.

*

Luke felt exhausted as he climbed back into the Beemer, a familiar feeling when he'd visited his mother.

She'd been hard work before she became ill, but now she was almost impossible to interact with. It wasn't just that she repeated herself, and he had even become used to her sudden angry outbursts. No, what was upsetting was the fact that she couldn't engage in any kind of meaningful conversation.

It was awful to see her deterioration and his father was taking it very hard. Hugo had always been a strong man who hid his emotions, but the way he was feeling was now evident on his face. He was a shadow of his former self.

Luke turned his attention to the afternoon ahead.

Fred had asked him to be there by 1:30 pm ahead of guests arriving at 2 to 2:30. He wanted to brief the hosts on what was expected of them, though what that meant, beyond smiling and making sure they were fed and watered, Luke wasn't sure.

He clicked his audiobook on, hoping that the latest from the pen of JD Kirk would keep him interested. Sure enough, Angus King's narration, and especially his interpretation of Bob Hoon, soon had him laughing out loud, the worries of the world forgotten for a few precious minutes.

Chapter 15

Fred Tanner was already in Filchers' private box when Luke arrived. He was chatting to Cora Evans, the Fortune Group Client Director, whom Luke had met on a couple of occasions. She was an attractive brunette in her early forties, known for her strong people-management skills, though what he had liked most about her had been her dry sense of humour.

Standing beside Cora was a man Luke was sure he'd met, possibly at the Executive Conference back in the Spring. He was the shortest in the group, slightly overweight, with glasses and a greying beard. After a few seconds, it came back to him. His name was Wilbert Longsmith and he was Client Director for Global News and Entertainment, better known as GNE. The man had bored him half to death at the conference talking at length about sector budgets and revenue.

He walked over. "Hi, Fred." He nodded to the other two.

"Hi," Fred said. "You know Cora and William, don't you?"

"Yes, of course." He smiled across at them.

William, that was it, not Wilbert. For some reason, the man was instantly forgettable.

"The others should be along at any moment," Fred went on. "Ah, here they are."

Luke turned as two men he knew only too well walked towards them. He smiled to see James McDonald, Head of Human Resources, who he'd known was on the list, but the other man, built like Mr Universe with a swagger to match, was both a surprise and a disappointment.

"Cora, William," Fred said. "Do you know James and

Glen?"

"I do," William said, with a smile at James and a grimace at Glen as if something with a bad smell had just come into the room.

"I know James," Cora said, then looked at Glen and held her hand out. "But I don't think I've had the pleasure."

Glen took her hand and pumped it up and down. "No, you haven't," he said with a beaming smile that showed all his teeth, "but I'll make sure that you do."

"Do what?"

"Have the pleasure." He saw that she was still confused and added, "...of me."

She pulled her hand away, raised her left eyebrow and then turned to Fred. "So," she said, glancing back at Glen for a second before returning her attention to the Head of Marketing. "Now that we're all here, what's expected of us?"

"I've had to juggle the assignments," Fred said, handing them each a revised greet sheet. "Ivan Pritchard's had a family bereavement so he had to drop out last night, which is why Glen's here. Maurice Brown from Gambet had an accident at home and has had to go to A&E."

"What happened?" Cora asked.

"Fell off a ladder apparently. However, another of Gambet's Non-Execs, Jeremy Ellis, is coming in his place. Also, as you're probably aware, Edward Filcher's attending a freemasonry event and Luke's stepped in to take his place."

"There's not a lot to it," he went on. "Make sure your assigned guests enter the competition to guess the first try scorer. It helps to break the ice and the winner will win a signed Bath Rugby ball. The main thing during the game is to make sure their drinks are topped up."

"And afterwards?" Luke asked.

"There's a three-course hot buffet after the game so food's taken care of. A couple of the Bath players will come up to chat with everyone once they've showered and dressed."

"What time will it all end?"

"We'll finish here around six, and we usually head off to The Boater afterwards."

Luke nodded. "Sounds good." He turned to Cora. "Thanks for agreeing to swap Adrian Critchley with me."

"No problem," she said. "Do you know him?"

"Not exactly. There's something we're looking into and…"

"I'm Head of Security," Glen said, interrupting Luke mid-sentence.

Luke sighed and turned slowly to face him. "I know," he said.

Glen grunted. "Yes, but she doesn't." He nodded his head sideways indicating Cora.

"I'm not the cat's mother," Cora said.

"Uh."

"I'm standing right next to you and I can hear what you're saying," she went on.

He turned to face her and smiled his all-too-white grin. "And standing very nicely too," he said.

"Standing very nicely?"

He nodded, pleased with himself. "Very nicely. That's a pleasant dress."

"A pleasant dress?"

"Yes. It shapes you very well."

She turned to face him and, despite being eight or nine inches shorter than his 6ft 2, the look on her face made him back away slightly.

"Isn't there something you have to go and secure?" she asked.

"Eh? Oh, you mean because I'm Head of Security. Ha, ha. No, I've got a team for that."

"Over fifty staff," Luke said.

Glen nodded and his grin transitioned to smugness. "Fifty-two," he said.

"Perhaps I should explain myself more clearly," Cora said. "Why don't you bugger off and leave us in peace for a minute or two?"

Glen looked at her and his smugness reverted to a grin before transforming into little-boy-told-off. "Ah, right," he said. "I'll do that, then. Not literally, of course, that would be, uh…"

He edged away.

"Let's talk over there," Luke said, indicating a group of chairs in the corner of the box.

"Do you know Adrian well?" he asked, once they had sat down.

"Not really. I've only met him three times. I see his wife at least once a week though."

"Yvonne?"

"Yes. I'm her line manager. Why did you ask to be his host?"

Luke decided to share part of the truth. "His name came up on a project we're working on, and when I got roped into this I thought it would be good to meet him."

She smiled. "Come on, Luke. There's got to be more to it than that. Didn't I hear you're ex-police? My nose is telling me you suspect him of something."

He returned her smile. "I couldn't possibly comment."

"In that case, you won't be interested in what I've heard about him."

She started to stand but he put his hand on her arm to restrain her. "Okay, okay," he said with a laugh as she sat back down. "There's a possibility he's involved in something odd. Not necessarily criminal, but certainly worth looking into. What have you heard?"

"I'll tell you on one condition."

"What?"

She turned to face him and looked him in the eyes. "We go out for dinner."

"Are you asking me on a date?"

She smiled again. "Now I understand how you became a detective."

"I'm flattered, but we hardly know each other."

"Call it an almost-blind date if you like."

Luke realised that the idea appealed to him. He found her good-looking but there was more to it than that. Cora was independent and forthright, and that always attracted him in a woman. *What would Jess think?* flashed through his mind, but the answer came almost as quickly: *She'd want me to be happy.*

"Okay," he said. "You're on. What about tomorrow evening?"

"Suits me."

"I'll choose the venue."

It was her turn to laugh. "I'd rather not go to KFC."

"Burger King it is then."

"What I've heard…" she started to say, only to be interrupted by a loud cough. She turned to see Glen looking down at both of them, teeth bared in an almost rictus smile.

"Not interrupting a budding romance, am I?" he asked.

"Yes, you are," Cora said.

"Ha, ha." He pointed his finger over his shoulder. "Our guests are here. It's time to mangle."

"Mingle," Luke corrected, but Glen had already turned towards the visitors, making a beeline for the only woman in the group.

"I'll have to tell you about Adrian later," Cora said in a whisper, "but if I were you I'd avoid talking about gambling."

Chapter 16

"Adrian's the younger one," Cora said, pointing to two men who were helping themselves to drinks.

"Interesting," Luke said, half to himself.

In his mind, a Head of Strategy was plain and staid, dressed sensibly and had neat short hair. If anything, Critchley was the opposite of this with a barrel chest, full ginger beard, curly locks to match and a booming laugh that could probably be heard at the other end of the stand.

He was laughing at something the older man was saying.

As he approached, Luke recognised the gravelly voice of Spencer Howell, having heard it many times before on the television.

"Hi," he said. "Sorry if I'm interrupting. He held his hand out. "I'm Luke Sackville. You're Adrian aren't you?"

Adrian grasped his hand but it was Spencer who spoke first.

"I remember you well, Luke," he said, then turned to direct his next words to Adrian. "Probably the fastest winger around when he played for Bath."

"That's very kind of you to say so, Spencer," Luke said.

"It was a real shame when you were injured. Wasn't it a torn ligament?"

Luke nodded. "Well remembered. I had reconstructive surgery but it put paid to my playing days." He smiled. "But today's not about me, it's about Bath's new rising stars." He turned to Adrian. "Are you a rugby fan, Adrian?"

"Very much so. Bath's my team, though I don't get to games as often as I'd like. I used to play as well, not to your standard but in one of the minor leagues."

Luke had already guessed the man was an ex-rugby

player. He had the stocky, powerful build of a hooker, a key role in any team.

"I was a hooker," Adrian went on, confirming Luke's suspicions. "Talking of which, Bath's new hooker is something special, isn't he?"

"I must admit I don't follow the team as much as I ought to," Luke admitted.

"His name's Brian Shepherd," Spencer said, "and he's come on no end in the last twelve months. People are starting to talk about him being an England pick for the next Six Nations."

"He was disappointing last week," Adrian said, shaking his head. "Very disappointing. He let a lot of people down."

"I thought he had a good game," Spencer said.

They continued talking about Bath's previous game for a few minutes, only stopping when Cora appeared accompanied by a man of fifty or so in a tweed blazer. He had matt black hair without a hint of grey and Luke had the sense that it might be artificial.

"Luke," she said. "I'd like you to meet Jeremy Ellis. Like Spencer, he's a Non-Exec on the Fortune Group Board."

"Hi, Jeremy," Luke said, shaking the man's hand. "Good to meet you."

"Good to meet you too," Jeremy said and Luke could have sworn his wig moved slightly as they shook hands. Jeremy nodded to the other two men. "Adrian, Spencer."

"We were saying Bath are strong favourites today," Spencer said.

Cora pulled Luke to one side as the men continued their discussion. "We need to ask them to guess the scorer of the first try," she said in a low voice before pointing to the only other woman in the box who was standing on her own gazing out at the playing area. "That's my third guest. I'll bring her over."

"I'll see if I can find my other guests," Luke said.

He walked over to Fred.

"Any sign of my other two?" he asked.

"Vernon Lancaster's pulled out." He laughed. "Stupid sod did the same as Filcher. Accepted this invitation forgetting about their masonic whatsit."

"And Patrick Casey?"

"He arrived a few minutes ago. I was going to bring him over when his phone went and he stepped outside to take it."

"Who is he anyway?"

"He's Risk Director for Thorney and Budge." He saw Luke's blank expression and added, "They're a hedge fund company. Not a client but they'll be going out to tender soon and Ambrose is keen that we treat them well."

"Right," Luke said.

He was still none the wiser as to what Patrick Casey did for a living, but if Ambrose Filcher, the CEO and founder of Filchers, wanted him looked after then so be it.

"Ah, here he is," Fred said and Luke turned to see a man in his late thirties walking towards them. "Patrick," he went on, "this is Luke."

They shook hands.

"I'm a rugby virgin," Patrick said. "I know it's a game of thirteen a side and that's about it."

"Fifteen a side," Luke said.

"Aye," Fred said. "Unless you're from Yorkshire."

Patrick looked from one to the other, clearly confused.

"Don't worry about it," Luke said and laughed. "I'll explain the basics as we go along. Come and meet the others."

He led Patrick over to Adrian, Spencer and Jeremy who had been joined by Cora and her third guest.

"Maddy," she said, "this is Luke."

"Hi," Maddy said. She was a petite woman of forty or so and had to crane her neck to look up at him. She smiled as she put her hand out. "I thought Adrian was a big lad but you take the biscuit."

Luke shook her hand and returned her smile before introducing Patrick to everyone.

Cora handed each of the guests a match programme. "There's a prize for the person who guesses the scorer of the first try," she said.

"Dinner with the giant?" Maddy suggested, looking up at Luke again.

"No, that prize has already been taken," Cora said with a sideways glance at Luke. "The winner gets a signed rugby ball."

Chapter 17

Brian sat on the edge of the changing room bench and tried to stop his hands from shaking.

Some of his teammates had already changed and were into their warm-up routines. He swallowed, stood up and reached for the familiar blue and white striped shirt and black shorts.

Normally he would be proud to be wearing team colours but today he felt ashamed. He told himself he had no option, but was that genuinely the case? This was his fault, he should never have agreed to what Mr Smith asked in the first place.

"Are you okay?" Ricky said.

"I'm fine," Brian said as he pulled the shirt over his head. He attempted to smile as he put his shorts on. "Nerves before a game as usual. You know how it is."

"Try not to worry. Hopefully, we'll have the edge."

"Right, men," Phil called. "Can I have your attention?"

A hush descended and everyone turned to look at the team coach as he walked to the centre of the changing room.

Brian had a lot of respect for Phil Tudor. He had been a hooker himself for Bristol, but had been Bath Rugby coach for four years since retiring as a player. The team, and Brian personally, had improved no end in that time. This year it was believed that they were in with a chance of winning the Premiership.

"Gloucester are a strong team," Phil began. "They beat Leicester comfortably last week and it's vital there are no fumbles, especially early on. We can't afford to give away easy points."

Phil looked at Brian as he said this and for a frightening

moment he thought he'd been rumbled, but the coach's eyes moved on to others and he realised he was looking at everyone equally.

"A strong start is essential," Phil went on. "I want to see us in their twenty-two from the off." He looked at his fly-half. "Ricky, you're pivotal. You need to get quick ball out to both wings."

"Right you are, Phil," Ricky said.

"And forwards…" Phil looked around at Brian and the other members of the pack, "you're bigger and better than them. Make your strength count."

A few minutes later, Bath's captain led the fifteen players onto the pitch to cheers from the crowd of over 15,000. There were a few boos from visiting Gloucester fans but they were very much in the minority.

Brian looked around the sea of faces. The first ten minutes were what had him on tenterhooks. Once they were out of the way he'd be able to relax.

*

The man that Brian knew as Mr Smith debated whether to turn the television on.

He liked to keep a distance between himself and whichever sports event one of his syndicates was betting on. However, the bets placed on Bath versus Gloucester were high, among the highest ever, and his cut was 30% which meant he stood to win over £100,000 from this one game alone. Only once before had a bet been worth that much to him, a tennis match at Wimbledon where the number seventeen seed had served five double faults in a row.

He also had worries that Shepherd might chicken out again. If the man let him down he wouldn't only lose his cut of the winnings, he'd have to provide a sweetener to his syndicate members. He would also suffer a loss of credibility, and credibility was everything. As things stood, he had people flocking to join the famous Smith syndicates. He had a waiting list, for goodness sake.

No, Shepherd had to meet his end of the bargain.

He relented and clicked the remote control. The screen flickered into life revealing the teams in position ready for kick-off.

*

Luke was standing with Adrian, Spencer, Jeremy and Patrick as Gloucester kicked off to start the match. The fly-half drop-kicked the ball from the centre line into the Bath twenty-two, where it was neatly caught and passed quickly from player to player to the right wing.

For a self-proclaimed Bath fan, Adrian was very quiet as the winger dodged first one tackle and then a second before diving in for a try at the corner.

"Remarkable," Jeremy said. "Good score."

"He gets five points for that," Luke explained to Patrick, "and Bath can get two more points if they kick the conversion between the posts."

"Do they always score so quickly in rugby?" Patrick asked.

It was Spencer who answered. "Not very often," he said. "Under a minute for the first is impressive."

"He did well," Adrian said grudgingly.

"I'm guessing he wasn't your guess for the scorer of the first try," Luke said with a smile.

"Actually, I think he might have been."

The conversion was successful and Gloucester's kick-off was again caught high, this time by the Bath number four. He passed the ball backwards to his scrum-half while still in the air, and the scrum-half threw a long pass right, missing out two players. The outside centre took it cleanly but his pass to the right wing was slightly behind the player and fell into touch.

"Ah," Adrian said, seeming to brighten up. "The first line-out will be a test."

"It shouldn't be," Spencer said. "Brian Shepherd's very reliable."

*

Brian was relieved. There were less than five minutes on the clock and he had his opportunity.

He positioned himself on the sideline as both sets of forwards lined up, then raised the ball above his head with both arms.

He had to get this right. It was the most important line-out of his life.

This is for Kim, he thought as he pulled his hands back and then forwards over his head, launching the ball into the air. It sailed over the heads of the players, but there was a gasp from the crowd as it veered off course.

"Not straight!" The referee called, holding his hand in the air.

Thank goodness, Brian thought but said, "Sorry, guys," and held his hand up in apology.

The players lined up again, this time with Gloucester awarded the throw-in. Brian crouched down about three yards from the line, his usual position for an opposing team's lineout. As the ball was sent over his head he stepped forward a few paces so that he was in line with the Gloucester forwards.

He was now in an offside position and a penalty should have been awarded to the opposing team, but the referee had eyes only for the players leaping for the ball and hadn't seen him. Brian glanced at the touch judge but he was also looking elsewhere.

"Brian!" one of the Bath props hissed. "You're offside."

He had no option but to step back, his chance gone. He glanced up at the clock. Six minutes had gone. He still had time.

*

"That was uncharacteristic," Spencer said. "Shepherd rarely puts a foot wrong, so to make two errors of judgement in quick succession is not like him at all. Moving into an offside position in that situation was an amateur mistake."

"Offside?" Patrick asked.

Spencer nodded. "The referee missed it, but Shepherd encroached into Gloucester territory before the lineout had ended. It should have been a penalty."

"It wasn't as if he had anything to gain," Luke said. "The ball wasn't likely to come to him."

"He must have been ball-watching," Adrian said.

As he was talking, one of the Gloucester players knocked the ball on and the forwards readied themselves for a scrum in front of the Bath posts. Bath scrummaged well, but when their inside centre received the ball he was tackled heavily to the ground by Gloucester's number eight. Players from both teams engaged above him and attempted to ruck the ball back with their feet.

"Oh no!" Spencer said as the referee blew his whistle, pointed at the players and moved his hand and arm horizontally from side to side.

"What's happened?" Patrick asked.

"Shepherd went into the ruck at the side and gave away a penalty," Spencer said. He shook his head. "He's showing a complete lack of discipline."

"It should be an easy kick," Adrian said.

"You seem pleased," Luke said.

"I'm making an observation, that's all."

Gloucester's fly-half placed the ball on a tee, stepped back, looked up at the posts and then kicked the ball cleanly over the crossbar for three points.

"Eventful start," Spencer said. "Twelve minutes gone and it's already 7-3."

"Twelve?" Adrian said. "Surely they haven't been playing for that long?"

Spencer pointed to the digital display below the roof of the stand opposite. "Almost thirteen minutes now," he said. "The coach will be having a word with Shepherd at half-time," he went on. "He's going to be in trouble, that's for certain."

Chapter 18

He turned the television off and his phone rang immediately.

It was going to be a long afternoon.

He looked at the name on the screen and accepted the call. "Hello, Mr Charteris," he said.

"You said this was guaranteed, Mr Smith," Charteris said angrily.

He bit his tongue. It was tempting to snap back, but Charteris was a wealthy syndicate member and he didn't want to lose him.

"What happened was most unfortunate," he said, "and I assure you I will be taking steps to ensure it doesn't happen again.

"I trusted you."

"You were right to."

"That's two weeks running."

Don't you think I know that you blithering idiot, he thought but said, "Please allow me to offer you a sweetener."

Charteris perked up at this. "What kind of sweetener?"

He sighed. It was against his better judgement to do this, but Shepherd had left him with no option.

"There's a major cycling event in Italy in two weeks. I have a recommendation for you and I'm willing to fund half of your bet."

"And I take all the winnings?"

"Of course."

"This is your final chance."

"I fully understand, but I am 100% certain this will come through."

Charteris considered this for a moment. "Okay," he said. "What's the event and what am I betting on?"

He ran through the details.

"I expect to get odds of 6 to 1," he said when he'd finished. In reality, he anticipated 10 to 1 but there was no reason why his punters had to know that.

"Mmm. Put me down for £20,000."

"I will, Mr Charteris."

"To be clear, that means the bet will be £40,000 at odds of 6 to 1."

The man was driving him up the wall. "Yes," he said, barely able to contain his anger.

"I assume you'll waive your commission, Mr Smith."

"Indeed I will."

The line went dead and less than a minute later the phone rang again.

*

An hour later he was apoplectic with rage, having spent all that time mollifying angry syndicate members.

It had cost him financially and it pained him to creep and crawl. However, what worried him most was the damage to his reputation. He had failed to deliver on his promises for two weeks running, and if word spread around that he couldn't be relied on he could kiss goodbye to everything he'd worked so hard for.

Finding match-fixers wasn't the problem. There were plenty of sportsmen and sportswomen who were desperate for money and prepared to put their principles to one side. However, once recruited he had to be certain they would deliver. It was crucial that they fully understood the implications of letting him down.

He'd thought Darren Jackson's so-called suicide would be enough to guarantee compliance, but he'd been wrong. He needed to send an even stronger message.

And besides, Shepherd had let him down big style and

he deserved to suffer for it.

He could kill two birds with one stone.

He called Artem's number.

"Good afternoon, Mr Smith," Artem said when he answered.

"Shepherd didn't deliver. He needs to pay."

"You mean like Jackson?"

He said it calmly and matter-of-factly, as if he had been asked to run an errand at the supermarket. The man was unbelievably cold and callous, but then that was why he had him on the payroll.

"The message has to be stronger. I don't want a hangman's noose this time." He paused. "His wife too."

There were a few seconds of silence and he thought that he may have misjudged the man, that perhaps this was a step too far even for him.

"That will be forty thousand," Artem said when he came back on the line.

He smiled. He hadn't misjudged him after all. It was a lot of money, but it would be money well spent.

"Very well," he said. "Twenty now and twenty afterwards. I'll transfer the first twenty after this call."

"How quickly do you want it done?"

"As soon as possible."

There was a short pause. "I may be able to do it today," Artem said, "but I cannot promise."

"He'll still be at the ground, but his wife's probably at home with their son."

"Good to know. This is what I am thinking…"

"I don't want the details. Report back when the job's done."

"I will do that, Mr Smith."

Chapter 19

Bath had won the game 35-11, but as they queued for the buffet it seemed to Luke that Adrian Critchley still bore the look of a man disappointed.

"A good win for Bath today," Luke said.

Adrian grunted, reached for some chicken and then sidled off to Spencer's table.

Luke turned to see Patrick standing next to him.

"Thanks for guiding me through the game," he said as he helped himself to some of the beef casserole. "I wouldn't have known what was going on if it hadn't been for you."

"No problem," Luke said, deciding the steak looked too well done and reaching for the lamb instead. "Why did you come today given you're not a rugby fan?"

"My CEO asked me to, well ordered me to really. We're looking to outsource our support functions and he wants me to build a relationship with Filchers, Bannerdown and CNH."

"He's already decided on his short list then?"

Patrick laughed. "He has indeed. He's very much like that."

Plates filled they took them back to a table.

"Fred told me that you're a hedge fund manager," Luke said as they sat down.

"Not quite. I'm Risk Director for Thorney and Budge which is a hedge fund company. We manage portfolios for investors who pool their money. It's the high-risk, high-reward approach that marks it out as a hedge fund."

"I see."

"So what's your role in Filchers, Luke?"

"I'm Head of Ethics."

"Now it's me that's lost."

It was Luke's turn to laugh. "Believe me, you're not alone. My team and I ensure that everyone in Filchers upholds ethical principles in their actions. We deal with accusations of harassment, bullying and misconduct among other things." He decided against adding kidnapping, international terrorism and murder.

"It sounds challenging."

That's an understatement, Luke thought, but said, "It can be."

"Mmm." Patrick put his knife and fork down. "I wonder if you might be able to give me some advice?"

"Of course."

"One of our fund managers has been unbelievably successful in the last few months. On the face of it, that's a good thing, and the sun shines out of his you-know-what as far as our CEO is concerned."

"I sense a 'but' coming."

"You're right. As I said, he's been making incredible profits, but I'm worried that he's investing money unethically or possibly even illegally. I've looked at his portfolio, and everything appears to be above board, but the results are too good to be true. I'm at a loss as to what to do next."

"I take it you can't raise it with your Chief Executive?"

Patrick shook his head. "He likes the profits too much and would prefer to turn a blind eye."

"Why don't I ask one of my team to give the portfolio a once-over?"

"I'm afraid I haven't got a budget."

Luke smiled. "No problem. I'm happy to help, and Filchers is keen to build our relationship with Thorney and Budge, so we'll fund the cost from our sales budget." He wasn't aware that there was such a thing but knew he'd be able to persuade Edward Filcher that the investment was worthwhile.

"Thanks, Luke. I appreciate you helping out. I'll email details of the portfolio to you when I get home."

They had just exchanged contact details when Luke felt a tap on his shoulder. He turned to see a familiar face, albeit one that he hadn't seen for the best part of two decades.

"Good to see you, Phil," he said as they shook hands. He turned to Patrick. "This is Phil Tudor. He's Bath Rugby's coach."

"Hi," Patrick said. "Well done, today."

"Thanks," Phil said as they shook hands.

"How do you know each other?"

Phil smiled. "We played together when we were students and then opposite each other when we turned professional."

Patrick addressed his next comment to Luke. "You didn't tell me you played professionally."

"It wasn't for long," Luke said.

"I still feel bad about that," Phil said.

"No need. It was destined to happen and it was simply bad luck that it happened after your tackle." Luke smiled. "In any case, things turned out pretty well for me after that."

"I'll leave you guys to reminisce," Patrick said. "Thanks for helping, Luke."

"Did you end up marrying that gorgeous blonde you were dating?" Phil said once Patrick had left them. "Jess, wasn't it?"

Luke swallowed and tried to smile. "Well remembered," he said. "I did, yes. But hey, this is about you and today's success. You must be pleased with your team's performance."

Phil shrugged. "Yes and no. It was good to beat Gloucester, but one of our players was a big disappointment."

"I assume you're talking about Brian Shepherd?"

"It was that obvious was it?" Phil shook his head. "I

don't know what got into him. His discipline is normally excellent. I gave him a severe dressing-down at half-time I can tell you."

"I saw he didn't come back for the second half."

"No, I substituted him."

"How did he take it?"

"Pretty badly. He'd already left for home when I got back to the changing room after the game finished."

"Are you going to give him a second chance?"

"Oh yes. He's a good player. Better than that, actually. He's up there with the best hookers in the country."

"It was a surprise to see you, Phil. We were told it would be two players coming up."

"Brian was supposed to be one of them which is why I've come up. Ricky Eastman, our fly-half, is here though. Come and meet him."

Chapter 20

Brian held his phone in his hand as he stared through the car windscreen. He had parked near the racecourse, in a parking area set high above Bath. It was somewhere he and Kim had often visited when they were first going out.

The view was stunning but his thoughts were elsewhere as he anxiously awaited the call that he knew had to come. He'd already checked twice that his phone wasn't on silent but he checked again, then looked at his messages in case he'd missed it.

Still nothing.

He had words ready in his head for when Mr Smith called. He'd say that he'd tried his hardest, that ten minutes was always going to be a major challenge.

Okay, he hadn't managed to concede the penalty within ten minutes but he'd only been two minutes late. Surely, the man would understand that he'd done his best.

Wouldn't he?

He couldn't face seeing Kim until he knew how things stood. He needed to have an answer for her, a way forward. He owed her that much.

His phone rang and he saw that it was his wife.

He hesitated.

This was the fifth or sixth time she'd tried to get hold of him. Should he reject the call again? She was bound to be worried so he ought to answer. He'd have to keep it brief though, so that Mr Smith could get through when he rang.

He accepted the call and put his phone to his ear.

"Hello, Kim," he said.

"Hello, Brian," Artem said.

Brian squeezed his eyes closed. Not again, he thought,

recognising the voice immediately.

"Where's Kim?" he demanded.

"With me."

"Leave her alone."

"Do not worry, Brian. She is fine. We have been having a nice chat and trying to ring you. You are being very evasive."

"Can I speak to her?"

"That will not be possible, no. Not until you come here."

"Where are you?"

"At your home. It is very nice. I am drinking tea."

"What about Max?"

"Your son is asleep upstairs."

"What do you want? Did Mr Smith send you?"

Artem ignored his questions. "Where are you, Brian?" he asked. "You need to come here quickly for the sake of your family. For their health and welfare."

"Let them go. They have nothing to do with this."

"You have disappointed Mr Smith and you must explain yourself. How far away are you?"

"I can be there in ten minutes."

The line went dead.

Brian threw his phone onto the passenger seat and started the engine.

Why, oh why, hadn't he gone straight home?

If that man did anything to Kim or Max he didn't know what he'd do.

He was breathing heavily, his heart thumping against his chest, as he drove down the hill towards the centre and then up to the Bear Flat.

A few minutes later he pulled up outside his house and practically ran to the front door.

"Kim!" he called as soon as he opened it.

His call was met with silence.

"Kim!" he repeated, louder this time.

Still nothing, and he'd shouted so it ought to have woken Max. Had the man been telling the truth, or was he now holding his son prisoner alongside his wife? Or worse, had he hurt one or other of them?

He raced down the hall to the kitchen, pushed the door open and wrinkled his nose as a smell hit him. It was oddly sweet, sickeningly dry, and almost metallic.

He glanced around the room, saw nothing and was about to leave to look in the lounge when it dawned on him that he couldn't see the floor behind the kitchen island.

She couldn't be there, could she? The man in the balaclava mask had said she was fine, so surely...

Brian swallowed as he took a step forward.

What he saw took his breath away.

He put his hands to his mouth as the prone figure of his wife came into view. Her face was facing away but the back of her head lay pooled in blood.

He started to bend to her when he heard a voice behind him and turned.

"I bring a message from Mr Smith," Artem said. He was holding a gun and raised his arm so that it was aimed at Brian's forehead.

"You bastard," Brian said.

They were his final words.

Chapter 21

The Boater was busy when they filed in after leaving the Recreation Ground. Luke waited to be served at the bar while Fred led the group to the garden to find somewhere to sit.

Fred returned a couple of minutes later.

"Not easy fitting a dozen of us in," he said, "but I've found a couple of tables. They're not reet big but they'll do and I've got everyone's order. How are you getting on with your guests?"

"Adrian Critchley's hard work," Luke said. "The game seems to have got him down for some reason, even though he's a self-obsessed Bath fan and they pretty much thrashed Gloucester."

Fred nodded. "I noticed that. What about Patrick?"

"I like him, but I could do with your advice. He's asked if I can help with an issue at his company but he's got no budget."

"I'd run it past Ambrose if I were you. As I said earlier, he's keen to court them so I'm sure he'll give you the go-ahead."

"Good idea. I'll do that."

"What can I get you?" the waitress asked.

They placed their order and Luke and Fred took a tray each into the beer garden at the back of the pub.

The others had divided themselves across two picnic benches. Fred joined his group and Luke squeezed in next to Cora. On her other side was Patrick, while Adrian, Spencer, Maddy and Jeremy sat opposite.

"Spencer was telling me more about your playing days," Cora said as she took her glass of red wine from the tray and passed the other drinks out. "He said that it was the

Bath coach who put an end to your career with a vicious tackle."

"I'd say it was over-eager rather than vicious," Luke said. "Phil Tudor was a great player and it was bad timing rather than anything else. In any case, it turned out for the best. Becoming a police officer was one of the best moves I've ever made."

Adrian, who had been looking into his drink, lifted his head as Luke said this, but it was Patrick who spoke.

"You didn't mention you'd been in the police," he said. "That must have been a complete change of direction from professional rugby."

Luke smiled as he took a sip of his cider. "It was, yes."

"And now you've made another leap, this time into the private sector," Spencer said. "That must have come as a shock."

"You'd be surprised how similar it can be. What about you though? Going from being a sports commentator to owning your own betting company was a dramatic change."

Spencer frowned. "You've been doing your research," he said.

"It sounds like gamekeeper turned poacher," Patrick said and laughed.

Spencer glared across at Patrick. "Not at all," he said angrily. "Are you suggesting betting is like poaching?"

"No, I…" Patrick started to say.

"I always put a tenner on the Grand National," Maddy said in a clear attempt to lighten the mood.

"Do you study the form and choose that way?" Cora asked.

"No. I look for a name that appeals. This year I went for a horse called 'I am Maximus'."

Cora laughed. "Let me guess," she said. "Was it because you like Russell Crowe?"

Maddy returned her laugh. "Got it in one."

"That's not a very scientific approach," Adrian said.

"My horse won though," Maddy said with a smile, "and in any case I only do it for fun. Gambling can be addictive, can't it?"

"It can," Jeremy said, "but we have a helpline and support structures if it becomes an issue."

"We?" Patrick asked.

"Adrian, Spencer and Jeremy work for Gambet," Cora said. "It's one of the UK's leading gambling companies."

Patrick nodded. "I see." He turned back to Adrian, tapped the side of his nose and smiled. "So when you said Maddy wasn't being scientific, was that because you use insider knowledge when you bet?"

It was Adrian's turn to glare. "What are you suggesting?" he demanded.

Patrick held his hand up. "Sorry," he said. "I didn't mean to offend you. It was a joke."

"Accusing me of being a cheat is not very funny."

There was an awkward silence for a few seconds before Maddy again stepped in. "So what's your job at Gambet, Jeremy?" she asked.

"Spencer and I are Non-Executive Directors. It's a part-time role. I spend most of my time running my organisation."

"Is that also a gambling company?"

"No, we're in financial services."

"That's interesting," Patrick said. "I work for a hedge fund company so perhaps our two organisations have worked together. What's the name of your company?"

Jeremy snorted. "It's highly unlikely we've worked together. I work in the upper end of the sector."

"The upper end?"

Jeremy looked pointedly at his watch. "It's time I was off. Thank you, Cora." He stood and walked away without another word.

"Spencer," Adrian said as he also got to his feet. "Shall we?"

"Yes, I think so," Spencer said.

"Was it me?" Patrick said after the two men had left.

"I wouldn't worry about it," Luke said. He turned to Maddy. "You work for Supracom don't you, Maddy?" he asked. "What's your role?"

The next thirty minutes passed pleasantly enough and it was approaching seven o'clock when Patrick stood up.

"I need to leave," he said, "or I'll miss my train. It's been good talking to all of you. Luke, I'll email you as soon as I get home. Thanks for saying you'll help."

"No problem. I'll give you a call on Monday."

"I'll walk to the station with you if that's okay," Maddy said. "Are you on the London train?"

"Yes. You too?"

"No. I live in Oxford but my train's at half past."

Cora turned to Luke once the others had left.

"I've been thinking about our arrangement for dinner," she said. "I don't think tomorrow night's a good idea."

Luke felt his heart sink and he realised how much he'd been looking forward to their date. "That's okay," he said, trying to keep the disappointment from his voice.

Cora put her hand on his, looked into his eyes and smiled. "No," she said. "I don't think I could bear to wait another twenty-four hours."

"Am I interrupting summat?" Fred asked.

Luke looked up to see the Head of Marketing beaming down at him.

"Just popped over to say goodbye and thanks for hosting today," Fred went on. "My lot have gone and I'm off now as well. Have a good evening, you two."

"Your choice then," Luke said, once Fred had left. "KFC or Burger King?"

Chapter 22

Sam was nervous. What if this guy was boring like Elmo or, worse still, totally self-obsessed like her ex-boyfriend Tony? He'd sounded pleasant enough on the phone, and he was definitely eye candy, but the photo could be a decade old for all she knew.

She stopped a few yards ahead of The Salamander, turned to look at her reflection in a shop window, and brushed away an invisible bit of fluff from her shoulder.

Come on Sam, she thought. *You can do this.*

She took a deep breath then walked the short distance to the pub, put on her best smile and pushed the door open.

Ollie was standing at the bar, a pint glass in his hand as he talked to the barman. He was exactly as he'd looked on his Hinge entry, more handsome if anything.

He turned and smiled. "Hi, Sam," he said and put his hand out. "I guess, do we... Oh, what the hell." He bent down and kissed her on the cheek. "What will you have?"

She returned his smile. "Prosecco, please."

He ordered her drink, handed it to her and led the way to a small table at the back of the pub. She sat with her back to the wall and Ollie took the chair opposite.

There was an awkward silence for a few seconds and then they both spoke at once.

"I wonder..." she began as he said, "These first..."

They both stopped mid-sentence and laughed.

"After you," Sam said.

Ollie smiled. "All I was going to say was that these first dates are always difficult."

"It's not easy, is it? Have you had many then?"

"Three."

"Oh. I'm a…" She almost said 'virgin' before thinking better of it. "I'm a first-timer."

"I guess it's a case of talking and seeing if we click. You know, whether there's any chemistry."

"And was there? With the other three, I mean?"

"Oh yes," he said, a sincere look on his face. "I married all of them."

Sam chuckled. "But seriously?"

He held up the thumb of his left hand. "Number one talked about nothing but her ex the entire evening." He raised his index finger. "Number two declared after five minutes that she couldn't cope with my accent."

Sam raised an eyebrow. "But you don't have much of an accent."

Ollie smiled and shrugged. "What can I say?" He raised his middle finger to join the other three. "And number three didn't want a relationship."

"What did she want?"

"What do you think?" He smiled wryly as he waved his hand up and down in front of his body.

"Oh. I see."

"That's enough about me." He took a sip of his lager. "Your profile said you're an ethics accountant. What's one of those?"

"You wouldn't rather talk about my ex-boyfriend?"

It was his turn to chuckle.

"I'm not really an ethics accountant," she went on. "I work in an ethics team, and I'm an accountant by trade, but my job is more about people than numbers." She explained about Filchers, and how the team dealt with accusations of harassment, bullying, misconduct and so on.

"It sounds like interesting work," he said when she'd finished. "Have you got a good boss?"

"Ah…"

"You don't seem sure."

"No, he's excellent. Very supportive."

"That's good. Is the job at all dangerous?"

Sam shook her head. "Not at all," she lied, thinking back to her broken leg and her relationship with a potential terrorist. "What about you? You were very vague on Hinge about your job."

"I'm a professional masseur."

"You are?"

Ollie laughed. "No. I'm a cyclist."

"That's your job?"

"Don't sound so shocked."

"I'm not shocked. A little surprised, but not shocked."

"I've been pro' for over a decade. It hasn't made me rich, but I do okay." He shrugged. "Of course, that won't last. I'm thirty-five so I've probably got another five years at the most."

They continued talking and Sam found herself warming to Ollie. He had a great sense of humour and was a good listener. What he wasn't was self-obsessed which was a relief.

She realised that he'd finished his drink.

"What are you drinking?" she asked, pointing to his glass.

He looked at his watch. "We ought to be going," he said. "The table's booked for eight and it's eight now."

"Is it far?"

He smiled. "Not very, no." He led her to the front where he opened the door to let her through. "Thanks," he said to the waiter as he followed her out.

"Which way?" she asked.

He walked to the door of the building next to The Salamander, opened the door and bowed. "Dopo di voi, signora."

"She stood back to see the sign above the window read 'La Terra'."

"Italian, I assume," she said.

"That's okay, isn't it? I should have asked."

She shook her head. "I don't eat Italian food on principle."

"Sorry, I…" He saw the look on her face and the corners of his mouth turned up. "Come on," he said and grabbed her hand to take her inside. It felt odd for a second but it also felt comfortable and she realised that she was already growing to like him.

"I booked a table for two for eight o'clock," Ollie said to the waiter, "in the name of Ollie Green."

While the waiter looked his name up, Sam cast her eyes around the restaurant. It was simply decorated and classy but in an understated way. She moved out of the way as a waitress passed with two plates of delicious-looking pasta and carried them to a corner table where a couple were laughing as they clinked glasses.

Sam thought she recognised the woman. She was forty or so with wavy dark brown hair and was smiling adoringly at the man facing her. She could only see him from the rear but…

She put her hand to her mouth.

Of all the restaurants in Bath, why did he have to come here?

"Are you okay?" Ollie asked, putting his hand on her shoulder.

"Sorry. Yes, I'm fine."

"We're over here."

He led her to a booth and she took the banquette facing Luke and his date.

No, date wasn't a strong enough term for it.

She was a long-term girlfriend. You only had to see the way she was looking at him to know that. She kept leaning forward to touch his hand as well.

They were serious about each other.

He'd certainly kept that a secret.

She remembered who the woman was now. She was fairly high up in Filchers, a Client Director perhaps. A lot more senior than Sam, that was for certain. Her name was Keira. Or Corrine. Something like that.

"I said shall we order some wine?"

She blinked her eyes and looked across at Ollie. "Sorry," she said again. "I was miles away. Yes, that would be great."

"You look like you've seen a ghost." He half-turned in his seat. "One of your ex-boyfriends isn't here is he?"

"No," she said quickly and laughed. "Definitely not. I was daydreaming, that's all."

The waiter approached and handed them each a menu.

"Shall we have a bottle of the Pinot Grigio?" Ollie asked.

"Yes," she said. "That would be lovely."

Ollie passed the order on and Sam lifted the menu to her face.

She stared blankly at the main courses.

Should she have told Ollie her boss was in the restaurant?

No, of course not. What would be the sense of that?

What if Luke saw her? What should she do then?

She shook her head.

This was stupid. She needed to stop thinking about her boss and focus her attention on her date.

She leaned over the table and put her hand on his. "I'm enjoying this evening, Ollie, and this restaurant is lovely."

"I try my best," he said and squeezed her hand. "I think this might be a case of fourth time lucky."

Chapter 23

Luke walked Cora back to her apartment on Julian Road. She looked up at him and smiled as she fumbled for her keys.

"Do you want to come in?' she asked.

He hesitated, but only for a second. "I won't thanks. It's late and I need to get a taxi home."

"You can stay, you know."

"Cora, it's been a lovely evening, but…"

"You don't find me attractive?"

"No. It's not that at all." He paused for a second. "I'm sorry, but I don't think I'm ready for a relationship."

She smiled up at him and stood on tip-toe to kiss him on the cheek. "Don't worry. I understand, but if you change your mind I'd love to do this again."

"Thanks, Cora. Goodnight."

"Goodnight, Luke."

He watched as she walked to the door, turned to smile at him and then disappeared inside.

As Luke headed for the taxi rank on George Street he wondered if he'd done the right thing. He liked Cora, he liked her a lot. She was attractive and good fun so why had he rejected her? Was he really not ready for a relationship, or was there something else?

Or someone else?

His thoughts turned to Sam.

She was every bit as attractive as Cora, more so if anything, but there was something else. He felt a genuine connection, a bond. She was someone he could share confidences with, who understood him and cared what happened to him. He cared for her too.

He stopped in his tracks.

This was stupid. He needed to make his feelings for Sam clear. What was the worst that could happen? He'd almost asked her on a date at Josh's flat-warming party but had chickened out.

He needed to act, and there was no time like the present.

He pulled his phone out and was about to retrieve Sam's number when there was a ping and he saw he had a message from Cora. Was she upset after what he'd said?

He clicked to open it but the text wasn't at all what he had expected.

'*Have you seen the news?*'

He frowned, closed the message, opened the BBC News app and read the headline.

Breaking News
Rugby star and wife found dead…

He clicked to read more.

Two people found dead from gunshot wounds earlier this evening have been named as Brian and Kimberley Shepherd. Brian Shepherd played professional rugby for Bath.

Their families have been informed.

Police have said that they are not looking for anyone else in connection with their deaths.

More information as we receive it.

He was appalled. He hadn't met Brian Shepherd but the way Phil Tudor had talked about him made him seem well-grounded. If that was the case then this was totally out of character.

The police weren't looking for anyone else which suggested to Luke that it was either a joint suicide or a murder-suicide. Either way, the reason had to be a lot more than poor performance in a rugby game.

Perhaps Brian and his wife had a major falling out and the situation escalated, possibly because they had financial difficulties or one of them was having an affair. It would be important to hear views from friends and family on the state of their marriage and their general well-being.

Evidence from the crime scene investigators would be crucial. He'd be wanting to know what they'd concluded based on things like the nature of the injuries, blood spray patterns and the positions the bodies were found in.

The gun had to be still at the scene so it would be imperative that they find out how it had been obtained, whether through a license or illegally. If illegally then who was the intermediary? He'd want his team out talking to the usual suspects and also tapping up informants.

Then there was the post-mortem. That would reveal whether there had been injuries before the fatal shots, suggesting a confrontation or a fight in the lead-up.

Luke half-smiled as he realised he was thinking as if he was the SIO.

Those days were long gone.

He was Head of Ethics in a private sector company and major investigations were part of his past.

It was only when he climbed into a taxi that he remembered he was going to call Sam. He looked at his watch, saw it was nearly half past ten and shook his head. No, much better to leave it until Monday when he could ask her face-to-face. It wasn't the kind of thing to do over the phone, and in any case it was late on a Saturday night and she was doubtless out enjoying herself.

Chapter 24

"Thanks for walking me home," Sam said. "I had fun this evening."

Ollie shrugged. "It was one of my better first dates," he said.

She punched him on the arm. "Hey, I'm a black belt, remember. You'd better be careful." She pulled her key out of her bag.

"Sam," he said. "I was wondering…"

Please don't ask if you can come in. I'm looking for a relationship not a fling.

"I know we only met this evening," he went on, looking suddenly nervous, "but do you want to meet up tomorrow?"

She raised an eyebrow. This wasn't what she had expected him to say.

"Sorry," he said quickly. "It's too soon. I'm being forward."

She stood on tiptoe and kissed him on the lips. After a few seconds she pulled away and smiled up at him. "That would be lovely," she said. "Where were you thinking?"

"Do you know Stockhill Woods?"

"Is that where mad axemen take their victims?"

"That's the one. It's also great for a walk, particularly at this time of year. As long as you like moss and toadstools that is."

"I love them."

"Great. Pick you up at two?"

"It's a date."

This time it was Ollie who leaned in for a kiss.

*

Sam hadn't long been awake, and had only just made herself a coffee, when Hannah rang.

"Well," she said as soon as Sam answered. "How did it go with Ollie?"

"I like him. We had a good time and he's got a great sense of humour and he's...."

"...as fit as he looked in his photos?"

"Hannah!"

"Well?"

"He looks good, yes."

"How does he compare with Luke?"

"That's hardly relevant."

"Mmm. I'll take your word for that." Hannah paused. "So, next step Joe or are you going to see Ollie again first?"

"I'm seeing Ollie this afternoon."

"Wow! You must have got on well."

*

It was twenty past two and Sam was beginning to fear that Ollie had changed his mind. Either that or he'd had an accident. She had just decided to give him until two-thirty when the doorbell went.

"I'm sorry," Ollie said when she opened the door. "A friend of mine's having a crisis. I'll explain in the car."

She followed him out to his silver Audi.

"Subtle," she said when she saw '*Oliver Green, Professional Cyclist, Sponsored by Savills*' emblazoned on the side of the car in large red script.

"My sponsor insisted but it does mean I get the car for free."

"Worth it then," she said. "And the bonus is that you

can become an estate agent when you retire from cycling."

"Ha, ha." He put the car into gear and they set off. "We should be there inside forty minutes."

"So, what's happened to your friend?"

"He's been stupid." Ollie sighed. "He bet on himself in a race earlier this year."

"Isn't that allowed?"

"It's completely against the rules. What's worse is that it was a spot bet and he fixed it so that he'd win."

"You've lost me. What's a spot bet?"

Ollie laughed. "To be honest, I didn't know until Sean explained it to me. Apparently, a spot bet is where you bet on a detail of the game rather than the overall result. What Sean did was to bet on himself to come in the top twenty but outside the top ten in one of the stages."

"That sounds ambitious."

"Not for Sean. He's very good and chose a stage where he expected to come in the top ten. All he had to do was slow down towards the end."

"Has someone noticed and reported him?"

"No. It's more complicated than…"

Ollie stopped as his phone rang and the message 'Sean Abbott calling' appeared on the console. "That's him now. Do you mind?"

"Not at all."

Ollie clicked the button on the steering wheel to accept the call.

"Hi, Sean," he said. "I'm in the car and Sam's with me."

"Hi, Sam," Sean said. "Ollie told me all about you earlier."

"Hi," Sam said and then mouthed "All about me?" to Ollie.

Ollie smiled, shrugged, then said, "So what's up?"

"Mr Smith has rung me again, and he's putting pressure on."

"What's he said?"

"He's offered me £4,000 to stage an accident in the last hour of Il Lombardia. There have to be at least five cyclists involved."

"You need to say no."

"I tried to but he knows what I did at the Tour de Pologne and he's threatening to tell the UCI."

"You know what I think, Sean."

"But it's my career on the line."

"If you do this, he'll ask again. There'll be no end to it."

There was a pause before Sean replied. "You're right. Of course you are. I'll contact him now."

"Let me know how you get on."

"I will."

Ollie ended the call and shook his head. "What an idiot."

"UCI and Il Lombardia?" Sam asked.

"UCI's the world governing body for cycling and Il Lombardia is the final race of the season. It's on Saturday week."

"I see."

"Sean's a good mate and I've known him since Uni. If this Mr Smith guy tells UCI then he's done for. They have zero tolerance for cheating."

"You were right to tell him to say no."

"He has to. Slowing down in a race is one thing but bringing down other cyclists by staging an accident is totally out of order." He paused. "I bet your friends are a lot more straightforward."

"I don't know about that. Hannah's going out with someone from Sesame Street."

"Kermit?"

"No, Bert. And I once had a date with Elmo."

They continued talking and before she knew it they were pulling into the parking area at Stockhill Woods. Ollie put the handbrake on and had just undone his seatbelt when the phone rang.

"It's Sean again," he said. "Sorry."

"Don't be silly."

He accepted the call.

"Christ, Ollie," Sean said and he sounded much more fraught this time. "This is getting heavy."

"What's happened?" Ollie asked.

"He's made threats."

"You said that before."

"No, he's…"

The line went silent.

"What has he said?" Sam asked.

"Oh, Sam. I forgot you were there. I'm sorry to bother you with my problems."

"Don't be silly. What's happened?"

"He started talking about Kirsten, my partner. About how…" The line went silent and Sam and Ollie exchanged a look as they waited for him to continue.

After a few seconds, Sean came back on the line and there was a quaver to his voice as he continued. "He said Kirsten was beautiful and it would be awful if her face was scarred."

Sam put her hand to her mouth.

"That's awful," Ollie said. "What did you say?"

"What could I say? I had to say I'd make the accident happen."

"You need to go to the police."

"I can't. He warned me what would happen if I did."

"It might be a long shot," Sam said, "but I could ask my boss if he can help. He used to be a detective."

"I don't know if that would be a good idea."

"Believe me, Sean, he's excellent and he's very discreet."

"It's a good idea," Ollie said. "What have you got to lose?"

There was another silence. "Why would he want to help me?" Sean asked after a few seconds.

"It's the sort of thing he does," Sam said. "He's

wonderful like that. I'll talk to him in the morning."

"Are you sure your boss won't mind?" Ollie asked, once the call had ended.

"Not at all. Luke was in the Major Crimes Unit at Avon and Somerset Police so he's got experience of this kind of thing."

"It sounds like you've got a lot of time for him."

"I have, yes. He's been very helpful. I had a rough time at work and when he joined Filchers he was kind of landed with me but he's been incredibly supportive."

"Does he live in Bath?"

"No, he's in Norton St Philip. Do you know it?"

"It's got one of those pubs that claims to be the oldest in England, hasn't it?"

"That's right. The George." She laughed. "Mind you, Luke's house is almost as old. It's a rambling farmhouse called, aptly enough, 'The Old Farmhouse'. It's a massive place given it's just him that lives there."

"He's single is he?"

"Yes. His wife died last year. Anyway, enough about him. Let's go and see these fungi you were raving about."

Chapter 25

Luke was pleased to be able to park directly outside the Good Bear Cafe in Hayes Place. He went inside, ordered two coffees and took them to one of the tables at the side.

True to form, his friend and ex-colleague Detective Inspector Pete Gilmore appeared a few minutes later at precisely 8:30.

"Thanks," he said as he took the chair opposite Luke and picked up his latte. "Good weekend?"

"Interesting," Luke said, electing not to mention his date with Cora. "I went to see Bath on Saturday. It was a good game but completely overshadowed by what happened to Brian Shepherd and his wife afterwards."

"Tell me about it." Pete took a slurp of his coffee and grimaced. "Believe me, Janice was none too pleased when I got the call to come in on Saturday evening."

Luke thought that might have been the case. Pete Gilmore was in Avon and Somerset Police's Major Crimes Unit, and as such was highly likely to be summoned in if there was a potential double murder.

"The media seem to think it was a murder-suicide or double suicide," he said.

Pete nodded. "It looks that way."

"Did they have any children?"

"A son aged two. He was out of the house when it happened, on a play date. It was his friend's mother who found the bodies."

Luke shook his head. "Poor kid."

"Yes, it's terrible." After a short pause, Pete called over to the waiter. "Can we have our usual breakfasts please, Mauro?"

"Of course, Pete," Mauro replied. "With you in ten."

"Have you had reports from scene of crime and the post-mortem?" Luke asked.

"We've had an interim summary from the SOCOs and the pathologist, and they've promised their full findings by close of play tomorrow. The gun's being analysed by the lab today."

"That's good. So I guess your next step will be to delve into the couple's relationship and their financial situation to try to uncover the motive."

Pete laughed. "You're not my boss any more, Luke."

Luke held his hand up. "Sorry. I guess old habits die hard."

"However," Pete went on, "you're right of course. The team will be on that today. From what the preliminary reports say my guess is murder-suicide."

"Brian Shepherd killed his wife and then turned the gun on himself?"

Pete nodded. "Her position on the floor suggests she wasn't a willing victim."

"Did either of them leave a note?"

Pete laughed again. "Close friends we might be, Luke, but you know I can't share that kind of information with you. Ah, here's our grub."

Luke smiled to himself as Mauro placed their full English breakfasts in front of them. He felt sure from Pete's reaction that there had been a note. What's more, its content must have been crucial in persuading him, and presumably the rest of the team, that no one else was involved.

He'd like to know more but Pete was right. He wasn't in the police any more and should stop asking questions as if he was the senior investigating officer. He had enough challenges facing him at Filchers and needed to concentrate on those.

Chapter 26

Luke turned into the corridor leading to the Ethics Room and almost literally ran into Josh.

"Sorry, guv," Josh said. "I'm getting the drinks. Double espresso?"

"I'd love one thanks. Is everyone else in?"

Josh nodded. "Certainly are." He lowered his voice a touch and looked both ways before continuing. "Do you want to hear some gossip?"

"No."

Josh ignored him. "I overheard Sam telling Helen about this guy she's been seeing. It sounds like she's smitten."

"Is she?"

"It seems like it. I got the impression they've been going out for a while but she's been keeping it quiet in case it didn't go anywhere."

"Really?"

"It's good news given everything she's gone through, isn't it guv?"

"Yes, Josh. That's excellent news."

Josh smiled up at him. "I thought you'd be pleased. I don't think she's telling everyone though so best to keep schtum."

"Don't worry. I won't tell a soul."

"Me neither," Josh said, completely disregarding the fact that he'd just done that very thing.

As Josh walked away, Luke reflected on how lucky he was that his most junior team member couldn't keep a secret. It would have been highly embarrassing had he asked Sam out only to be rebuffed because she was in a serious relationship.

"Hi, Luke," Maj said when he entered the Ethics Room.

"Good morning, Maj," Luke said.

He noticed Sam was sitting on the edge of Helen's desk. She looked over when she saw him and beamed. Josh had been right. Her relationship was clearly doing her the world of good.

That was great news.

Wasn't it?

"Could we have a word when you've settled in?" she called.

"Of course."

A few minutes later Sam wandered over and pulled up a chair.

Luke thought of asking her how her weekend had been but decided it would be better to concentrate on work. The last thing he wanted to hear was what a fantastic time she'd had with this man she was seeing.

He hoped the guy was decent and good to her. Her previous partners had not been the best and she deserved better.

"I'd like to accept," she said.

He was momentarily confused before realising she was talking about his offer to make her his deputy.

"That's great," he said. "I'll speak to HR and get the ball rolling."

"There's something else as well," she went on. "A friend of, ah…" She hesitated for a second then seemed to come to a decision. "A close friend of my boyfriend is in trouble."

There it was.

Her 'boyfriend'.

It dawned on him that Sam had to have been going out with this guy for many weeks. Ben hadn't been prepared to call Pippa his girlfriend until they'd been going out for over three months.

"What sort of trouble?" he asked.

"He's being threatened."

She told him about Sean's bet on himself and the

subsequent invitation to cheat from a man calling himself Mr Smith.

"And yesterday," she concluded, "this Mr Smith said he'd harm Sean's partner if he didn't do as he asked."

"I take it Sean's not prepared to go to the police?"

"No. He's scared as hell." She hesitated. "I said you were ex-police and very discreet. Is there any chance you could help him? It would mean a lot to me and I know Ollie would appreciate it."

"Ollie?"

"My boyfriend."

Luke nodded and attempted a smile. "Ah. I see. Of course."

Ollie, eh? That was a trendy name.

"Ollie and Sean have known each other since University," Sam went on, "and now they're on the Tour together they've become especially close."

"The Tour?"

"They're both professional cyclists."

"Right."

This Ollie character had to be ultra-competitive which would mean he was only out for himself. That had better not extend to his attitude towards women.

"So, what do you think?"

"I'll see what I can do."

"Thanks, Luke."

She gave him Sean's contact details and was about to get up when Luke put his hand on her arm to stop her.

"There's something I'd like you to do for me if you wouldn't mind."

She smiled. "Of course. Anything."

Dump Ollie and go out with me was what he wanted to say but instead he told her about Patrick Casey.

"Patrick is Risk Director for Thorney and Budge."

"The hedge fund company?"

Luke nodded. "Patrick's concerned that one of their

fund managers is investing money unethically or illegally. He's making unbelievable profits but Patrick can't see anything untoward."

"Do you want me to look into his portfolio?"

"Yes, please. I suggest you spend today on it. If you think it warrants more time let me know and I'll ask Ambrose for approval. Patrick's emailed me all the details and I'll forward it to you now."

Chapter 27

Luke forwarded Patrick Casey's email to Sam and was about to contact Sean Abbott when his phone rang.

"Hello, Luke Sackville."

"Hi. This is Yvonne Critchley. You went to the rugby with my husband at the weekend."

"How can I help?"

"I'd like a word if possible. I don't suppose you're free now, are you? I work on the second floor."

"Of course."

Yvonne was standing at the top of the stairs when Luke emerged. A slim, petite woman with a black bob, he found it hard to imagine her alongside the barrel-chested Adrian.

"Hi," she said as they shook hands. She tried to smile but it was a weak attempt and it was clear she was on edge. "I've booked one of our meeting rooms."

She led him along the corridor and opened the door to a typically bland Filchers space with a table, four chairs and magnolia walls on which were three poster-size advertisements for Tom Crowther's summer collection.

Yvonne noticed him looking at them. "They're a nod to the Fortune Group," she said with a nervous laugh.

"So what can I do for you?" Luke asked once they were seated.

She dropped her hands to the tabletop, clasped them together, stared down for a few seconds and then let out a deep sigh. "This is so difficult," she said before lifting her eyes to look across at Luke. "I feel like I'm going behind his back but I'm worried sick about him."

"I assume you're referring to Adrian?"

She nodded. "Yes. Tell me, did you find his behaviour

odd on Saturday?"

"It's difficult to say. It's the first time I've met him."

Yvonne continued looking at Luke and her lower lip started to tremble. She reached into her bag for a tissue and dabbed beneath her eyes. "I'm sorry," she said. "This is hard, but I don't know who else to turn to."

"What's the problem, Yvonne?"

She looked away, fixed her eyes on one of the wall posters and then said, so quietly that Luke could only just make out the words, "He's an addict."

"A drug addict?"

She turned back to face him and shook her head. "To be honest, treatment would be more straightforward if his problem was drugs. No, Adrian has ICD."

"ICD?"

"Sorry." Another nervous laugh. "I've talked to so many consultants that I've got used to their jargon. ICD stands for Impulse Control Disorder. He's a pathological gambler."

"I see. Has he sought treatment?"

"Countless times. He's tried cognitive behavioural therapy, self-help groups, mood stabilisers, anti-depressants, even a residential programme."

"He admits there's a problem then?"

"Oh yes, he knows. It's like alcohol addiction though. The problem never leaves you, all you can do is learn how to live with it." She dabbed at her eyes again. "About six months ago we agreed on a budget for his gambling and I manage the money so that it doesn't spiral out of control. It's still a lot of money each month, but we're both on healthy salaries and with no kids and no holidays it's been manageable."

"What's changed? Has he found additional money?"

"I don't think so. He's had a run of luck lately so he's got plenty of money to bet with. No, something happened on Saturday that left him traumatised. When he left home in the morning he was happier than I've seen him in years, but when he returned he was distraught. I asked him what was wrong but he shouted at me and shut himself away in the study. I've only seen him twice since, both times when he's been grabbing food from the fridge, and both times he refused to speak to me. He slept in our spare room Saturday and Sunday night but I heard him going out this morning."

"Do you know where he is now?"

She shook her head. "That's the problem. I'm worried he's going to do something stupid. I've phoned his office but he's not there and his phone is going straight to voicemail."

She pulled a piece of paper out of her bag and passed it to Luke with shaking hands. "I found this in the waste paper basket in the study after he left."

The note had been crumpled up. Luke flattened it out on the table and read the contents.

HARVEY'S MRS

Sats

Burn free five

Batex pen twenty

Live throw two

He looked up at Yvonne. "Is this Adrian's handwriting?"

She nodded. "Yes. I don't know what it means and I don't know anyone called Harvey let alone his wife, but I thought it might be useful."

"I'll hang on to it if I may."

"Yes, that's fine."

Luke slid the note into his pocket. "Have you told the police he's missing?"

"Not yet. That's one of the reasons I wanted to talk to

you. You used to be a detective, didn't you?"

"Yes, I was in Avon and Somerset Police."

"So, if I tell them will they take me seriously? He's only been gone a few hours."

"They will if you explain the background and that you're worried he might harm himself."

Yvonne sighed. "I'm worried but I'm probably being overzealous. In all likelihood, Adrian is sitting in his car mulling things over and he'll ring me as soon as he's calmed down. If I tell the police, and they barge into his office asking everyone where he might be, he'll go up the wall."

"Have you any idea where he might have gone?"

She shook her head. "Not really, no."

"I take it he took his car?"

"Yes."

Luke sat back in his chair. After a few seconds, he came to a decision.

"I can see you're genuinely concerned," he said, "and I trust your judgement. My view is that you should report him as a missing person. However, if you want me to, I can ring one of my contacts first and ask him to keep an eye on the investigation to ensure they don't go in too heavy-handed."

"Thanks, Luke. That would be very helpful."

"I'll give him the basics then ask him to transfer the call and you can provide all the background information."

He picked up his phone and retrieved Pete Gilmore's number.

"Hi, Pete," he said. "I've got a favour to ask."

"No problem. How can I help?"

"I'm with a colleague and…"

"Just a second," Pete said.

Luke heard Pete say, "It's ended?" There was a pause, then he said. "Oh no. Is she okay?"

Pete came back on the line. "Sorry about that, Luke. I've just heard that one of our officers tried but failed to talk someone out of jumping off the Clifton Suspension Bridge."

Luke felt a sinking feeling in his stomach. "Just a second," he said then covered the mouthpiece and looked over at Yvonne. "I need to talk to Pete about a case we're cooperating on. Would you mind if I step outside for a moment?"

"No, of course not."

Luke left the room and walked a few yards down the corridor to be certain he couldn't be overheard.

"What case is that?" Pete asked when he put the phone back to his ear.

Luke ignored the question. "Is the jumper dead?" he asked

"I believe so, yes."

"Do you know anything else?"

"Just a second. I'll ask."

Pete came back on the line a few seconds later.

"They're still making their way to the body. It was a man. A big guy by all accounts."

"Red beard and curly hair?"

"Why?"

"Please ask, Pete."

Luke paced up and down while he waited, but he knew in his heart what the answer was going to be.

"You were right," Pete said when he returned. "Do you know him?"

"I'm pretty sure it's Adrian Critchley. I'm with his wife now."

"Christ." Pete's next words were to someone else. "Any id yet?" A short pause, then, "Okay. Thanks."

"Well?" Luke asked.

"It's him."

Luke sighed as he glanced down the corridor to the room he'd left Yvonne in. He'd thought the days of breaking bad news to relatives were behind him.

She was going to take it hard.

"His wife will need to identify the body," he said. "Will he be taken to Flax Bourton?"

"Yes."

"Okay. I'll make sure she gets there."

Luke returned to the meeting room. He dreaded what was coming but he had to tell her and he had to do so in a way that left no doubt in her mind. This was not the time to sugar-coat anything.

Yvonne gestured to the phone in Luke's hand as he walked in. "Weren't you going to keep the call open for me?" she asked.

Luke sat down opposite her. "I was, yes," he said, "but I'm sorry to say I've received some very bad news."

She looked across at him and her eyes started to well up. "About Adrian?"

"I'm sorry, Yvonne. His body's been found beneath Clifton Suspension Bridge."

She put her hand to her mouth. "No! It can't be!" She continued staring. "Are you sure? Could it be someone else?"

"They found his wallet. It's definitely him."

She started breathing heavily, the tears falling freely.

"Is there anyone I can call?'" Luke asked. "Have you got relatives nearby, or close friends?"

"My sister lives in Bath. I, ah…" She fumbled for her phone, searched for a name and then passed it over. "Sheila," she said in a shaky voice. "My sister's name is Sheila."

Chapter 28

The man who called himself Mr Smith swivelled in his black leather office chair, put the lead crystal glass to his lips and took a sip of whisky. It was an 18-year-old Macallan that retailed at £300 a bottle but was worth every penny.

As he swirled the liquid gold around his mouth he looked up in admiration at the dark mahogany panelling of his library. There was no doubt it was elegant and epitomised grandeur, but there was more to it than that.

It spoke of a man who had made it in the world and that was him down to a tee. He was self-made and proud of it.

He reflected on the moniker he had chosen for himself. It was suitably anonymous but also felt a touch downmarket. He would have preferred a name that conjured up a position of superiority, a sense of someone who sat above it all but had their finger on the pulse.

He laughed as he remembered that he had briefly considered 'M' as an option. He wasn't the head of a secret intelligence service but he had an empire and it would have sent the right message to his subordinates. Unfortunately, he had been forced to rule it out. It wouldn't have worked for his clients.

The name wasn't enough on its own of course. He worked according to three fundamental business principles.

First and foremost, he believed in delegation rather than micromanagement. He was careful to recruit people of the highest calibre, people who could perform independently without continually presenting him with problems.

His second principle was accurate and regular reporting.

He insisted on detailed weekly updates so that he could ensure he received his fair share of the profits.

Last, but not least, he believed in transparency and decisiveness. If there were problems they needed to be flagged up and action taken. He did not tolerate people who tried to hide things from him.

His phone pinged and he saw that he had a message from Davison.

'*Now finalising this week's update*,' it said. '*Will email it this afternoon.*'

Davison had performed excellently over the previous few months and he looked forward to analysing his report.

The UK gambling syndicate, on the other hand, was in trouble. Brian Shepherd's failure to deliver on the two preceding weekends had created problems.

He placed his glass carefully on the desk, picked up his phone and retrieved Artem's number, smiling to himself as he did so. He might not be M, and he might not control MI6, but his longest-serving and most loyal subordinate had a track record of success with a very different secret service, having spent seven years in the FSB reporting directly to the Kremlin.

Artem picked up after three rings.

"Good evening, " he said.

"Artem, how did everything go?"

"It went to plan. I took great care and the police have concluded that Brian Shepherd killed his wife and then turned the gun on himself. As you know, I have experience in these matters."

"Good. I plan to use the Shepherds' deaths to encourage others where necessary." He hesitated. "Using violence to reinforce the encouragement may also be necessary."

"For the normal payment?" Artem asked.

"Of course."

"Then that will not be a problem."

Chapter 29

Sam began by researching Patrick and his employer.

She discovered that Thorney and Budge was the fifth biggest hedge fund company in the UK with assets of over £70 million under management.

Patrick Casey's LinkedIn entry revealed that he had worked exclusively for hedge fund companies since leaving university. He had been with Thorney and Budge for two years and had been their Risk Director for six months.

She reread the email from Patrick that Luke had forwarded.

Hi Luke,

Thanks for saying you will ask your expert to cast an eye over the attached investment portfolio.

As I said on Saturday, I am concerned at the profits that one of our fund managers, Adam Davison, is reporting. I fear that he may be investing money unethically or illegally.

Regards
Patrick

Sam smiled to herself when she saw she'd been described as an expert. She was good with numbers but knew little about hedge funds and how they operated aside from the fact that they focused on higher-risk investments.

However, she'd do her best. That was all she could do and it would have to be good enough.

She began by googling hedge funds to find out more about them, then called up Davison's LinkedIn entry. He was thirty-one and had been with Thorney and Budge for nine months, joining them from LAQ Partners where he had risen rapidly through the ranks after joining their Graduate Programme in 2014.

Next, she opened the spreadsheet attached to the email to find it had numerous tabs, forms, tables and entries. It was complex but that was to be expected and she relished the challenge of getting to grips with it.

She began by finding her way around, making notes as she went.

An hour had passed when she realised Maj was talking to her and looked up to see him staring at her laptop screen.

"That looks complicated," he said.

She smiled. "It is, but I'm beginning to get a handle on how it works. This…" she pointed to one of the tabs titled 'Summary', "…summarises the long and short positions, using factors in this tab…" she clicked another tab titled 'AUM', "…to identify undervalued and overvalued assets. There are some clever macros which…"

"Can I stop you there and ask a question?" Maj asked.

"Of course."

"Do you want a latte, cappuccino or flat white? I'm going to the canteen."

Sam laughed. "Flat white, please." She pointed to the spreadsheet again. "Too much for you?"

"And some." He returned her laugh. "I'd rather wade into those IT reports that Josh and I have been avoiding. Maths has never been my favourite subject."

He returned fifteen minutes later and put Sam's coffee on her desk, grimacing as he glanced at her screen. "Rather you than me," he mumbled as he made his way to his desk. "Rather you than me."

It was another two hours before Sam felt she had got to grips with the myriad of tables, sophisticated formulae and macros. It didn't help that she hadn't heard of any of the sixty-four different organisations that the investments were spread across.

What she needed to do next was review the performance of each company in the portfolio. She'd then be able to review Adam Davison's conclusions and how he had determined whether assets were undervalued or overvalued.

It was clear that this was going to take much more than a day. She needed to flag as much to Luke and decided to have a word with him when he returned from his meeting.

Chapter 30

Luke waited until Yvonne had left for Flax Bourton with her sister and then returned to the meeting room.

He stood at the window, watching cars entering and leaving Filchers' car park as he tried to make sense of everything that had happened.

Three people had died over the previous forty-eight hours. On the face of it, there was little connecting the deaths of Brian and Kimberley Shepherd and the suicide of Adrian Critchley. However, his gut was telling him there was a link, that it was more than a coincidence.

But what was that link?

Both Brian Shepherd and Adrian Critchley had been at the rugby game on Saturday, but in very different capacities and as far as he was aware they had never met.

If there was a connection it surely had to be something to do with the match.

It could be that the pressure and stress of Brian Shepherd's money problems, or difficulties in his relationship with his wife, had driven him to despair, so much so that he killed her before taking his own life. Presumably, these worries also caused him to underperform in the game itself.

Or could it be the other way around?

Was it his disappointing performance in the game that caused him to go off the rails? Phil Tudor had said he was normally reliable and likely to be considered for England soon. Had he thought he'd ruined his chances?

Luke shook his head.

No. Losing the chance of playing for his country surely wouldn't have that much impact on a person.

It also didn't link his actions to those of Adrian.

According to Yvonne, Adrian had Impulse Control Disorder and was a pathological gambler. Had he killed himself because of the condition, or was it because he'd lost a lot of money? Yvonne controlled his budget, but had he borrowed more, placed a large bet on the game and then lost it all, leading him to want to end his life?

He rang Pete.

"Yvonne Critchley is on her way to the mortuary with her sister," he said when his friend answered.

"Okay. Thanks for letting me know."

"Pete, I've been wondering if there's a connection between the Shepherds' death and Adrian Critchley's suicide."

"I don't see how that can be the case. Hell, Luke, I'd be surprised if they even knew each other. One was a rugby player and the other a business manager of some kind."

"Adrian was Director of Strategy for the Fortune Group."

"There you go then. Connecting their suicides is a bit of a long shot."

"They were both at the Rec on Saturday."

Pete laughed. "So were you and fifteen thousand other people." He paused. "We've had Sally Croft's report and she's concluded that Brian Shepherd killed his wife and then turned the gun on himself."

Luke had a lot of respect for Sally who was a pathologist with decades of experience.

"Plus," Pete went on, "and I shouldn't be telling you this so keep it to yourself, his reason came over clearly in the note he left."

"What did it say?"

Pete laughed again. "I've said enough."

Luke ended the call and continued staring out of the window.

His ex-colleague was probably right that the deaths were a coincidence. Sally Croft had concluded that the

Shepherds' deaths had been a murder-suicide, and Adrian had been talking to a PC before he jumped off the bridge, so there was nothing suspicious about his demise.

The fact that they had both been at the game was neither here nor there.

He looked at his watch to see it was almost lunchtime and remembered that he'd promised Sam that he would ring Sean Abbott.

He retrieved her email and entered Sean's number.

"Hello."

"Hello, Sean. My name's Luke Sackville. I work with Sam."

"Oh, hi. Thanks for calling." He hesitated and Luke could sense his edginess. "Sam said you're ex-police but I'm not sure what you can do to help."

"I have to be honest with you, Sean. It may be I can't do anything, but why don't you tell me exactly what's happened and we'll take it from there?"

"I can't go to the police so please don't suggest that."

Luke chose to ignore the comment. "Why don't you start by telling me about this bet you had on yourself?" he asked.

"Did Sam tell you I'm a professional cyclist?"

"Yes, although I have to admit I don't know much about the sport."

"I'm on the World Tour and there are events from January to October each year. Sometimes there's just one race but usually there are a few separate events called stages."

"Like in the Tour de France?"

"Exactly." Sean swallowed before continuing. "In August I was confident of coming in the top five in stage 3 of the Tour de Pologne."

"Top five. You must be good."

"I'm ranked sixteen in the world but that particular stage is very hilly and hills have always been a strength of mine." He paused. "Anyway, the day before the event a man rang me asking if I wanted to make £10,000. All I had to do was finish outside the top ten but in the top twenty on stage 3. He said he'd put a bet on for me at £2,000 and could get odds of six to one. He'd then give me £10,000 of the winnings and keep £2,000 as his commission."

"So you trusted him with £2,000?"

"No. He said he'd place the bet using his money as a gesture of good faith."

"What made you say yes?"

There was another pause. "Greed, I suppose. It didn't seem like I was doing anyone any harm and I thought, why not?"

"And now he's asked you to do it again?"

"Demanded rather than asked. He's told me to stage an accident in Il Lombardia which is a single-race event in Italy the weekend after next. I tried to say no and he said he'd tell the governing body what I'd done in the Tour de Pologne. I called his bluff and that was when he threatened Kirsten."

"Kirsten's your partner?"

"Yes. We've been together six years and we've got a five-year-old daughter."

"What exactly did he say?"

"He said that it would be terrible if there was ever an accident. I asked what he meant and he said there had been an awful acid attack on another woman in London and Kirsten needed to be careful. It was obvious what he meant."

"What can you tell me about him?"

"Not a lot. I've talked to him on the phone a few times and that's it. He calls himself Mr Smith and he sounds English. No real accent though."

"How old would you say he was?"

"Difficult to say, but I'd hazard a guess that he's in his fifties or sixties."

"Sean, try to cast your mind back to the first time he contacted you. Did he say anything about himself?"

"Not really. He said he was a fan, although I can see now that he was just buttering me up. We talked about my top ten finishes for a while and then he said he'd been talking to someone else on the tour and was aware of how expensive it is."

"Did he say who?"

"I'm afraid not. It was when I agreed about the high cost of entering tour events that he broached the subject of the bet."

"Okay. Can you text me his phone number, please? Don't worry, I'm not going to contact him."

"Will do."

"And if you remember anything else about him, no matter how trivial, please let me know."

"I will, Luke. Thanks for this."

Luke hung up and shook his head as he looked down at his negligible notes. All he knew about Sean's blackmailer was that he was possibly in his fifties or sixties, English and called himself Mr Smith. Aside from that and a number he had nothing.

Chapter 31

Luke returned to the Ethics Room and went over to Sam who was flicking through the tabs of a spreadsheet and making notes as she went.

"Is that the document Patrick Casey sent through?" he asked.

She nodded. "I'm getting somewhere but there's at least a week's work in this if I'm going to do a proper job."

"Don't worry, I'll have a word with Ambrose. I've just spoken to your, ah…" He couldn't bring himself to say 'your boyfriend's friend' and concluded with, "…to Sean Abbott. I'm not sure if I can help him, but I'll do my best."

"Thanks." She turned to smile up at him, then her face dropped when she saw his expression. "Are you okay?" she asked. "You look upset."

"It's not been a good morning. I could do with telling the whole team what's happened." He turned around. "Maj, Helen, Josh, could you spare me a moment please?"

They turned around.

"What's wrong?" Helen asked, immediately sensing that he was unhappy.

"I've just come out of a meeting with Yvonne, Adrian Critchley's wife," Luke said. "She asked to see me because she was worried about him. While we were talking we found out that he committed suicide this morning."

There was a collective gasp.

"Where is she now?" Helen asked.

"I called her sister and they've left to identify the body."

"Does this mean we stop work on Project Barney?" Josh asked.

"I forgot," Luke said. "You've been researching him, haven't you?"

Josh nodded. "I've found out quite a lot too."

"Was it definitely suicide?" Maj asked.

"Beyond doubt," Luke said. "A police officer was trying to talk him down when he jumped off Clifton Suspension Bridge."

"How dreadful," Sam said, shaking her head. "His poor wife."

Luke considered this for a few seconds and then turned and glared at Josh. "You're wrong," he said.

"About what?" Josh asked, suddenly on the defensive.

Luke ignored his question and continued, almost to himself. "So's Pete. There's a connection, there has to be. One coincidence I could believe, but two…"

"Eh?" Josh started fidgeting. "Is everything all right, guv? You're scaring me."

Luke continued staring at him for a few seconds and then flicked his fingers. "Sorry, Josh," he said. "I was thinking about what you said."

"About learning a lot?"

"No, about stopping Project Barney. I think we should do the opposite and extend it. Let me explain." He wheeled out the whiteboard. "Did you all hear about Brian Shepherd and his wife?" he asked as he picked up a dry marker and started writing.

"I read about that," Maj said. "Double suicide wasn't it?"

"The police are positive it was a murder-suicide," Luke said, "but I have my doubts."

He finished writing and stood back so that the others could see the whiteboard.

1. *Brian Shepherd, professional sportsman, underperforms, kills himself and his wife.*

2. *Adrian Critchley, gambler, upset during rugby match, kills himself.*

3. *Sean Abbott, professional sportsman, underperforms,
   wife threatened.*

"Are you saying that Sean's problem is linked to the three deaths?" Sam asked.

"Sadly," Luke said, "I'm beginning to suspect that may well be the case."

"Just a second," Josh said. "Who's Sean Abbott?"

"He's a professional cyclist Sam knows," Luke said. "Someone calling themselves Mr Smith is threatening to hurt his partner if he doesn't cheat in a race."

"Shouldn't he go to the police then?"

"Mr Smith has warned him off doing that. I spoke to Sean this morning and he's very scared."

Luke pointed to where he'd written Brian Shepherd and Adrian Critchley. "The police are convinced that these two aren't connected but I had my doubts, and now," he said, pointing to what he had written about Sean Abbott, "I think this confirms my worst fears."

"The obvious connection is sport," Sam said.

"And underperformance by both Shepherd and Abbott," Josh added.

"Good spot," Luke said. "However, unlike Shepherd, Sean's failure to perform was deliberate. He did it to finish outside the top ten because he'd placed a bet on himself."

"Are you certain Shepherd didn't play badly intentionally?" Maj asked.

"I suppose it's possible, although I'm not sure why he would do that. Rugby's a team game and it would be nigh on impossible for a single player to directly influence the outcome." He thought about this for a few seconds. "It would be good to rule it out though. Shepherd was taken off at halftime. Can you look at the footage for the first half, Maj, and see what you think?"

"Will do."

"Why are the police so convinced that Brian Shepherd killed his wife and then himself?" Helen asked.

"A combination of things: they found no evidence of a third party, the gun was in Brian's hand, murder-suicide was confirmed by reports from the post mortem and scene of crime officers…"

"CSIs," Josh added without thinking.

Luke glared at him for a second before continuing. "He left a note as well."

Helen nodded. "That does sound conclusive. I wouldnae mind seeing that wee note though."

Luke gave a dry laugh. "I'd like to see all the evidence," he said.

"Isn't the pathologist a friend of yours?" Sam asked. "Couldn't you ask her to share her report with you as a favour?"

Luke smiled. "Good idea. I'll phone her this afternoon."

"We're going to need a crazy wall for Project Barney," Josh said.

"I hate to admit it, Josh, but I think you're right. Helen, would you mind?"

Helen walked to the whiteboard, rubbed out what Luke had written then wrote 'BARNEY' in the centre in capital letters and next to it 'Mr Smith'. At the top she wrote 'Brian Shepherd', held the pen next to it and looked at Luke questioningly.

"Kimberley," he said.

Helen wrote 'Kimberley Shepherd' next to her husband's name and drew a line between them. She then wrote 'Adrian Critchley' at the bottom left of the board, 'Sean Abbott' at the bottom right and drew a line from Sean's name to Mr Smith. Lastly, she drew a large dotted circle connecting the four victims.

"I'll find photos online and print them off for the board," Josh said.

Helen pointed at Adrian Critchley's name. "What do we know about Adrian?"

Josh immediately put his hand up.

Luke raised an eyebrow. "You're not at school now, Josh."

Josh pulled his arm down and grinned. "I found loads out online," he said. "I even know his shoe size."

"His what? Why would you even…"

Josh started to answer but Luke held his hand up to stop him. "I suggest we work separately now," he said. "Helen and Josh, you complete what you can on Adrian. Oh, I nearly forgot."

He reached into his pocket, retrieved the piece of paper Yvonne Critchley had given him and laid it on the table.

HARVEY'S MRS
Sats
Burn free five
Batex pen twenty
Live throw two

"Yvonne found this in the bin in Adrian's study," he said as they gathered around to read the note.

"Josh and I will see if we can make sense of it," Helen said.

"Thanks." He turned to Maj. "Maj, once you've looked at footage of the Bath Gloucester game can you do some digging to see if you can find anything out about Kimberley Shepherd? At present, we know nothing about her."

"Yes, sure," Maj said, making a note on his pad.

Luke turned to Sam. "I guess you'll need to continue with the Thorney and Budge portfolio, Sam," he said. "I'll speak to Ambrose and ask him to approve your time."

"There's also Douglas Woods," she said. "I need to meet him again."

"Oh yes." Luke turned to Helen. "That reminds me.

Woods and Martin Ribble need to be on the board too with a dotted line to Adrian Critchley."

"Martin was the person who found Adrian's name in the Gambet database, wasn't he?" Helen asked.

"That's right, but when he looked a second time it had been replaced with another name. Martin told me that Douglas Woods was one of only four people who could have made that change."

Helen wrote 'Martin Ribble' and 'Douglas Woods' next to Adrian Critchley's name and drew lines connecting all three.

"It's already looking impressive, guv," Josh said.

Luke stood back and looked at the whiteboard. "There's a lot there," he agreed. "However, we must remember that the police could be right and all we're looking at are coincidences. We have to use the evidence to develop a theory and not force it to fit any preconceived ideas."

Josh nodded knowledgeably. "EBP," he said.

Luke turned to glare at him again. "What?"

"Evidence-based policing, guv. We covered it on that detecting course I did."

Luke frowned and shook his head. "You were misled there, son. Your instructor was well out of date. We dropped EBP a few years ago and now we use LFWFO."

"Gucci," Josh said. He opened his notebook and reached for his pen. "What does LFWFO stand for?"

"Look for what's fucking obvious."

"Look for…" Josh looked up from his pad. "Eh?"

Luke walked to the office door and opened it. "Good luck, everyone," he said. "Let's catch up later."

Chapter 32

Helen was relieved when she saw Ronnie emerge onto New King Street. She looked at her watch, surprised to see it was still only ten to one. She'd been so worried he wouldn't turn up that she'd assumed he'd be late and here he was ten minutes early.

"Hi, Mum," he said as he approached. "Thanks for coming." He gave her a peck on the cheek and then looked around nervously. "I might have chickened out if you weren't going in with me."

"Try not to worry," Helen said. "They won't bite. Remember, you need to tell them everything if they're going to help you." She pointed to the building opposite. "It's over there."

The offices of the charity were somewhat at odds with the other Georgian houses on the street. There was a single door set back between two floor-to-ceiling windows behind which were closed Venetian blinds. Above all of this was a sign with *'Help your Family'* in large blue letters on a white background and beneath that, in a lighter colour blue, *'The Centre for Support and Counselling'*.

Ronnie swallowed. "I don't know. I…"

"Come on." Helen grabbed his hand and led him across the street. She pressed the door handle and they walked in.

A woman in her early forties looked up from her laptop and smiled as they approached her desk.

"Hi," she said. "I'm Fay. How can I help?"

"Hi," Helen said. "I'm Helen and this is my son Ronnie. He's having difficulties at the moment and we're hoping your charity can help. Is there any chance of seeing someone now?"

"Of course." She stood up and opened a door at the

back of the office. "Please take a seat in here and I'll be with you in a minute. Can I get either of you a drink?"

"I'd love a tea," Helen said.

"Nothing for me," Ronnie said.

The room was relaxing, with pale cream walls and three comfy-looking red velvet armchairs around a small coffee table. Helen and Ronnie sat down and a few minutes later Fay returned with a tray and placed it on the table.

She looked at Ronnie "I brought three cups in case you changed your mind," she said as she passed a cup to Helen and then took a cup for herself and sat down to join them. "Help yourselves to milk and sugar." She paused before continuing, her face suddenly serious. "Now then, what's the problem?"

*

It was over an hour later by the time Helen and Ronnie emerged onto New King Street.

She felt the session had gone well. Ronnie had clammed up on a few occasions, but Fay had been skilled at drawing him out and he had given her his full history, some of which had been news to Helen and shocking news at that.

"Well done in there," she said, putting her hand on her son's arm. "That can't have been easy for you."

"She's nice," he said. "I'm pleased you suggested coming."

"Are you okay with a session a week?"

Ronnie nodded. "Yes, I think so." He pulled his phone out of his back pocket. "I'll send Becky a message to let her know how it went."

"I'll walk to your office with you," Helen said when he'd finished.

Ten minutes later they reached Argyle Street and saw Ronnie's boss, Simon Abrahams, standing outside the office speaking on his phone. He was sixty-two, Helen knew, and not much taller than herself, though he carried considerably more weight. She'd met him twice and had a lot of time for him. Although he was an elder, Simon had been very understanding when her son elected to leave the Jehovah's Witnesses, and had allowed him to remain working for him as a clerk.

Simon hung up as they approached, looked at his phone and nodded to himself, apparently pleased with the way the call had gone.

"I'm sorry that took a while," Ronnie said.

"No problem," Simon said. He smiled at Helen. "Hello, Helen."

"Hi," Helen said.

Simon's smile broadened and he held his phone up. "I have had some good news," he said. "Do you have any savings, Helen?"

"A little. Why?"

"I found an excellent investment advisor and I can't recommend him enough. If you don't mind me asking, is your money in a bank account or do you dabble in stocks and shares?"

"In a savings account. Why?"

"You ought to consider what I've done." He lowered his voice. "I invested £20,000 two months ago and it's already earned me £3,600 which I've ploughed straight back in. That's almost 20% profit already."

"Very impressive."

"My advisor gave me a couple of spare business cards. Just a second." He took his wallet out of the inside pocket of his suit jacket, extracted a card and passed it over.

The name on the card was Harvey Robinson, described as 'Investigator and Financial Advisor'. Below the title were his contact details including an address in Oldfield Park.

Helen raised an eyebrow. "Investigator?"

Simon smiled again. "I know it seems an odd mixture

of jobs but believe me he knows his stuff." He leaned forward and tapped the card with his index finger. "Well worth giving him a call if you ask me."

"Thanks, Simon. I might do that." She put the card into her bag but had already decided to throw it away when she had the chance. She was too canny a Scotswoman to risk her hard-earned savings on stocks and shares.

"Excellent," Simon said. He turned to Ronnie. "Come on. We ought to be getting back to work."

Chapter 33

Sam felt that she had finally got to grips with the Thorney and Budge spreadsheet.

The 'Transactions' tab contained details of all the stocks and shares purchased and sold since Adam Davison had set the hedge fund up in early May. They were in chronological order and there were over 5,000 entries with daily transactions for most of the sixty-four companies in the portfolio.

It was clear that he was a skilled Microsoft Excel practitioner. Davison had set up a variety of macros to assess whether shares in the companies were undervalued or overvalued. The results drove further calculations with the output being decisions on whether to hold onto the shares or sell them.

Sam had looked at nine companies so far to check his decisions. She'd tried to minimise the time taken on each one, but had already spent over an hour and a half. At that rate, she'd need more than ten hours to get through the rest, and once she'd done that she needed to cross-tabulate, ensure everything tallied, look back at their performance over the five months, check that against the 'Transactions' tab, then reconcile...

She shook her head.

There had to be a better way of approaching it.

Her phone pinged and she called up the message, pleased to be temporarily distracted. She smiled when she saw it was Ollie.

'Fancy a trip to a pub tonight?'

She did, but she needed to get to grips with the portfolio and it was likely to be a late one. She sent a message back.

'Too much work. Perhaps at the weekend?"

His reply took a while and when it came she was surprised by the tone.

'Sounds like your wonderful boss is a hard taskmaster'

What did Ollie mean by that? She tapped out a message of her own, adjusted it slightly to temper her language, then hit send.

'It's my choice to work late. Cross Keys on Friday?'

The reply came back almost instantly.

'Okay'

Sam sat back and stared at the phone for a few seconds before deciding it was probably nothing to worry about. The reference to Luke as 'your wonderful boss' was most likely a joke, and she already knew that Ollie had a great sense of humour.

She picked up her phone again and sent another message.

'Looking forward to seeing you x'

Again his reply was immediate.

'Me too x Can't wait x'

Two kisses.

That was interesting.

She smiled to herself. Things were moving on apace and why not? He was lovely and they had lots in common. She deserved a serious relationship after all the...

Her thoughts were interrupted by the ringing of her phone and she picked it up to see 'Number Withheld' on the screen. Shrugging, and assuming it was going to be a scam call of some kind, she put it to her ear and waited for the voice to say they were from Santander, or Amazon Prime, or HMRC or some such nonsense.

There was silence at the other end for a few seconds and then she heard a noise that sounded like giggling but could just as easily have been gerbils squealing.

"Hello," she said. "Who's this?"

The giggling continued and she was about to hang up

when she heard, "Say it, Jazelle. Say it."

Sam sighed as she recognised the voice of her ex-boyfriend. She'd removed him from her contacts but hadn't blocked him from calling. An error she would have to remedy.

"Tony," she said. "Is that you?"

There were further small rodent sounds then his girlfriend's voice came on the phone.

"We're tranced," Jazelle said in a voice that mixed gravel with smoke in a none-too-desirable way.

"You're what?"

"Tranced," she repeated. "In Torremolinos."

"You're tranced in Torremolinos?"

"Yeah. Mediation. Hang on…" Sam heard Tony mumble in the background and then Jazelle came back on the line. "My bad. Meditation not mediation. Tantrics too. Like Sting. You should try it, Sammy."

Sam closed her eyes and pinched the bridge of her nose. She had always hated Tony calling her Sammy, and now he had his girlfriend doing it.

"It's hot here," Jazelle went on. "Tony put my bikini on."

"Tony's got your bikini on?"

More cheeping. "Nah, silly. He put it on me."

"Why are you phoning, Jazelle?"

"Is it raining there?"

"No, it's not raining here."

She heard Jazelle move away from the phone and say, "It's not raining there," and then Tony came on the line.

"Hi, Sammy," he said. "I've got my speedos on. They're very tight, know what I mean. I more than fill them."

"At the back?"

"No," he said, taking her question literally and missing the sarcasm completely. "At the front, you know, where my…"

She ended the call.

What had she ever seen in him?

There had been a time when she'd thought Tony attractive, but now the thought of him waltzing around in tight bathing trunks made her feel sick.

It was with renewed energy that she dived back into the spreadsheet, the thought of analysing the performance of another fifty-five organisations suddenly much more enticing. However, she had to find a quicker way. Looking at each company individually was very time-consuming and would take her a couple of days.

Tony's statement 'I more than fill them' made her think about the spreadsheet tab titled 'Diverts' that she had been unable to understand. It was linked in some way to the table of investors, but was jam-packed full of long sets of letters and numbers rather than whole words or formulae. Davison knew what he was doing, so it had to be there deliberately and had to have a purpose.

The title itself was intriguing. Was the tab used to tell him when funds should be diverted from one company to another?

Sam decided she would spend thirty minutes looking at the 'Diverts' tab, and if she was still getting nowhere would revert to the slowly, slowly, catchy monkey approach.

Chapter 34

Ellie, Ambrose Filcher's Personal Assistant, had said that he was free at 2:30 which gave Luke time to ring Sally Croft, Avon and Somerset Police's pathologist.

He found a spare office and was pleased when he got through straight away.

"Luke, my darling," she said. "Long time, no speak. Is my ravishing beauty too much for you to countenance?"

He smiled as he pictured her lounging back on her office's Chesterfield, her curly pink hair clashing with one of her many outlandishly-coloured outfits.

"Definitely too much," he said. "You're also too quiet and withdrawn for my taste."

"Ha, ha. Very funny. So what can I do for you if you don't want my body?"

"I'm ringing to ask a favour. I've got an interest in the Shepherds' case."

"I see." She paused. "A little DI Gilmore-shaped bird told me that you're now a part-time consultant for A and S. Is that what this is about?"

Luke hesitated. "I'll come straight with you, Sally," he said after a few. seconds. "This is my own investigation. Are you performing the post-mortem on Adrian Critchley?"

"The man who jumped off Clifton Suspension Bridge? I am, yes. His widow's just been in to identify the body and I'll be starting on him tomorrow. Why?"

"I believe that the Shepherds' deaths and Adrian Critchley's suicide are connected."

"I take it the police don't?"

"No. However, there are links between them that I believe are more than a coincidence."

There was silence for a few seconds before Sally

continued. "Your own investigation, did you say?"

"That's right."

"I fear there's a chance, Luke, that I misheard you. As a result, I may accidentally email you a copy of the post-mortem reports thinking that you're part of the police investigation."

"That would be terrible."

"It would be, yes."

"Thanks, Sally."

"No problem. Don't be a stranger."

Luke hung up and looked at his watch. It was still only ten past but he decided to return to the Executive Floor in case Ambrose was available before 2:30.

As he approached Ellie's desk, he saw his boss Edward Filcher standing behind her chair glowering at her computer screen. She looked up and heaved a sigh of relief when she saw Luke.

"Perhaps Luke can help," she said.

"Eh! What?" Filcher stood upright and for a second Luke could have sworn his hooked nose wobbled slightly as he glared across at his subordinate. "Bone to pick with you," he said.

"The summary," Ellie reminded him.

"Mmm. Yes." Filcher jabbed his index figure at her monitor. "Do you know, Luke?"

"Know what?" Luke asked.

Filcher sighed in exasperation. "The summary. Where is it?"

"I can't find last month's summary report for Mr Filcher's department," Ellie explained. "I'm sure I filed it but it doesn't seem to be in the folder."

Luke thought about this for a second. "Will it still be attached to Gloria's email?" he suggested.

"Good idea." Ellie clicked a couple of times and then smiled. "Got it! Thanks, Luke."

"I told you it would be somewhere," Filcher said. "Her

email was the obvious place to look."

"Then why…" Ellie started to say before changing her mind. "Is there anything else, Mr Filcher?"

"When will my uncle be free?"

"In the next few minutes but, as I told you, he's seeing Luke."

"Exactly." Filcher turned back to Luke. "That's the bone."

"The bone?" Luke asked, genuinely confused.

Filcher nodded. "Bone of contention. Between us." He pointed at Luke. "You." He gestured to Ambrose Filcher's office door. "Our CEO." He then turned his finger to his own chest. "Me. I'm in between. Not cricket."

"Not cricket?"

"Exactly." Filcher nodded as if Luke finally understood what he was talking about. "You work for me. I work for him."

"I know."

"I need to be there."

"Where?"

Filcher harrumphed and indicated Ambrose's office again. "In there of course. With you."

"I don't think so, Mr Filcher. It would be a waste of your time."

"Not your decision. I decide how to waste my time."

"And mine," Ellie said.

"Eh?" Filcher glanced briefly at Ellie then returned his attention to Luke. "Well?"

"I take it you want to be in my meeting with Ambrose?"

Filcher nodded again. "Yes. In addition, I need a pre-briefing to prepare me."

Luke smiled through gritted teeth. "Okay. I want to see him about…"

Filcher held his hand up to stop him. "In writing."

"In writing?"

"Twenty-four hours in advance."

"But…" Luke was saved from replying by Ambrose emerging from his office.

"Ah, Luke," Ambrose said with a broad smile. "I'm sorry to have kept you. You can come in now." He spotted his nephew. "Edward, do you need to see me as well?"

"Naturally," Filcher said, and there was the slightest hint of a bow as he spoke.

"Naturally?" Ambrose prompted.

"Luke works for me and I, ah… I work for you. You are the Chief Executive."

"I know I'm the Chief Executive. What's your point?"

"It's probably easier if we both come in," Luke said. '*And certainly quicker*' was his other thought but he decided not to voice it.

"Very well," Ambrose said.

Filcher raced forward, almost pushing past his uncle as he dived into the visitor's chair beside the desk.

Ambrose gestured for Luke to go in. "Take a seat on one of the sofas," he said, prompting his nephew to leap out of his chair and rush to the nearest settee.

Ambrose waited until they were all seated, then asked, "Do you want a coffee, Luke?"

"I'm fine thanks," Luke said. "This won't take long."

Filcher nodded approvingly. "Not long," he said.

"It's about Thorney and Budge," Luke began.

"Thorney and Budge," Filcher repeated, nodding his head up and down knowledgeably.

"That's interesting in itself," Ambrose said. 'As you're probably aware, I'm hoping we'll be getting some business from them soon."

"I met Patrick Casey at the rugby on Saturday," Luke said, "and he expressed concern about one of their portfolios. I put Sam onto it this morning."

"Sam's a woman," Filcher said, tapping the side of his nose.

Ambrose ignored him. "Good idea," he said. "She's an excellent accountant."

"The thing is," Luke went on, "she's already spent nearly a day on it but it's clear she's going to need more time. Probably another five to ten days."

"Can't afford that," Filcher said, frowning and shaking his head. "Time is money."

"That won't be a problem," Ambrose said. "They're an important prospect."

Filcher's head faltered mid-shake and he rotated it in a circle once before changing its trajectory to the vertical. "Hot," he said, now nodding again.

Ambrose turned and stared at his nephew as if seeing him for the first time. "Do you need a window open, Edward?"

"Eh?"

"If you're hot…"

"Hah! Not me. Thorney and Budge. Hot prospect. Worth any amount of investment."

"Within limits."

"Exactly. Any amount up to, ah…" He hesitated for a second and then added tentatively, "…limits."

Luke stood up. "Thanks, Ambrose. If it looks like Sam will need more than ten days I'll let you know."

"Me!" Filcher exclaimed. He saw the other men's confusion and added, "Let *me* know."

"So that you can pass the information on to me?" Ambrose asked.

Filcher smiled. "Exactly. Line of command. Good discipline. Otherwise, it's not cricket. Must always…"

"Stop whittering, Edward," Ambrose said without looking at his nephew. "Thanks for taking this on, Luke. Please will you pass on my thanks to Sam?"

"I will."

Chapter 35

Josh and Maj were staring at the whiteboard when Luke returned.

"Any more progress?" he asked.

"We're struggling with that," Maj said, pointing at the note Yvonne Critchley had found.

HARVEY'S MRS
Sats
Burn free five
Batex pen twenty
Live throw two

Luke noted that there were now several photos on the board as well as a few more post-its. "Let's return to it later. First, can you update me on what you've found out?"

"Sure thing, guv," Josh said. "I've been looking into Adrian Critchley. We already knew he was linked to a large bet and that he had a gambling problem. Unfortunately, his social media presence is limited. There are a few photos and no posts on Facebook, absolutely nothing on Instagram and the only entries on LinkedIn are about his career."

He hesitated and Luke could see he was pleased with himself.

"However," Josh went on, grinning broadly, "we're ninety-nine per cent certain he's 'strattyman'."

"Strattyman?" Luke asked.

Josh nodded. "On Reddit. It's an online forum."

"I know what Reddit is, Josh."

"Gucci. Well, Maj and I combined a few things we knew about him to do a smart search and that's how we found 'strattyman'. We're pretty sure it's him aren't we, Maj?"

Maj nodded. "Looks like it," he said. "He's been very active over the last month or two."

"Here's the thing though, guv," Josh said. "His questions have all been about spot-betting."

Sam looked up from her laptop when she heard this. "That's what Sean's involved in," she said. She stood up and joined them at the board. "Was he asking about cycling?"

Josh shook his head. "No, nor about rugby. He was asking about football."

Luke turned to Maj. "Did you get anywhere looking through footage of the Bath game against Gloucester?"

"Kind of," Maj said. "Brian Shepherd was almost hyperactive for the first fifteen minutes or so. He was involved in every play, then he seemed to go off the boil until halftime when he was substituted."

Luke considered this for a moment. "When was the first penalty?"

Maj referred to his notebook. "After twelve minutes."

Luke nodded his head and smiled. "That's got to be it."

"Got to be what?" Josh asked.

Rather than answer, Luke turned back to Maj. "Did you get anywhere researching his wife Kimberley?"

"She was very active on Instagram and posted photos every day. They're family photos and from her comments, and her friends' responses, I think she and her husband were very close."

"Mmm. I suspected as much. I wonder if the Shepherds had financial difficulties and he was promised money if he gave that penalty away deliberately. Look." Luke pointed to the third line of Adrian Critchley's handwritten note.

"You think 'pen' means 'penalty'?" Maj asked.

"It's got to. I'm not sure what 'Batex' means though. Unless…" He smiled again. "Josh, can you look up Bath Rugby's fixture list on your phone and see if they've played Exeter yet?"

"Sure." Josh clicked his phone a couple of times and then nodded. "Yup. Played them in Exeter a couple of weeks ago."

At that moment Helen came in. "Sorry, I'm late getting back, Luke," she said. "I had to go to a meeting with Ronnie." She glanced at the whiteboard and spotted the note. "What's that?" she said, pointing at it.

"It's a note Adrian Critchley wrote," Luke said. "We think it refers to bets he's placed. I'm guessing there was a penalty inside twenty minutes when Bath played at Exeter which explains why he wrote 'Batex pen twenty'."

"I'll check it out," Maj said.

"No, I meant what does that top line mean?" Helen said.

"It's kind of weird isn't it," Josh said. "The wife of someone called Harvey must have been giving him tips, or I guess she might have been his bookie."

Helen pulled a business card out of her bag and passed it to Luke. "It could be a coincidence, but look at this," she said.

"Who's it for, guv?' Josh asked.

"A Harvey Robinson," Luke said as he read what was on the card. "He describes himself as an investigator and financial advisor and he's based in Bath." He looked up. "Where did you get this, Helen?"

"Ronnie's boss, Simon Abrahams. It's nothing to do with gambling though. Harvey Robinson is Simon's investment advisor and Simon recommended I use him for my savings."

"Mmm. It could be a coincidence but it's certainly worth looking into. Josh, could you…"

"On it, guv."

"Football," Maj said triumphantly. He pointed at the note. "Burn is short for Burnley and Live is Liverpool. It's got to be. That would explain Adrian Critchley's Reddit questions."

"That makes sense," Luke said. "Adrian must have been betting on a free kick in the first five minutes of a Burnley game and a throw-in in the first two minutes of a Liverpool game."

"I'll check it out," Maj said.

"Sats must mean Saturdays," Josh said.

"I'm sure you're right," Luke said. "And I suspect," he pointed to the top line of the note, "that 'MRS' is not Harvey's wife. It's more likely that it's 'Mr S'."

"Mr Smith?" Sam said. "The man who's threatening Sean?"

Luke nodded. "Good work, guys. I'll leave you to it. Sam, can you spare me a moment please."

He led Sam back to his desk, leaving Maj, Josh and Helen talking at the whiteboard.

"How are you getting on with the Thorney and Budge portfolio?" he asked.

She smiled. "So-so. It's slow work."

"Ambrose has approved more time. Up to two weeks if you need it."

"That's good. I think I need to meet Adam Davison so I'll give Patrick a call to arrange it if that's okay?"

"Of course it is. I'm sorry, but I haven't had a chance to follow up on Sean Abbott yet."

"Don't worry, Luke. There's no immediate urgency. It's over a week until his race."

Chapter 36

Luke's phone rang.

"Hello, Luke Sackville."

"Hi, Luke," Leanne said. "There are three men in reception asking for you."

"Really? I wasn't expecting anyone."

"They're from The Fortune Group and they say it's important that they see you as soon as possible."

"Okay. Please can you book them in and I'll come down. Do you know if there's a meeting room free?"

"I'll have a look."

"Thanks, Leanne."

Luke ended the call and made his way downstairs, wondering who it could be and what they wanted.

When he arrived at reception the three men were standing in a line facing him as they attached visitor badges to their lapels. He recognised Spencer Howell and Jeremy Ellis but not the third man. He looked in his late fifties and had neatly trimmed salt and pepper hair, although his most memorable feature was a thick handlebar moustache.

"Hello, Luke," Spencer said with a smile when he saw him. They shook hands. "You know Jeremy of course," he went on, "and this is Maurice Brown. He's another Non-Exec."

So this was Maurice Brown, co-owner of SCHBet.

"Hi, Maurice," Luke said, shaking the man's hand. "Good to meet you."

"Good to meet you too," Maurice said. He twisted one end of his moustache. "Thank you for seeing us."

"Not a problem," Luke said. "It was a shame you couldn't make it to the rugby. I heard you fell off a ladder."

Maurice hesitated for a second before replying. "Yes,"

he said. "I was trying to clear a gutter and lost my footing. Still, no damage done."

"I heard you had to go to A&E."

Maurice laughed. "Fortunately, it turned out to be no more than bruising."

"The Royal Crescent Room is free," Leanne said.

"Thanks, Leanne," Luke said.

He led the way to what was Filchers' largest meeting room. It was on the ground floor and had seating for sixteen around a rectangular glass-topped table.

Luke opened the door and gestured for the others to go in first. "Please," he said, "take a seat."

They sat beside each other along one side while Luke seated himself at the head of the table.

"This is quite a delegation," he said. "How can I help you?"

It was Spencer, who was seated nearest to Luke, who answered. "This is a sensitive matter," he said. "It concerns poor Adrian."

"We are aware," Maurice said from the position next to him, "that Adrian's widow shared some confidences with you yesterday."

Luke raised an eyebrow. "Confidences?"

Jeremy, the man at the end of the line of three, nodded. "Yes," he said. "We believe that she told you that Adrian was addicted to gambling."

Luke nodded. "She did, yes."

"He was our Director of Strategy," Spencer said.

"A very senior position in the Fortune Group," Maurice added.

"Very senior indeed," Jeremy chipped in.

This was beginning to feel like a triple act. Luke automatically looked back to Spencer for the next comment and was duly rewarded.

"We cannot afford for that information to get out," Spencer said.

"Awfully bad form," Maurice added.

"Not good for business," Jeremy said.

It was Spencer's turn again. "We came to ask for your assurance you will keep his affliction a secret," he said.

"We're sure you understand," Maurice said.

"It was after all told to you in complete confidence," Jeremy added.

Luke turned back to Spencer but he merely raised an eyebrow and said, "Well? Do you agree?"

"You have my assurance I won't tell anyone," he said.

"Excellent," Spencer said.

"That's good," Maurice added.

"We appreciate it," Jeremy said.

Luke had to bite back a smile as he led them back to reception, shook their hands and watched them leave the building.

He turned to Leanne. "Have you ever seen the film *The Three Amigos*, Leanne?" he asked.

She shook her head, "I can't say I have, no."

"You should watch it," Luke said. "You should definitely give it a try."

Chapter 37

Artem finished the burger, licked his lips and then used a napkin to wipe his mouth and hands. When he'd finished he stood up from the bench to throw the tissue in the waste paper bin. He didn't like litter, never had. He liked everything to be tidy and precise.

He returned to his seat and watched as Sean Abbott's partner continued pushing her daughter, the little girl giggling as she swung backwards and forwards.

His phone rang and he clicked the button on the earphone cable to accept the call, his eyes still on the playground some thirty yards away.

"Are you still at the park?" the caller asked.

"Yes, Mr Smith," Artem said.

"Have you done it yet?"

"No. Do not worry, everything is in hand."

"And she will be suitably frightened?"

Artem gave a dry laugh. "Oh yes. I believe the appropriate English expression is 'scared shitless'." He watched as the only other mother in the playground wheeled her pushchair towards the exit. "Ah, I think now is the time. I will ring to update you."

He ended the call and sent a text with the single word 'Go'.

A few seconds later there was movement in the bushes to his right and he watched as a thin, acne-covered boy of about sixteen emerged. The lad looked over at him, nodded and then headed towards the swing, pulling the hood of his jacket over his head as he drew near.

Kirsten looked up as he approached. There was a short exchange and then the boy passed her a white envelope and turned to point at Artem. Artem smiled and waved and saw her raise an eyebrow before tentatively waving back.

The boy returned to the bushes and Artem watched as she opened the envelope, pulled out the piece of paper he had placed inside and unfolded it.

She read what was written and looked momentarily confused before realisation dawned.

Kirsten looked back at Artem who continued smiling as he pointed to the little girl and slowly drew his index finger across his throat. Her eyes widened and she rushed to her daughter and began pulling her out of the swing.

Artem stood up and walked away, his job done. The message had been simple but eloquent and he was proud of it.

> *Sean must choose*
> *Accident in Lombardy*
> *Or a childless couple*

Ten minutes later, Artem climbed off his motorbike at Tooting Common car park and set off towards the cafe. He would have an ice cream before his journey back, he decided. He had earned it.

He looked forward to returning to the city he now called home. Bath was a beautiful place, and he was pleased to have settled there. It was largely Georgian and had none of the 70's high-rises that blotted the streets of Moscow where he was born and raised.

At first, he had thought he would have to live in London, where there was likely to be more call for his services. However, since he had linked with Mr Smith work had been plentiful.

Most of his commissions were what he thought of as 'soft work', using his skills of persuasion to encourage people to do what Mr Smith required of them. Artem was a master at that kind of thing. In his experience, it was rarely necessary to torture or maim someone. Words were usually enough.

As, he was sure, would be the case with Sean Abbott.

Occasionally, he was rewarded for ending someone's life, but that wasn't a problem either. It was a tough world and if a person failed to fulfil their promises then they had to pay the consequences.

That had been the case with Brian Shepherd. He had let himself down and he had let his wife down. Artem had been clinical about their termination. He liked to think of himself as a considerate man, and there had been no need to cause them any more pain than was necessary.

He upped his pace to draw ahead of an elderly couple and called up Mr Smith's number.

He answered immediately. "Is it done?" he asked.

"Yes, Mr Smith. It is done. I gave her a note. Do you want to know what it said?"

"No."

This reply disappointed Artem. He was proud of what he had written and did not feel that Mr Smith should distance himself in this way.

"I am confident it will have the desired effect," he said.

"100 per cent confident?"

"I can never be 100 per cent confident."

"Then after a few days you must do it again. I cannot afford for another of these sportsmen to let me down. I will pay the same."

"Very well, Mr Smith."

Chapter 38

Luke opened Sally Croft's email and was pleased to find that she had attached the scene of crime conclusions as well as her post-mortem report. He decided to start with the summaries before diving into the detail.

As Pete had indicated, both Sally and the SOCO's team leader had concluded that Brian Shepherd had shot his wife and then turned the gun on himself. Their findings were based on positive evidence, such as the distribution of blood and the positioning of the bodies, as well as negative evidence, principally the complete lack of anything pointing to a third party being present.

The SOCO's report included an image of the note Brian Shepherd had left. It was brief.

I'm sorry Max. The money
worries were too much.

Luke could understand why Pete had said it made the motive clear, but he was left wondering why it was written at all. His son was only two so what purpose did it serve?

Unless it was written to put people off the scent.

Luke smiled to himself. He was falling into the trap of making evidence fit a theory rather than the other way around.

His thoughts were interrupted by Josh who exclaimed, "Wowza!" before adding, "Take a look at this, guv."

Luke stood up and walked over to see a familiar red logo in the top left-hand corner of Josh's screen. "Reddit again?"

Josh nodded. "Not Adrian Critchley this time though.

Harvey Robinson."

"He uses it?"

"No, I don't think so, but I found a thread about him and he sounds a bit iffy. Look." Josh pointed to a post from someone calling themselves *antisocialsquid*. "About a year ago this guy asked if anyone had come across a PI called Harvey Robinson and he got two replies. The first said no, then talked about another investigator he'd used, but look at this one."

Luke read what was written on the screen.

carcrazywurzel - 1y ago

I would find someone else. I'm a serving police officer and he's well-known to us. Nothing's ever been proven but it's an open secret that he's involved in some shady stuff.

"Good work," he said. "I'll make a call and see if they know about him at Avon and Somerset."

He returned to his desk and called Pete who answered straight away.

"Hi, Luke."

"Hi, Pete. I hope I'm not interrupting your work on the Shepherds case."

Pete laughed. "There's no case as you well know. It was a murder-suicide, open and shut."

"I thought you'd say that. Actually, I'm ringing about something else entirely. Have you come across a private investigator called Harvey Robinson?"

"I can't say I have, no. Why?"

"Something we're working on. Do you think you could put some feelers out and see if he's got any sort of reputation?"

"Sure. I can do that. I'll let you know if I find anything out."

"Cheers, Pete."

Luke hung up and returned to Josh's desk. "Did you find anything else?" he asked.

"I found his Facebook page," Josh said. "It doesn't mention financial advice though, just the investigating side of the business. It seems to be just Robinson and an assistant and it'll be just him soon."

"Why's that?"

"She's leaving. There's a link to a recruitment company for anyone interested in the role. He'll be lucky to find anyone though given the pay he's offering. Plus, he might not be very pleasant to work for."

"What do you mean?"

"The phrasing in the ad makes it clear what his main selection criteria are." He clicked a couple of buttons and read from the screen. "It says *'applicants must be dependable, empathetic and supportive with preference given to recent graduates'*." Josh chuckled. "It doesn't take much reading between the lines to see that he wants to recruit an attractive young woman."

Luke smiled as a thought occurred to him. "Did you say an attractive young woman?"

"Yes." Josh hesitated and the corners of his mouth turned up. "Oh. Are you thinking what I'm thinking?"

"I am indeed, Josh. I am indeed. I'll give her a call."

Chapter 39

The others had long gone, and it was already dark outside, when Sam decided she'd done enough for the day and closed her laptop. Besides, she'd agreed to meet Patrick Casey at Thorney and Budge's office at 9 am the next day which meant an early start.

She had worked through twenty-three of the organisations in Adam Davison's portfolio. It was a good start, but if she was honest she had to admit that she didn't feel like she'd got very far. She certainly wasn't much closer to understanding the secret of his success.

Her thoughts went back to the 'Diverts' tab. She was sure there was a clue in there somewhere. She lifted her laptop screen and was about to enter her password when something told her not to.

This was stupid. She needed to stop work for the day and relax.

A thought occurred to her and she bashed out a message to Ollie and hit send before she could change her mind.

'I've finished work for the evening. Still fancy the pub? xx'

There you go.

Pleased with herself, she waited for what seemed like ages, but was probably only a couple of minutes, and then his reply arrived.

'Let you off early, has he? Lucky me!'

She stared at the screen, trying to work out whether this was more evidence of Ollie's sense of humour or if there was some deeper meaning. In the end, she gave up on trying to decide and sent a simple two-word reply.

'The pub?'

This time his response was immediate.

'*The Salamander - I'll be waiting xx*'

Sam smiled to see the two kisses were back.

She put her laptop in her bag and headed out, deciding that she'd go straight to the pub rather than home and change. After all, this was their third date and it was about time he saw her all stinky and smelly.

True to his word, he was at the bar when she walked into The Salamander. He turned and smiled as he handed her a glass of Prosecco.

"Thanks," she said. "It's been a long day. You'll have to excuse what I'm wearing. I came straight from work."

"You look beautiful," he said as he bent down and kissed her lightly on the lips. He took her hand in his. "Come on, let's find a table."

He led the way to the same small table at the back of the pub that they had sat at a few days earlier.

"This seems familiar," she said with a smile as they sat down.

She sipped her bubbly and wondered if she should ask why he'd suggested Luke was a problem boss. However, to her surprise it was Ollie who raised it first.

"I was only joking," he said with a laugh, "when I suggested your boss might be a hard taskmaster."

"I know," she lied.

"I've been worrying that I offended you."

"No, not at all." She hesitated. "So, anyway, how's your day been?"

"The usual regime. Training, study, lunch, training, study."

"What are you studying?"

"Advanced midwifery."

"Advanced…" She saw the smile on his face and jabbed his side. "What are you really studying?"

"I'm doing a Level 4 Diploma in Personal Training. I need something for when these bones are too old for pro cycling."

"Good for you."

"Yes, well…" He stopped as his phone rang and pulled it out of his pocket. "It's Sean. Do you mind?" She nodded and he accepted the call. "Hi, how's it going?"

There was silence while Sean talked and Sam saw Ollie's face grow more serious.

"He did what? Sean, that's awful. How is she?"

There was another silence, then Ollie said, "Sam's with me now. I'll ask her."

He put his hand over the microphone and addressed his next words to Sam. "Sean's had more threats and they're even worse this time. What did your boss discover?"

"I'm not sure he's found anything out yet."

Ollie stared at her for a few seconds then took his hand off the microphone. "Nothing yet, Sean. Give my best to Kirsten."

He ended the call and put the phone back in his pocket.

"What's happened?" Sam asked.

"Another threat. Directly to Kirsten this time."

"That's awful."

"It was already awful. Did you tell your boss about the first threat?"

"Of course I did."

"Then why hasn't he done anything? I thought you said he was 'wonderful'." He made air quotes with his fingers as he said the last word.

"These things take time and there's not a lot to go on."

"Yes, well I hope that when he does finally get going he doesn't put his foot in it and make things even worse."

"Luke isn't stupid, Ollie."

"No. Just slow."

Sam didn't know whether to cry, storm out or let him have two barrels of vitriol.

But in truth, she was part to blame. She'd told Luke there was no rush because the race was over a week away.

She also had to take into account the fact that Ollie was

upset. His best friend had dug himself a hole, a very dangerous hole, and she had told him that Luke would help. His lashing out was understandable given what was happening.

Sam placed her hand on top of Ollie's.

"I'll have a word with Luke," she said. "Believe me, he's very good. Don't let this ruin our evening."

Ollie smiled. "You're right. I'm sorry if I had a go. Hey, have you eaten?"

"No, and I'm ravenous."

He stood up and grabbed her hand. "Come on then."

"What about my drink?"

"Leave it. I know a fantastic tapas place and their cocktails are to die for."

Chapter 40

Luke decided he'd rather talk face to face than over the phone and arranged to meet Lily at The George in Norton St Philip, a short walk for each of them from their homes.

She had helped the team in two previous investigations, putting her acting skills to good use both times. Smart as hell and cool under pressure, she had been an invaluable asset. He hoped she would agree to join them again.

Lily was already there when he arrived and smiled when she saw him. An attractive woman, and only twenty-two years old, she managed to look both chilled and glamorous in a white sleeveless crop top and faded denim jeans, her brown hair falling in curls down her back.

"So, what's this about?" she asked, once Luke had ordered them both a drink and they were seated at a table.

"Are you busy at the moment?"

"Not desperately. I was in an advert for toothpaste a week ago, but aside from reading, studying and watching *Loose Women* I'm pretty much free."

Luke smiled. "In that case, I may have a job for you. It's another position which will need your acting skills."

"I'm intrigued."

"Let me fill you in on some of the background. One of Filchers' clients is Gambet, an online gambling company, and we believe that someone linked to them is fixing sports events." He showed her a photo on his phone of Adrian Critchley's note. "This note was written by a man who committed suicide a few days ago. He was addicted to gambling and these…" He pointed to the bottom three lines. "…are bets we believe he placed on two football matches and a rugby game."

He swiped to a photo of Harvey Robinson's business

card. "We need to find out if this man is the 'Harvey' at the top of the note and, if so, what he's up to."

"And that's where I come in?"

"Exactly." Luke drank a little of his cider. "He's looking for an assistant and I was thinking you might fit the bill, particularly if you adopt a somewhat innocent demeanour."

Lily slipped effortlessly into an Essex accent. "Do you mean I gotta be all flirtatious and fick?"

Luke laughed. "Perhaps not quite so over-the-top, but we want him to be comfortable when you're around. If you can come across as not totally on the ball that might help."

"Not a problem. Subtly stupid is definitely in my repertoire."

"Before you say yes, I should warn you that Robinson may be mixed up with some nasty sorts so there could be an element of danger."

She sipped her water. "That makes it sound all the more exciting. Count me in. Are Sam and the others involved?"

"The whole team are working on the investigation in one way or another. They're mainly office-based, but if you need to pass on information it would be good to line Josh up to play the role of your boyfriend."

"Oh, that would be fun. Should I use a fake name?"

"I don't think that's necessary."

She nodded. "Lily Newport it is then. When do I start?"

"You've got to get the job first. However, he's paying a very low wage so it's unlikely he's deluged with applicants." He held up the phone so that she could see Harvey Robinson's business card. "You could ring him now. Or do you need time to prepare for your role?"

Lily took out her phone. "You'd be surprised how easily I can slip into not-so-bright."

She entered the number, tapped the green button and looked over at Luke as she waited for her call to be answered. After ten rings she was thinking she would have to leave a message when a gruff voice said, "Harvey. What do you want?"

"Hello," Lily said. "Is that Mr Robinson?"

"Yeah."

"My name's Lily, Lily Newport. Someone told me you're looking for an assistant."

"Too right. How old are you?"

"I'm twenty-two."

Harvey grunted. "That's good. It's in Oldfield Park, £11 an hour, cash in hand."

"That's fine." Her eyes widened and she mouthed *"It's below minimum wage,"* to Luke.

"Send me a photo and if that's okay you can come in tomorrow."

"Do you mean I can start tomorrow? That sounds wonderful."

"Yeah, call it a trial run. It depends on whether you're suitable."

"How will you know that?"

"The photo. I already said. Message it to me now."

The line went dead.

Lily looked at the phone for a few seconds and shook her head. "I don't think I'm going to like that man. Why do you think he needs a photo of me?"

"Why do you think?"

Lily shuddered. "He sounds gross."

"Sorry. Do you want out?"

"Of course not." She started tapping on her phone. "I'll have to find a suitable photo." After a few seconds she showed one to Luke. "What do you think?"

It was taken in Bath. Lily was leaning against a stone wall and smiling at the camera with Pulteney Bridge in the background.

"I'm sure that'll do the trick," Luke said.

She sent the photo and Harvey's response came back after less than a minute.

'*10am tomorrow. 26a Moorland Road, Oldfield Park, Bath. Be on time.*'

She showed it to Luke. "It looks like I'm in."

Luke nodded. "I'd better tell you everything we know."

He explained why he thought Brian Shepherd, Adrian Critchley and Sean Abbott were connected, and how Helen had got hold of Harvey Robinson's business card.

"That reminds me," Luke said when he'd finished. "Excuse me while I make a phone call." He called up Pete Gilmore's number but it was his wife who answered.

"Hello," she said.

"Hi, Janice. It's Luke. How are you?"

"I'm fine. Pete's busy at the moment."

"That's okay, I'll…"

"Just a second…" He heard her say, "It's nearly eight," followed by a response from Pete that he couldn't make out after which she said, "Make it quick then."

"Hi," Pete said a few seconds later.

"Hi, Pete. Sorry to interrupt your evening."

"Don't worry about it." He lowered his voice to a whisper. "She's in one of her moods."

"I was ringing to see if you'd found anything out about Harvey Robinson?"

"I did actually. Just a second, I'll get my notebook." The phone went quiet and it was a minute or so before Pete came back on the line. "I'll have to be quick," he said. "She's kicking off." Luke heard pages being turned. "Here it is. He's forty-six and a private investigator, although most of his work seems to be process-serving. We've come across him twice according to his file, both times when people complained he was stalking them."

"Was he?"

"No." Pete laughed. "He was spotted while trying to do a covert investigation. Seems he's more Inspector Clouseau than Sherlock Holmes."

"Anything else?"

"He's got a criminal record for ABH. He broke someone's nose outside a pub four years ago and received a community order. I'll have to go, Luke."

"That's fine. Thanks, Pete."

He hung up and told Lily what Pete had said. "ABH stands for actual bodily harm," he clarified. "It means he caused hurt or injury without it being serious. He was in a pub fight."

"It confirms my suspicion that he's an arsehole," she said. "Wish me luck."

Chapter 41

The alarm went off and Sam reached out her hand to turn it off, concerned that it might wake Ollie.

She needn't have worried. He stirred for a second and then his breathing returned to steady inhalations and exhalations.

He was zonked.

She lay on her back, looked up at the ceiling and smiled as she allowed herself a moment of reflection. It had been a lovely evening, and night for that matter, and she was already growing to like him. Okay, he'd been disproportionally annoyed over Luke's lack of action concerning Sean, but the irritation hadn't lasted. They laughed together over their meal, and back at the pub afterwards, and it seemed like they had a lot in common.

He was certainly a vast improvement on Tony, but that wasn't difficult.

Once he had walked her back to her apartment it had seemed natural to invite him to stay. It was early, only their third date, but she had thought why not?

You only live once.

She slipped silently out of bed, grabbed some clothes and crept to the bathroom for a shower.

Ten minutes later she wrote Ollie a note, left it on the bedside cabinet and bent to peck him on the cheek before leaving. He mumbled something, which might have been 'bye', but his eyes remained closed and it was clear he was still heavily asleep.

Smiling again, she let herself out and set out for the bus station. Once seated, she sent Luke a message telling him about the threat made to Kirsten, then turned her attention to the meeting with Patrick Casey.

*

Fortunately, Sam's bus ran to schedule and it was just before nine when she arrived at Thorney and Budge's offices.

They weren't what she had expected. In her mind, a hedge fund company was trendy and would have an ultra-modern head office, all tinted glass and sharp angles and designed by an up-and-coming architect. Thorney and Budge's building was as far removed from that as you could get, a drab red-brick building just outside Bristol's city centre.

Once inside, the reception area was brighter, if no more modern, and she was greeted warmly by the young woman on the reception desk.

"Good morning," she said. "Have you got an appointment?"

"My name's Sam Chambers. I'm here to see Patrick Casey."

"That'll be me."

Sam turned to see a smiling man in a royal blue Armani suit. He had designer stubble and sparkling blue eyes and she put him at thirty-five, maybe slightly older.

"Thanks for coming in," he said as the receptionist passed her a visitor badge. "I've booked a room. We'll have a quick word and then I'll introduce you to Adam."

"That'll be great. Thanks."

He led her upstairs and opened the door to a meeting room that was a step up from those at Filchers' head office, but not by much. It was the mid-century modern prints on the walls that raised the stakes, she thought. They were almost abstract, but not quite, and the bright colours helped to brighten the space.

The table and chairs, meanwhile, were standard office issue, chrome and black leather and evidently designed by someone in Sweden who delighted in making people uncomfortable.

"So," Patrick said, once they had sat down, "What have you discovered so far?"

"Not a lot, I'm afraid. That was the reason for wanting to see Adam. A couple of his tables confused me and I could do with him explaining what they're for."

"The 'Diverts' tab?"

"You guessed it. Have you any idea what it's for?"

Patrick smiled. "Not the faintest I'm afraid." He paused. "Look, I have to be straight with you. Adam isn't aware that I've asked a third party to look at his portfolio. I'm sure he'll be fine about it but I'll sit in on the meeting if that's okay?"

"Of course it is."

"Good. If you wait here I'll ask him to join us."

Patrick returned a few minutes later with a man of similar height and build to himself but almost a decade younger. He was also dressed in what looked to be an expensive suit, though his was dark grey and he was jacketless. His green and white checked tie was tied loosely three or four inches below the collar of his white shirt and he looked like he'd been sweating.

"Uh, hi," he said as he shook Sam's hand. He was fidgeting and looked from Sam to Patrick and then back again. "I'm not sure what this is about. Something about a check?"

"It's nothing to worry about, Adam," Patrick said. "Please, take a seat."

Adam sat on the edge of his chair at one end of the table as if poised to run. Patrick sat opposite Sam.

"This is Sam Chambers," Patrick went on. "She's an accountant and I asked her to cast an eye over your fund to help me understand how it's been set up."

"I'm sorry to have interrupted you," Sam said with a smile. "You're obviously busy."

Adam looked at her for a second but didn't return her

smile. He turned back to Patrick and started to stand up. "I don't have time for this," he said.

"This won't take long, I promise," Sam said. "It's your 'Diverts' tab that I'm struggling with."

Adam's eyes widened and he stared at her, evidently shocked by what she'd said. "What do you mean?"

"I can't understand how it works. There's…"

"How did you access it?" His words were coming out more quickly now. "I set a password."

"There's no password," Patrick said. "I had the same problem as Sam. I opened it, but I couldn't fathom how it worked."

Adam opened his mouth but no words came out.

"Are you all right?" Sam asked.

He stared at her for a few seconds then ran his fingers through his hair and tried to form his face into a smile. "Can we do this on Friday?" he said. "I'm really up against it today."

"Up against it?" Patrick said, raising an eyebrow. "Why's that?"

Sam held her hand up. "It's okay," she said. "Friday's fine with me. Shall we say eleven-thirty, Adam?"

"Uh…" He swallowed, looked at Patrick then back to Sam. "Yes, that's okay."

"Great. I'll see you then."

Chapter 42

Luke turned his chair around and stared across at the whiteboard.

Helen had done a good job, and it was easy to understand the main characters in Project Barney and the links between them. The problem he had was that there was too much supposition and guesswork and very little in the way of concrete evidence.

The names of the victims were around the outside and connected with dotted lines. At the top were Brian Shepherd and his wife Kimberley, while Adrian Critchley and Sean Abbott were at the bottom left and right respectively.

The centre of the board was reserved for the suspects, but so far all they had were two names: 'Mr Smith' and 'Harvey'. The name 'Mr Smith' was being used by Sean Abbott's blackmailer, and it seemed fair to assume that he was the 'MRS' on Adrian Critchley's discarded note which was stuck next to Adrian's photo.

Luke stood up and walked over to read the details on the note.

HARVEY'S MRS

Sats

Burn free five

Batex pen twenty

Live throw two

The idea that the 'Harvey' on the note was the 'Harvey

Robinson' on the business card that Helen had been given was a long shot but Luke's gut told him they were one and the same.

"Helen," he called, without looking away from the board, "Could you find out more about Simon Abrahams' involvement with Harvey Robinson please?"

"Aye, I can do that," Helen said.

"Get as much detail from him as you can. Try to find out exactly where he's invested his money and how he first came across Robinson."

"Will do."

"Maj?"

Maj looked up from his laptop. "Yes, Luke."

"Any joy checking out those football and rugby games?"

"I'm drawing a blank on the rugby game between Bath and Exeter. The first penalty was after thirty minutes and I can't see anything to suggest Brian Shepherd was behaving oddly either before or afterwards."

"What about the football games?"

Maj stood up and walked over with his notebook. He was smiling. "I've just been looking at footage of the West Ham game at Anfield a couple of weeks ago and I think I may have sussed it."

"What have you sussed?" Josh asked. He joined Maj and Luke by the whiteboard and watched as Maj wrote a name on a Post-it and stuck it next to the note.

"Alphonse Moreau?" Luke said.

Maj nodded. "He's West Ham's right-back. He was booked for a sliding tackle after four minutes of the Burnley game and gave away a throw-in inside a minute against Liverpool."

"Coolio," Josh said. "Is he French?"

"No," Maj said. "He's Japanese."

"Eh?"

"I was joking. Yes, he's French."

"Good work, Maj," Luke said. "Can you try to get hold of his contact details?"

"Will do."

Luke rubbed his chin and stared at the note. "Could 'Batex' mean something other than the Bath Exeter rugby game?"

"It could be Exeter City," Maj said. "They're in League One. Give me a second." He returned to his laptop and bashed away at his keyboard for a few seconds before turning back to the others. "Would you believe there are five teams in League One beginning with 'B': Barnsley, Blackpool, Bolton Wanderers, Bristol Rovers and Burton Albion?"

"You'd better check them out," Luke said. "Have a look at whether any of them have played Exeter City recently. It loses us our link to Brian Shepherd though."

His phone rang and he swiped to accept the call.

"Hello, Luke Sackville."

"Luke, this is Leanne." She lowered her voice to a whisper. "One of the three amigos is back and he's asking to see you urgently."

"Which one?"

"Mr Brown."

Two minutes later, Luke arrived in reception to find Maurice Brown twirling the end of his moustache and looking very much on edge.

"Good morning, Maurice," he said as he shook the man's hand. "How can I help you?"

"Can we talk somewhere more private?"

"Of course."

"There's no one in the Royal Crescent Room," Leanne said.

"Thanks," Luke said.

He led Maurice to the room and invited him to take a seat. However, instead of doing so, he walked down the side of the table then back again before leaning his hands against the back of one of the chairs and sighing.

"What is it, Maurice?" Luke asked.

Maurice looked across at Luke. "I need to know I can trust you," he said.

"Of course you can. If this is about Adrian's gambling addiction, please don't worry. The secret's safe with me."

Maurice half smiled. "No, it's not that. It's S."

"S?"

"Sorry. It's what I call Spencer. We've been friends for years, you know. We owned a company together. I feel like I'm betraying him, but it's important that I tell you." He paused. "Yvonne told me yesterday that she found a note written by poor Adrian."

"That's correct."

"She wouldn't tell me what it said other than it was something to do with his gambling."

Maurice waited but Luke merely smiled.

"She said she gave it to you," Maurice went on, "and I fear it may have mentioned S's contributions."

"Contributions?"

"Yes. I'm sure he meant well, and I know how horrified he was, as we all were, by Adrian's suicide. However, the fact is that he had been helping him out. Yvonne was limiting her husband's spend, but the poor man was out of control and close to a breakdown."

"I see."

"Yvonne told me she gave the note to you, but it would do no one any good at all, least of all Spencer, if it got out that he'd been giving Adrian money."

"Don't worry, I won't say anything."

"Thank you, Luke."

Chapter 43

Luke returned upstairs to find a grinning Glen Baxter standing outside the Ethics Room. He was holding a manila folder in one of his massive hands.

"Hi, Glen," Luke said. "How can I help?"

Glen opened the folder and extracted five sheets of paper. "Are all of your team in?" he asked.

"Not at the moment, and we're swamped with work." Luke gestured to the sheets of paper. "What are those?"

"Forms." Glen waved them in the air. "I need money."

"Money for what?"

"A lot of things. There's the runs for a start."

"You've got the runs?"

"Burpees too."

"Burpees?"

"Yes. In between the runs. It all ends with balls. And believe me, I'm talking a load of balls."

"You certainly are."

Glen nodded. "I have to do a hundred and each ball is six kilograms." He held the wad of paper out. "So? What do you think?"

Still none the wiser, Luke took the forms and scanned the content. "What's Hyrox?" he asked when he'd finished reading.

"It's a sport made for someone like me," Glen said, grinning again as he raised his left arm and flexed his bicep. "I'll have to use my two main assets."

"Charm and modesty?"

"Muscles and stamina," Glen replied, missing the sarcasm completely. "It's for a good cause too."

Luke looked down at the form again. "Isn't Rocky Road a type of chocolate cake?"

"It's a charity for steroid addicts."

"Oh, I see. So you're planning for the future?"

"What?"

"Never mind. Give them here and we'll see what we can do."

"Thanks, Luke." Glen started to move away and then turned back. "Don't forget to gift wrap it. Rocky Road gets an extra 25% if you do."

Luke glanced back at the form to see a section for Gift Aid at the bottom. "Right," he said with a smile. "I'll make sure we do that."

He watched as Glen disappeared around the corner and then opened the door.

"I heard you talking," Maj said as he walked in. "Was that Mr Steroid?"

"The one and only. He gave me these sponsorship forms." Luke passed one to Maj and a second to Josh. "He's doing something called Hyrox."

"A friend of mine does Hyrox," Josh said. "It alternates running with workouts. Things like sled-pulling, lunges and burpees."

"Glen mentioned burpees. What on earth are they?"

"They're a jump combined with a squat." Josh stood upright with his hands in the air. "Do you want me to show you?"

Luke gave him a withering look. "Not really. No." He saw Josh's hangdog expression and relented. "On second thoughts, I've changed my mind. This might be amusing. Go on, give us a couple of burpees."

But instead of launching into exercise Josh turned and fired a finger gun at Luke. "Got it," he said, and he was beaming from ear to ear. "You changed your mind. Maybe he did as well."

"Who did?"

"Brian Shepherd. I was thinking LFWFO. Like you told me, guv, look for what's, uh…" He lowered his voice to a whisper. "…fucking obvious."

"I was joking."

"I know, but what if he didn't do it, and then he did, only he was too late and…" He put his index finger to his temple. "…BOOM!"

"What on earth are you wittering on about?"

"Maj, you said that Brian Shepherd didn't do anything to give away a penalty in the Exeter game. Is that right?"

"As far as I can see," Maj said.

"So, what if that was simply because he changed his mind? Then the man offering him money, this Mr Smith, threatens him like he threatened Sean Abbott and says he has to give a penalty away in the Gloucester game."

"Which he did, don't forget," Luke said.

"Yes, but what if he was too late? When was the penalty?"

"After twelve and a half minutes."

"So maybe Mr Smith demanded it was within five minutes or eight minutes or ten minutes, which means Shepherd failed."

"Mmm. I wonder if you're onto something."

Chapter 44

Number 17 was Hot and Sour Soup and Lily decided it would make for a tasty starter. King Prawns in Black Pepper Sauce, number 78, sounded good as a main, with 213 as a side. Or should she have plain boiled rice? It was difficult to decide.

After half an hour of standing outside the Cheong Sing takeaway, Lily felt she knew the menu back to front and sideways. Whether the food was any good or not she hadn't the faintest, but it had helped pass the time while waiting for her prospective employer to arrive.

Her thoughts of whether to add prawn crackers were interrupted by the sound of cussing, and she turned to see a man in his late forties struggling to open a door adjacent to the takeaway.

"Fuck this lock," he said under his breath, and those few words confirmed her belief that Harvey Robinson wasn't born and bred in Bath, his accent more Ronnie Kray than Jane Austen.

"Are you Mr Robinson?" she asked, smiling as she held her hand out.

He stopped fiddling with his key, rose to his full height, though that didn't put him at much more than five foot eight, and blatantly looked Lily up and down before his eyes settled on her t-shirt. It was pink with the word 'Barbie' emblazoned in white across the front, but it wasn't the character's name he was focused on, his eyes flicking from the 'a' to the 'i' and back again.

"I've got Barbie and Ken earrings to match," she said, rotating her head slightly to show a two-inch Barbie swinging from her left ear and a similarly diminutive Ken swinging from the right.

He tore his gaze away from her breasts and his mouth opened in a grin that exposed every single one of his front teeth, top and bottom. She was reminded of the character Jack Torrance in *The Shining,* although Robinson was distinctly less attractive than Jack Nicholson, his looks not helped by a mass of grey chin hair that was more wiry hedge than designer stubble.

He was also wearing a suit that did nothing to improve his appeal. It was a couple of sizes too large for his slight build, but what marked it out was that it was pastel blue.

Where did you even buy a pastel blue suit?

He held his hand out. "You must be Livvy," he said.

She shook his hand, which was disturbingly moist, and managed to continue smiling. "Lily," she said. "Lily Newport."

"Oh yeah. Forgot your name. You're twenty-two, ain't you?"

He remembered her age but not her name. What did that say about him?

Everything!

"That's right. I'm here about the job."

"Yeah, right. Need someone, don't I?" He turned his attention back to the door, mumbling again. "Cock-sucker of a door this is, always sticking." He twisted a couple more times before finally managing to engage the mechanism. "About fucking time," he grunted before opening the door and marching up the stairs without another word.

Lily followed him up and into a room that looked like it had once been a bedsit. She was immediately hit by the all-pervading smell of heavily spiced oriental food and suddenly felt less keen on the idea of a Chinese takeaway.

There was a sink in the corner of the room, an old desk to one side and a cracked brown leather sofa that had seen better days set back against the wall facing the front window.

Harvey parked himself on a black leather swivel chair

behind the desk.

"Shall I sit here, Mr Robinson?" Lily asked, gesturing to a wooden kitchen chair.

Harvey nodded. "Yeah. Pull it up" He waited until she was seated before continuing. "Told you about the pay, didn't I?"

"Yes. £11 an hour."

"Cash in hand. Pay you at the end of every week."

"That's fine. What does the job involve?"

"Whatever I tell you to do," he said and smiled again, though he dialled *The Shining* down a couple of notches this time. "Answer the phone, do me copying, make coffees, check reports, all sorts of stuff."

"I can do all that."

"I like me coffee strong with milk and two sugars. Not too much milk though, don't want it washed out."

"Right." She paused but he didn't say anything else and she noticed his eyes slowly drifting from her face back downwards to her chest.

"Do you need to ask me any questions?" she asked and giggled girlishly. "You know, to check I can do those things?"

"Nah. You'll do. Make me a coffee."

She turned around. "Ah, where?"

"Through there." He gestured to a door next to the sink. "That's where your desk is. There are a few mugs and a kettle. You can fill it in the bog."

"The bog?"

"Yeah. There's a sink. Mugs are through there too."

"Okay. What do you want me to do first?"

"Like I said. Make me a coffee."

"Right."

Lily walked through to a smaller room to find a large kitchen table and a single chair against one wall, while against the adjacent wall was a fridge. On the fridge were five mugs of varying sizes and designs, a teaspoon, a jar of instant coffee, a kettle and a closed laptop. She could see a small cloakroom through an open door and used its sink to fill the kettle.

The walls were white and bare of any decoration, the only nod to design a pink tasselled shade over the single ceiling bulb. All in all, the room was unashamedly dreary and Lily decided to brighten it up as appropriate to her adopted character. She would stop at B&M on the way home and buy a Barbie and Ken calendar and matching accessories.

A few minutes later she placed Harvey's coffee on his desk, prompting him to look up from his computer. "Did you add two sugars?" he asked.

She nodded. "Yes. Is there kenough milk in it for you?"

"Kenough? Did you say kenough?"

"Sorry." She giggled. "It's a Barbie thing."

He grunted, glanced at his drink and then back at Lily. "Yeah. Milk seems about right."

"Great." She looked around the room blankly. "What do I do now?"

He handed her his phone. "If anyone rings you gotta answer by saying 'Harvey Robinson's office' and asking who it is. Then come and tell me and I'll decide whether I wanna speak to 'em. Got that?"

"Sure."

"Good. I'm gonna print out a report. Check it for typos but don't read the content."

How can I check it if I'm not allowed to read it, Lily thought but said, "Will do. What shall I do if I find mistakes?"

"Make a note. Here." He opened the top drawer of his desk, pulled out a notebook and passed it over. "Got a pen?"

Lily shook her head. "No."

"Fucking hell." He reached back into the drawer and pulled out a biro, handing it to her without looking up.

"Thanks, Mr Robinson. What time do I finish?"

"When I finish. Or six. Whichever's later."

"Okay. What about my lunch break?"

"I dunno. Take half an hour at one or summat. I may have to go out so…" he reached back into the drawer and passed her a key. "Don't lose it."

"I won't."

Chapter 45

Luke stared for the umpteenth time at the number that Sean Abbott had given him. He'd promised he wouldn't ring it, but what other way did he have of finding anything out about the mysterious Mr Smith?

Unless Lily came up trumps of course, but that was a long shot. An early update would be good though.

"Josh," he called. "Could you come over for a minute please?"

"Of coursio," Josh said, and reversed his chair over before spinning it around twice so that he ended up facing his boss. He beamed up at Luke. "What is it, guv?"

"I want you to be Lily's boyfriend."

Josh's expression changed in an instant from eager puppy to frightened wildebeest.

"I… but…" he spluttered. "What about Leanne?"

Luke held his hand up. "I'm not asking you to transfer your affections, son."

Josh shook his head. "I'm not being a bigamist. No, no, no." His voice rose an octave. "That's what it would be, wouldn't it? Not that Leanne and I are married, but if I… I mean Lily and me…" He shook his head again.

"Stop right there. I'm not some kind of pimp. I'm asking you to pretend to be Lily's boyfriend, that's all."

"Ah!" Josh's cheeks reddened as he finally caught on. He smiled but then, after a moment's pause, grew more serious again. "I don't have to pretend to Leanne that I'm Lily's boyfriend, do I?"

Luke sighed. "No, Josh." He closed his eyes and rubbed his temples, then took a deep breath before continuing. "I want you to go to Harvey Robinson's office later today on the pretext of needing to see Lily. She can pass on anything she's found out but, more importantly, I want you to build your own view of him."

"My view?"

"Yes. You've been involved in several projects now, and I value your perspective. He sells himself as a private investigator and financial adviser and I want you to gauge how the real Harvey Robinson matches up to that."

"Me, guv? You trust me with doing that?"

"Am I wrong to?"

"Definitely not." The smile returned. "Are you saying I'm an experienced investigator?"

"No."

"Ah. Right." Josh's smile faded slightly. "When should I go?"

"Why not take her some lunch? That'll give you the excuse to stay while you both eat, and you can use the time to get a feel for Robinson."

"Gucci."

Luke smiled as Josh wheeled himself back to his desk. The lad displayed a combination of maturity and immaturity that was unique in his experience. On the one hand, his opinion of Harvey Robinson would most likely be accurate and incisive…

…but on the other, if he said 'Gucci' one more time he was in danger of being throttled before he was twenty-three.

His thoughts returned to Mr Smith and he decided he had no option other than to ring the number that Sean Abbott had given him. He preceded it with 141, to withhold his number, and pressed the green button.

To his surprise, it was a female voice that answered.

"Kamusta," she said, her accent thick and almost, but not quite, Spanish.

"Hello," Luke said. "Who is this?"

"Dolores. Sorry! I not English."

Luke was wondering what to say next when she spoke

again. "Meester Smith back soon. You wait."

Before Luke could reply he heard a man's voice in the background though he couldn't make out the words. A few seconds later there was a loud bang and the phone went dead.

"Helen," he called. "I've got something to add to the crazy wall."

Josh immediately turned around, grinning from ear to ear, and Luke realised what he'd said. "To the whiteboard, I mean," he added.

"Aye. I've got a wee something as well," Helen said as she stood up and walked over.

Luke told her about his phone call and she had just finished writing 'Dolores (assistant?)' on Mr Smith's Post-it when Josh called over.

"I know where she's from," he said.

Helen and Luke looked over, eyebrows raised.

"I heard what you said, guv," he went on, "and I looked 'Kamusta' up." He waited, clearly wanting to make the most of his big reveal.

"And?" Luke asked.

"It's Filipino for 'Hello'." Josh paused for a few seconds before continuing. "What do you think about mousse?"

"Eh?"

"Mousse. What do you think?"

"I thought you used gel?"

"No, guv. Not for my hair, for Lily's, uh… mouth."

"Her mouth?"

Josh nodded. "I'll have an excuse to stay longer if I take a pudding. Do you know if she likes chocolate?"

"I don't know, Josh, and to be honest I don't care."

"I'll go with chocolate mousse then. Or maybe apple pie. Do you think…"

"Enough!" Luke said emphatically.

"Gotcha, guv." Josh grinned and mimed zipping his lips together.

Luke turned back to Helen. "You said that you had some news?"

"Aye. I spoke to Simon Abrahams. He was put in touch with Harvey Robinson by a friend who's made a lot of money based on his advice. I was about to ring his friend when you called me over."

"Good. Anything else?"

"Would you believe that Simon's investments are with Thorney and Budge? He's put £20,000 into their..." She checked her notebook. "...AOIF. He didn't know what the initials meant though."

Luke gave a rueful smile. "AOIF, eh? Somehow that doesn't surprise me."

"What do you mean? Have you heard of it?"

"It's the fund that Sam's looking into. AOIF stands for Alternative Opportunities Investment Fund."

Chapter 46

Josh was drawn to the yum yums.

Yum yums were deliciously moreish and he'd once polished off six in one sitting. His stomach had felt distinctly gurgly and rumbly afterwards but it had been worth it. However, were they likely to be Lily's dessert of choice? No, probably not.

He'd be better off going for the lemon cheesecake. Cheesecake was a safer option, and the slices looked a decent size. He eyed them up for a few seconds before grabbing the two biggest ones and popping them into his basket.

The most important part of lunch sorted, he turned to head for the sandwich aisle and immediately collided with someone.

"Sorry," he said, pulling away before realising he'd bumped into his girlfriend.

"I thought you had a working lunch," Leanne said after she'd pecked him on the cheek. "You said that was why we couldn't meet up." She pointed at his basket and smiled. "That's very thoughtful of you. Lemon cheesecake's my favourite."

"They're for Lily," he said before mentally kicking himself. He didn't have to say that, he really didn't.

"You've bought two slices for Lily?"

"No, ah…" He gulped as it dawned on him that the conversation was heading down a route he'd traversed before. It was a dangerous path full of potholes and precipices. He needed to step carefully, very carefully.

He smiled and tilted his head to one side. "Any thoughts about dinner tonight?"

But Leanne wasn't to be diverted. "Is Lily at this

working lunch with you?" she asked.

"Ah, yes." He tried to laugh but it came out more as a nervous bark. "That's why I bought cheesecake for us both."

"I see. But you're not buying anything for the other people at the lunch?"

"I, ah… I was just about to." He hesitated, returned to the display of desserts and stared at it before exclaiming, "Yes! The yum yums." He turned back and grinned. "I'll buy them yum yums." He grabbed a pack of four and dropped them into the basket. "There. Done."

"Who else will be there?"

"Who else?" he squeaked.

"Yes. Who else will be at the lunch? Or will it just be you, Lily, two slices of cheesecake and four yum yums?"

"Ah. Gosh. Is that the time?" He lifted his left arm and gazed at his watch.

"Yes, it is."

"It is what?"

She pointed to his wrist. "The time."

"Right. I, ah…"

He swallowed as he stuttered to a halt.

It was time to be honest.

"The truth is," he said. "I'm having lunch with Lily and it's just the two of us."

"Which is why you declined lunch with me?"

"Yes." He smiled and then saw the expression on her face. "Ah… I mean no. It's work."

"You're having lunch with her for work?"

He nodded. "She's undercover and I'm seeing her for lunch because I'm her boyfriend."

"You're her boyfriend?"

"Yes."

Leanne narrowed her eyes and put both hands on her hips, prompting him to change his answer for the second time.

"No," he squealed.

"Make your mind up."

"We have to pretend we're a couple, but we're not a couple. You and I are a couple, but Lily and me, no, never, not possible."

"So you won't have to hold her hand or kiss her or anything like that?"

"I, ah…"

"Joshy?"

"No. Definitely not. No way. Yuk. What a thought." He shook his head from side to side and grimaced. "She's not my type at all." He raised one eyebrow and his face transformed into a smile. "You're my type."

She tapped him on the nose with one index finger. "Yes. And don't you forget it. Any idea what time you'll finish?"

"Finish what?"

"Work, silly."

"Oh. I thought you meant the boyfriend-girlfriend things." He hesitated before adding hastily, "Not that there will be any, ah…"

"So what time?"

"Half-five, I think."

"Great. I'll see you in reception."

"Gucci."

She kissed him briefly on the lips, smiled and headed towards the exit.

Josh heaved a sigh of relief and reached down to retrieve the pack of yum yums. He placed them on the counter before changing his mind and dropping them back in the basket again.

He needed a sugar rush after what he'd just been through.

Chapter 47

Josh got off the bus on Moorland Road and wiped his lips to remove small pieces of sugar that had evaded his tongue.

Gollio, those yum yums were good. He briefly considered launching into the third one but decided to leave it for now. After all, he still had his BLT sandwich and cheesecake to consume.

Maybe he'd have the last two yum yums on the bus back.

He spotted the Cheong Sing takeaway on the opposite side of the road, crossed over and pressed the buzzer on the door to its left. After a few seconds, Lily's tinny voice came over the intercom.

"Hello," she said. "How can I help you?"

"It's Josh," he said.

"Hi, angel. I'll buzz you in."

As he opened the door and mounted the stairs he reflected on Lily calling him 'angel' and wondered how he should refer to her. Clearly 'Lily' wasn't good enough. He needed to come up with a suitable term of endearment, something that spoke of them being a close couple.

He knocked on the door at the top and she opened it, smiling and indicating with her eyes that the man himself, Harvey Robinson, was in the office behind her.

"Hi, Lil," he said.

"Lil?" she mouthed.

"Is that your boyfriend?" came a gruff voice behind her.

Lily grabbed Josh's hand and pulled him into the room.

"Yes, this is Josh," she said. "Josh, this is Mr Robinson."

"Hello, Mr Robinson," Josh said. "Nice to meet you."

"Yeah, right." He sniffed and returned his attention to

his laptop.

"Is it okay if we have our lunch in the other room?" Lily asked.

Harvey looked up again. "Thirty minutes then back to work."

"Okay." She looked at the clock. "We'll kensure we're done by one-thirty."

Josh cast a sideways look at her but Robinson seemed to take what she said in his stride.

"Did you say kensure?" Josh asked.

"Of course," Lily said, squeezing his hand so hard he thought she'd drawn blood. She pointed to the front of her t-shirt. "As you know, it's my Barbie thing."

"Right."

He hesitated.

Luke had told him to build a view of Harvey Robinson, but he couldn't do that if he was in another room.

"Your job sounds fascinating, Mr Robinson," he said. "What are you focused on at the moment?"

Harvey forced his eyes away from Lily's bust and looked at Josh. "A couple of things."

I noticed, Josh thought but said, "Lil told me you're a private investigator as well as a financial advisor. Which do you find most…" He paused and grinned. "…kenjoyable?"

"Fuck," Harvey said. "Are you Barbie-mad as well?"

"Not normally," Lily said between gritted teeth.

Josh swallowed and looked at Lily then back to Robinson. "I'd imagine being a private investigator is more challenging," he said in an attempt to recover.

Harvey sniffed again. "Yeah, can be."

"What are you working on at the moment?"

"This and that."

"Like?"

"What is this, a fucking interrogation?"

"Sorry, I, ah…"

"Come on, angel," Lily said, squeezing Josh's hand

tightly again. "Let's go and eat our lunch."

*

"Are you going to eat that?" Josh asked, pointing at Lily's cheesecake.

"Yes," she said. "I'll have it later this afternoon."

"Shame, I'm still…"

He stopped as he remembered he had two yum yums in the bag.

He'd have one of them on the bus back.

Or two.

Probably two.

"He's horrible," Lily said, "but I guess that's why I'm here."

"What have you discovered so far?"

"Not a lot. I've taken a couple of calls for him and reviewed two reports."

"Who were the calls from?"

"People wanting a private detective, but I think he turned them both down."

"And the reports?'

"They were more interesting. They were for two people called 'Mr F' and 'Miss J'. I presume he took the real names out because he doesn't trust me. With any luck that will change once I've been here longer."

"What was in them?"

Lily smiled. "A lot. There were two sections in each report. The first described their movements over seven days in detail. Again, he disguised the names of everyone they were with, but nothing else."

"And the second section?"

"It focused on their financial status. He broke down their net worth, estimated their outgoings, described where they got their income from, that kind of thing."

"Was there any mention of gambling, sports events or Thorney and Budge in either document?"

"No, but there was one thing that struck me as unusual. Mr F and Miss J don't appear to be connected in any way, and as far as I can see they're the subjects of two completely separate investigations. However, in the summary he included a similar conclusion for each of them."

"Which was?"

"For Mr F, it said 'S zero, I five', and for Miss J, 'S zero, I nine'."

"What on earth does that mean?"

Lily shrugged. "I haven't the faintest."

Chapter 48

The man known as Mr Smith was old-fashioned and valued the feel of paper in his hands.

He took a sip of his whisky and looked over at the quietly whirring printer as pages were fed into the tray. When he heard the concluding beep he walked over, stapled the top six sheets together and then did the same for the second report.

Returning to his black leather Chesterfield, he flicked through both printouts and was pleased to see that Harvey Robinson had been as thorough as usual. He didn't like the man, never had, but behind that obscenely coarse exterior lay a lot more intelligence than you would have thought. His analysis was usually comprehensive, and his conclusions concise and accurate.

He decided to start with Gordon French, but was disappointed to see that Robinson had given him a syndicate score of zero and an investment score of five. That meant that French was of no value as a gambler, and his usefulness as an investor was borderline at best.

Rather than wade through the rest of the report, he placed it on the lamp table beside him, took another sip of his Macallan and picked up the document for Ivy Jessup, mentally crossing his fingers in the hope of a better result. He went straight to the conclusion and was delighted to see her investment score was nine.

Nine was very high and indicated that the woman was highly susceptible to persuasion and also, equally important, had significant funds. He settled back to read the report in full.

Miss Jessup, it turned out, was twenty-eight years old and had recently inherited almost a quarter of a million pounds from her grandfather. At the moment the money was languishing in her bank account and Robinson had overheard her saying to a friend, 'I really should do more with it'.

He smiled.

She was perfect fodder for Davison.

He pulled out his phone and was pleased when it was answered immediately.

"Hello."

"Adam, I have an excellent new prospect for you."

"Oh, uh… good." Davison's response was unusually diffident.

He could sense something was amiss. "You don't sound very interested. Is everything okay?"

"Yes. Everything's fine, Mr Smith."

"What's happened, Adam?"

"It's nothing."

He deliberately kept silent. He knew from experience that this was the best way to encourage people to open up.

"There's an external audit going on," Adam said after a few seconds, "but I'm sure it's nothing to worry about."

"I thought Thorney and Budge's Risk Director had approved your portfolio?"

"He has, Mr Smith, but he wanted a second opinion."

"Who's he brought in?"

"I'm not sure of the company she works for, but her name's Sam Chambers."

"Is there any risk?"

"I don't think so."

He sat up when he heard this. "You don't think so! That's not good enough, Adam. When will she finish and give her seal of approval?"

"I… I don't know. She's coming back to see me on Friday."

"Ring me with an update straight afterwards."

"What about the new prospect?"

"That can wait. Let's deal with this Chambers woman first."

He ended the call, drained his glass, and walked to the drinks cabinet. He surveyed the bottles for a few seconds, decided on the Glengoyne and poured himself a double.

As he took his first sip, he reflected on how quickly things could change. Only a few weeks earlier, everything in the garden had been rosy. The syndicates had been flying high while Davison's hedge fund gained new investors almost every day.

Now it seemed that both were in trouble.

Davison was bright though, and with luck he'd done enough to deceive this Sam Chambers, whoever she was.

If he hadn't, he'd need to act quickly.

Having Artem at his beck and call gave him confidence that termination would be clean and tidy.

Artem never left loose ends.

Chapter 49

"How did you get on?" Luke asked when Josh returned from Oldfield Park.

Josh wheeled his chair over to Luke's desk and sat down next to him. "Unfortunately, I didn't see much of Harvey Robinson," he said. "I'm taking lunch in again tomorrow though."

"What were your first impressions?"

"He's brash and rough, stereotypically cockney. The way he talks you might think he was dumb, but I suspect there's a lot more to him. I've a feeling he's a smart cookie."

"That's interesting. How's Lily settling in?"

"Okay, I think. He asked her to check for typos in two reports, and in the summaries he'd written this."

Josh opened his notebook and passed it to Luke.

"S zero, I five, and S zero, I nine," Luke said, reading out loud. He looked across at Josh. "Who were the reports for?"

"The reports referred to them as Mr F and Miss J. We're guessing Robinson did that because he doesn't trust Lily yet."

"Probably. Hopefully, that'll change once she's been in a couple of days."

"Shall I add it to the crazy wall?"

"Yes, please."

Luke whirled his chair around, took a slurp of his coffee and tried to make sense of the whiteboard as Josh added the new information. It was full of photos and post-its with dotted lines going here, there and everywhere. The answer was up there somewhere, he knew it was. But where?

His gut told him that Harvey Robinson was key. It was

Robinson who had advised Simon Abrahams to invest with Thorney and Budge, but was he the Harvey in the note that Adrian Critchley had written? Lily's placement as Robinson's assistant was vital to finding out the extent of his involvement.

Then there was the mysterious Mr Smith who had threatened Sean Abbott and was likely to be the 'MRS' on Adrian's note.

"Guys," he called. "Could you spare me a minute please?"

Luke stood up and walked over to Josh as Sam, Maj and Helen joined them. He pointed at the photo of Adrian Critchley.

"Adrian Critchley was the reason we kicked off Project Barney," he said, "and I think we need to go back to basics if we're going to unravel what's going on. Sam, when are you seeing Douglas Woods again?"

"Tomorrow morning," she said.

"I think you need to be upfront with him. With Sean Abbott now being threatened, and the possibility that Brian Shepherd and his wife were murdered, we can't afford to pussyfoot around. Drop some of the names on the whiteboard into the conversation and see what reaction you get."

"Will do."

"Actually, would you mind if Maj joins you? Two pairs of eyes and ears would be better than one."

"Four pairs," Josh said before Sam could answer.

Luke glared at him. "Eh?"

Josh smiled. "If Maj joins Sam there'll be two pairs of eyes and two pairs of ears. That's four pairs."

"And that's important is it?"

"I'm just saying."

"Well, don't."

"It'll be good to have Maj along," Sam said, coming to Josh's rescue.

Luke turned his attention back to the board. "We're still missing something. I'm sure we are."

"Spencer Howell and Maurice Brown," Josh said.

"What about them?"

"They're missing from the crazy wall."

"We've discussed this. There's nothing to link them to the case."

"There might be, guv." He held his finger up. "Un momento." He turned back a page in his notebook, tapped it with his index finger and smiled, clearly very pleased with himself. "I think I may be onto something."

"And?" Luke prompted. "Spit it out."

"Before I left this morning I was trawling the internet to learn more about SCHBet, you know, Howell and Brown's company that the Fortune Group acquired." Josh read from his pad. "6th March 2019, Balakrishnan and Sharma. 18th December 2019, Chatterjee." He paused as if waiting for applause.

"Those are dates and what sound like Indian names," Luke said.

"Exactly." Josh nodded his head and his smile spread across his face. "They're the dates that Balakrishnan, Sharma and Chatterjee were found guilty of cheating at cricket. I'm still on the case with the first two, but Chatterjee was found to have deliberately bowled four no-balls in succession. And guess what?"

"People put money on that happening with SCHBet?"

Josh fired a finger gun at Luke. "You got it."

"I'll add them to the board," Helen said.

"I hate to say it, Josh," Luke said, "but good work. See what else you can find out."

"Gotcha, guv."

Chapter 50

Sam smiled over at Ollie as he topped up her orange juice.

He'd stopped over for the third night in a row. Was she allowing things to progress too quickly? Possibly, but they had so much in common and she was growing to like him and felt sure the feeling was reciprocated.

"What are your plans for today?" she asked.

"The usual routine. I'll start my exercises at around ten, then cycle sixty kilometres after lunch."

"It's alright for some. I'm aiming to be in work for nine."

He smiled and reached across the table for her hand. "It's only seven. That gives us plenty of time for…"

He stopped when Sam's phone rang. It was on the worktop behind him and before she could say anything he winked, turned around to retrieve it, pressed the green button and said, in his sexiest voice, "Hello, this is Sam Chamber's *very* personal assistant." After a few seconds he added, his voice now back to normal, "Yes, she's right here." He handed the phone over, mouthing, "Sorry," as he did so.

"Hello," she said.

"Hi, Sam," Luke said. "Sorry to bother you so early."

She sat upright and ran her hand through her hair. "No problem."

"I'm out this morning, but I wondered if you could get in by eight so we can discuss a couple of things before I leave. It's not essential, though. I can tell you're busy."

"No, it's fine. I'll be there."

"Really, Sam, you don't have to."

"I'll see you at eight," she said, more abruptly than she had intended, and hung up.

"Eight?" Ollie said. "I thought you were going in for nine?"

"It's changed." She pushed her chair back and stood up. "I'd better get in the shower."

"Yes. You need to be with your boss."

"What do you mean by that?"

"Nothing. He's asked you to be in early. I understand that." He looked down at his bowl of cornflakes, dipped his spoon into it and added, almost under his breath, "It's clear what's important to you."

Sam glared at him and started to say something before thinking better of it and leaving for the bathroom.

Chapter 51

Lily wore a pale blue denim jacket over a pink top for her second day working for Harvey Robinson. It was an outfit, she hoped, that wouldn't lend itself as readily to his wandering eyes.

She'd retained the Barbie and Ken earrings though.

As on the day before, Harvey was again late, though this time by only fifteen minutes.

"You could have left me the spare office key, Mr Robinson," she said when he appeared, still sporting his pale blue suit.

He shook his head as he fumbled with the lock. "Don't wanna risk you losing it."

He opened the door and in a rare moment of chivalry gestured for her to go first. She darted up and turned, smiling, to greet him when he appeared in the office.

"You raced up those fucking stairs," he said as he trudged up the last step.

"That's me," she said. "Always full of kenergy. Make you a coffee?"

"Yeah."

A few minutes later she returned with two mugs and placed his on the desk in front of him. "Any plans for how to use me today?" she asked.

Harvey grinned in a way that suggested he could think of several. His eyes were focused on her face and she found herself growing increasingly uncomfortable and slightly nauseous.

It had almost been better when he'd ogled her breasts.

A few seconds passed before he pulled himself together.

"I'm going out today," he said. "Probably around

eleven. I want you to review another report now and then while I'm out you gotta sort that out." He gestured to an old metal filing cabinet against one of the walls. "Pull out any folders more than ten years old and tidy the rest. They need index cards with the client's name on, then putting in alphabetical order."

Wow, this is going to be fun, she thought, but said, "Not a problem, Mr Robinson. What do you want me to do with the old files?"

"Find a box and put 'em in it. They can go in the other room." He took a slurp of his coffee. "I'll be back between two and three. That boyfriend coming over?"

"Yes, he's bringing me my lunch again."

"Dunno what you see in him. Seems a bit dozy if you ask me."

"I think he's lovely. We've talked about getting kengaged."

Chapter 52

"Thanks for coming in early," Luke said when Sam walked into the Ethics Room. "Maj offered to get us all coffees. Ah, here he is now."

"Morning, Sam," Maj said.

She turned and saw that he held a tray with three styrofoam cups. "Hi," she said, adding, "Thanks," as he indicated which one was hers.

"That one's yours, Luke," Maj said, pointing to the smallest cup.

"Cheers," Luke said as he retrieved his espresso from the tray. "Please pull up a chair." He waited until they were seated before continuing. "I asked you both to come in because I've had some thoughts about Douglas Woods. I'm in a meeting with Filcher at nine which is why it needed to be early."

Sam's phone beeped.

"Do you need to get that?" Luke asked.

"No, it's fine," she said. "It's only a WhatsApp." *The fifth or sixth he's sent since I left home.* "I'll deal with it later."

Luke smiled. "Please can you remind us what we know about Woods?."

"Sure. He first came to our attention because he'd been harassing Teresa McNee, a younger colleague. However, we now suspect him of removing Adrian Critchley's name from the Gambet database." She gestured to the whiteboard. "That's why his name's up there. When I saw him last week he was very much on edge and I couldn't get him to open up. However, two things he did reveal were that he's separated from his wife and that his main hobby is playing online casino games." She paused. "I've talked to a few other people who know him, and they've told me his whole personality has changed recently. It could have been triggered by the break-up of his marriage, of course."

"It could," Luke agreed, "but if it was Woods who altered the Gambet database there could be another reason. He could be the missing link and I want you to go in hard in this morning's meeting. I don't think we can afford to waste time going softly, softly." He smiled. "I want the two of you to use the Mutt and Jeff technique, better known as good cop, bad cop."

"Interesting," Maj said. "Who gets to be the bad cop?"

"That depends. How did you get on with Douglas Woods, Sam?"

"Not bad. I wouldn't say we were best buddies but he did force a smile when I praised the biscuits."

"You'll be the good cop, then."

"How do we play it, Luke?" Maj asked.

Luke smiled. "Very carefully. If you're too blatant he'll see right through it." He turned to Sam. "Sam, you need to take the lead, do most of the talking and continue to be your normal positive and supportive self." He returned his attention to Maj. "Maj, you're going to be negative throughout, making it clear that you don't believe him, even when Sam leaps to his defence and shows herself to be on his side."

"Then what?" Sam asked.

"When you feel the time is right, Maj leaves the meeting at which point, if we're lucky, Woods will open up and provide the information we're looking for."

Chapter 53

It was five past eleven, but Douglas Woods had been late for their first meeting and Sam had expected a repeat performance. Maj was planning to join them at around twenty past.

With a sigh, she scrolled through Ollie's WhatsApp messages again. He'd said 'sorry' a total of seven times in the twelve messages he'd sent since she'd left home. He had been half-asleep, he said, and had been looking forward to their spending another hour together before she set off for work.

She could accept all that, but there was something about the way he had said, *'You need to be with your boss'* that had bugged her. She thought of messaging him to ask what he'd meant but that would only put him on the defensive. *'Sorry. I didn't mean anything by it,'* would probably be his reply and where would that get her?

There was a light knock at the door and then Douglas Woods opened it and walked in. He looked more hangdog than ever.

She stood, smiled and shook his hand. "We're in luck," she said, gesturing to the tray on the table. "Not only have we got jammie dodgers but there are some custard creams today as well."

"Lucky us," he said without returning her smile. He sat down. "Is this going to take long?"

"Shouldn't do. Coffee?"

"No. I'm fine. You said you wanted to talk about technical training and development?"

"That's right." She poured herself a coffee and smiled at him again. "You're sure I can't tempt you?"

"Oh, okay then." He produced the tentative half-smile

that she remembered from last time. "White, please."

"Great. I'm not very technical so I've asked a colleague to join us. He's running late, but I'm afraid he can be like that." She passed him his coffee. "So, how's your week been so far?"

"Thanks," he said as he put the mug to his mouth. "The week's been okay I suppose."

"I can't get over how technical your job is. It's way beyond my capabilities." She laughed. "Believe me, using a basic spreadsheet is about as technical as I get. When did you first start working with databases?"

"University."

"Really. Wow. Did you study Information Technology?"

He nodded. "Then I did a PhD in Data Science."

"Have you ever thought of being a trainer yourself? I bet you'd be good at it."

"I'm not sure I would." He smiled and it was a genuine smile this time. "Too much of a nerd."

They were both taken aback when the door opened and Maj flew in like a whirlwind. "Hi, Sam," he said, ignoring Douglas. He leaned over both of them, poured himself a coffee and parked himself at the end of the table.

"How far have you got?" he asked.

"We've only just started," Sam said. "We…"

"For heaven's sake! I haven't got all day." Maj sat back and folded his arms across his chest.

Sam raised her eyebrows and looked across at Douglas as if to say, *This is typical Maj behaviour*.

"So, Douglas," she said, "you were saying that you did a PhD in Data Science."

"That's right."

"And has that made it easy for you to do the job you're doing now, or have you had lots of top-up training?"

"I've been on courses and conferences to keep me current. There are always new techniques to learn, not to mention new products."

"And has that helped you with the Fortune Group databases?"

Douglas nodded. "Yes, we use Oracle across the board and sometimes problems can only be corrected if you know how to interrogate the raw data."

Maj sat forward. "Interrogate or alter?"

Douglas looked over at him and raised an eyebrow. "Interrogate."

"So you've never amended the raw data?"

"I hardly think that's relevant, Maj," Sam said. She turned back to Douglas. "How many courses have you been on in the last twelve months?"

Douglas looked nervously over at Maj before answering. "Three," he said.

"You haven't answered my question," Maj said, still sitting forward and now jabbing his finger in Douglas's direction. "Someone told me that the Gambet database had been changed and one name replaced with another. Adrian Critchley became Ray Thomas. Was that your work, Mr Woods?"

"Maj!" Sam said. "Please excuse my colleague, Douglas. He's obviously got a bee in his bonnet about something. Now where were we? Oh, yes. You said you've been on three courses. What were the topics?"

"Two were Oracle courses," Douglas said, with a glance over at Maj, "and the other was a Gambet conference."

"Did that improve your skill with online casinos?" Maj asked.

"How did you know…"

Sam held her hand up. "I'm sorry, Douglas. That's my fault. Maj asked to see my notes from our last meeting, though why he's interested in your hobby I don't know." She turned and glared at Maj. "Do I need to remind you, Maj, that we're here to talk about training and development, nothing else?"

"And can I remind you, Sam," Maj sneered, "That some

of us in Internal Affairs have a wider remit than people's developmental needs? Someone's been fiddling with Gambet's database and I believe the culprit's in this room."

Maj stood up and glared at Douglas before delivering his next words. They had rehearsed this and Sam watched closely for any reaction.

"Do the names Brian and Kimberley Shepherd mean anything to you, Mr Woods?" Maj demanded. "What about Dolores or Sean Abbott or Harvey Robinson?"

Douglas shook his head. "Never heard of them."

"Have you come across Mr Smith?"

"I, ah…" Douglas swallowed and looked at Sam and then back at Maj. "What's this all about?"

Sam stood up. "Maj," she said. "You need to leave. This is disgraceful behaviour."

Maj gave her a look that would have frozen burning coals before storming out of the room, slamming the door behind him as he went.

"I'm sorry about that," Sam said. "I don't know what got into him." She smiled. "Maj has a wider remit than me and…" She hesitated. "Are you all right, Douglas?"

Douglas's face had lost all colour and he stared at her open-mouthed.

"I had to do it for Megan's sake," he said after a few seconds, a pleading note in his voice. "I had no choice."

Chapter 54

Luke glanced at his watch and was shocked to see that he had only been in Filcher's office for twenty-five minutes.

He sighed.

It felt like he'd been there for hours.

Edward Filcher had called the meeting to discuss budgets for the next quarter, a subject close to his heart but which none of his team were interested in.

Luke sat next to James and opposite Glen and Fred, while their boss had taken his customary position at the head of the table.

"Balance sheet," Filcher said. "Vital. Hah. Only thing that matters." He hesitated as another thought came to him. "And profit. Those two are key. Nothing else."

"What about share value? Isn't it important to our investors?" Fred asked, a twinkle in his eye.

"Exactly. Good point, Fred. Balance sheet, profit and stock value. Those three. They are the only measures of importance."

James nudged Luke and indicated Glen with a nod of his head. Luke looked across the table to see the Head of Security struggling to stay awake, his eyelids gently closing every few seconds before springing open again.

"And capital," Fred added.

"Indeed. yes." Filcher nodded several times. "Good point, well made. Those five are crucial if…"

"Four," James said. "Balance sheet, profit, share price and capital. That's four."

"Of course. I meant four. They are important and only them."

"Unless you include brand," Fred said.

"Mmm. Yes. Important to consider our brand. That

means…"

He stopped speaking as Glen suddenly jerked upwards in his seat, grunted loudly, looked wildly around the room and then fixed his eyes on his boss.

"Yes," Glen said, now blinking his eyes. "Lots of them."

Filcher raised an eyebrow. "Lots of what, Glen?"

Glen was saved from answering by a knock at the door.

"Enter," Filcher called.

It was Gloria. "I'm sorry, Mr Filcher," she said. "Luke's needed urgently."

Luke tried to ignore James' whispered "Lucky sod," as he stood up to leave.

"I'm sorry about this, Mr Filcher," he lied, then compounded the lie by adding, "I'll try to keep it brief so that I can rejoin you."

"Mmm." Filcher turned back to the other members of his team, Luke already forgotten. "Where was I?"

"You were talking about the balance sheet," James said, trying unsuccessfully to stifle a yawn.

Luke closed the door behind him and didn't catch his boss's reply.

"What is it, Gloria?" he asked as he followed her to her desk.

"Sam needs to speak to you," she said, passing him her handset.

Luke put it to his ear. "Hi, Sam," he said. "Are you okay?"

"I'm fine. Could you come down to the Abbey Room, please? I'm with Douglas Woods."

"Of course." He handed the handset back to Gloria and strode to the stairs.

Two minutes later he walked into the small meeting room to see Sam sitting at the table while a man stood at the window, his shoulders slumped.

"This is Luke," Sam said.

Douglas turned around and Luke could see that his eyes were rimmed with red. He looked at Luke and sighed and his shoulders seemed to slump even further. "I had no option," he said. "I didn't know what else I could do."

"Why don't you come back to the table and tell us all about it?" Sam said.

Douglas shuffled back to the nearest chair as Luke sat down opposite Sam.

"As I said a minute ago," Sam went on. "Luke is very experienced and I guarantee he'll keep everything you say confidential." She turned to Luke. "I suggested we invite Maj back in, but Douglas wasn't keen."

"I never want to see that bastard again," Douglas mumbled.

"You told me you had to do it for Megan's sake," Sam said. "Is Megan your wife?"

Douglas nodded. "She doesn't know about any of this. You won't tell her, will you?"

"Of course not. You're separated, aren't you?"

"Yes, but I still care for her. Hell, I still love her. If I didn't I wouldn't have done what he demanded."

"What who demanded?" Luke asked.

"I don't know his real name, but he calls himself Mr Smith." He swallowed. "He helped me out when I got into debt."

"Was that through your online gaming?" Sam asked.

He nodded again. "Yes. I ran up a massive credit card bill. That's why Megan left me." He paused. "I should have known he was too good to be true, but he sucked me in and I was desperate."

"How did he suck you in, Douglas?" Luke asked.

Douglas sighed. "He rang me out of the blue and said he was looking for a database engineer for his company. He told me he'd heard I was the best in the business and that he'd be prepared to pay me way more than I earn here. I was flattered." He grunted. "Stupid too."

"Then what happened?"

"He asked about our Oracle system and whether I could write a program to manipulate the raw data, to prove I could get past the firewalls and other security layers. I resisted at first, but he said he realised what I was doing was time-consuming as well as being a tad unethical and he'd pay me a thousand pounds as a gesture of goodwill."

"What did he want you to change?"

"The names of a couple of people who had placed bets. I then had to send him images of the before and after records."

"When was this?"

"About two months ago."

"Did he offer you the job after that?" Sam asked.

Douglas laughed, but there was no humour in it. "There was never any job. After that first time, he claimed there'd been a glitch and could I change two more names. I fell for it again, received another thousand pounds in my bank account, and then the threats started."

"The threats?" Luke prompted.

"Yes. He started by saying that he'd expose what I'd done if I didn't continue, that I'd lose my job. I called his bluff. I mean he sounds so posh, I never dreamt he'd…" He put his head in his hands. "Christ," he said. "How did I get myself into this mess."

Sam put her hand on his arm. "What did Mr Smith do, Douglas?" she asked.

"It wasn't him directly. He sent someone else." He shivered. "He knocked on my door one evening and told me he had a message from Mr Smith. The things he said seemed ridiculous, but you only had to look in his eyes to see that he meant every word."

"What did he say?" Luke asked.

"He said he knew where Megan lived, that…" He wiped his left eye before continuing. "He said he would throw ammonia in her face if I let Mr Smith down, that she would be scarred for life."

"Can you describe him?"

"He's big. Not as tall as you but over six feet and strongly built. He wore a balaclava." He paused. "All I could see were his eyes but I'll never forget them. They were a vivid blue and so, so cold. They seemed to cut right through me."

"Was he British?"

Douglas shook his head. "Definitely not. He spoke excellent English but he had an Eastern European accent. I'd say he was Polish or maybe Russian."

"Maj listed a lot of names and asked if you knew them," Sam said. "Do you mind if I run them past you again?"

"No, I suppose not."

She looked down at her pad. "Brian and Kimberley Shepherd?"

Douglas shook his head. "No."

"Dolores?"

He shook his head again.

"Adrian Critchley?"

"Mmm." He thought for a second. "I think that was one of the names Mr Smith asked me to alter."

"Douglas," Luke said. "Did you keep a record of the changes you made?"

"No. I knew what I was doing was wrong and I deleted everything as soon as I'd made the amendments."

"Do you think if you tried you might remember more of them? This is very important, Douglas."

"I can try."

"Good. Sam, is it okay if I leave you with Douglas now?"

"Sure," she said. "Do you have to go back to your meeting?"

Luke smiled. "Not on your nelly."

Chapter 55

It was just before twelve-thirty when Lily buzzed Josh in.

"He's gone out," she said when he stepped into the main office. She was seated on the floor with documents and folders in piles around her.

"What are you doing?" Josh asked.

"Tidying and you need to help. Robinson's due back between two and three and he asked me to get all this mess sorted out. If I finish it early I can have a nosey around."

She pushed a stack of folders towards him. "More than a decade old, in there," she said, pointing to a large cardboard box. "If they're newer than that, pass them to me and I'll write the index cards. And don't bother trying to read any of the contents beyond the names. Nothing in the cabinet seems to be less than five years old. It's all his old cases."

"Gotcha." He pulled the first folder off the top of the pile. "So, found anything interesting out today?"

"He's asked me to review another report for him. Says he'll finish it this afternoon and wants me in on the dot of nine tomorrow to check it." She laughed. "Bit of a cheek given he's the one who's late every day."

"Who's the report for?"

"Lord V, he said."

"Lord Voldemort, do you think?"

Lily ignored the question. "I told him you're my fiancee."

"You did what?" Josh squealed. "But why?"

"To help my character. I said we were kengaged."

Josh chuckled. "That's kind of funny." His smile disappeared and his next words came out in a panicky rush. "But what if he tells Leanne?"

"He doesn't know Leanne."

"I guess not. Still, it's a bit risky."

"Your acting was good yesterday, Josh."

"What acting?"

"The way you played dumb. Robinson commented on how dozy you seem."

"But I wasn't... ah, right, yes, thanks."

*

It was almost an hour later when Lily announced that they'd finished.

"About time," Josh said. "I'm famished."

He pulled two packets of sandwiches out of his backpack and held one out in each hand.

"Prawn mayo or chicken and sweetcorn?"

"Prawn, please."

He handed the packet in his left hand to Lily, put his own down, peered into the backpack and stared sheepishly at her.

"Have you brought something sweet?" she asked as she began tearing into the sandwich wrapper.

"No, well, I, ah..." he reached into the bag and pulled out a clear packet with a slab of something inside it."

"Is that millionaire's shortbread?" she asked. "I love millionaire's shortbread."

"There's only one. Do you want to split it?"

"Isn't that a two-pack?"

"Ah..."

"Did you eat one on the bus?"

Josh laughed. "Possibly."

Lily held her hand out and he passed it over. "I'll have it with coffee later this afternoon," she said as she put it beside her and started her sandwich.

"I think you'd better leave as soon as we've eaten," she

added after she'd swallowed her first mouthful. "Don't want to risk you still being here when he returns."

"Shouldn't I stay to keep an eye out for him? You know, while you have your nosey."

"That's a thought. He's been late both mornings, so I'd be surprised if it's not nearer three or even afterwards before he's back, but it would be good to have a lookout."

"Are you searching for anything in particular?"

Lily shook her head. "Not really. He locks his desk drawers and that cabinet..." She pointed to a more modern-looking filing cabinet adjacent to the desk. "...but there's always the chance he's dropped something by mistake."

"I suggest you start with the bin."

"Good call." Lily retrieved the waste bin from under Harvey's desk, stuck her hand in and immediately screamed.

"Buggery-boo!" Josh screeched, fearing she'd found a severed finger or worse. "What is it?"

Lily turned to face him and pulled a sour face. "Chewing gum," she said. "It's disgusting."

Josh heaved a sigh of relief. "Thank goodness. I thought..."

"What's this?" She looked up at him, a bemused smile on her face, and then back into the contents of the bin. "That's the last thing I expected to find in Harvey Robinson's discarded rubbish."

Chapter 56

"It was the original passport?" Luke asked as he read the words on the screen of Josh's phone.

Josh nodded. "Absoluto. It had a red cover embossed with 'Pilipinas Pasaporte' in gold. Robinson must have dropped it in the bin by mistake."

"You did the right thing taking photos and leaving it there. I can't imagine he meant to throw it away."

"It has to be the same woman, doesn't it, guv?"

"Yes, has to be." Luke smiled and waved Josh's phone in the air. "This is proof that Harvey Robinson is working with Mr Smith." He read from the photo. "Dolores Buenavista, born in Manila."

"I saw that, guv, but her date of birth puts her at forty-two."

"What of it?"

"She doesn't look that old in her photo."

"What do you mean 'that old'? She's the same age as me."

"Sorry." Josh's cheeks began to turn pink. "I meant she doesn't look, you know, ah…elderly."

"Elderly?"

"No, no. Not elderly, I meant… I, ah…"

"What are you two looking at?" Helen said.

"Please help me out of this," Josh whispered.

"Ignore him," Luke said. "He was busy digging a hole and I was having fun helping him do it." He passed Josh's phone over. "Josh and Lily found this in Harvey Robinson's bin."

"Ach, that's a bonus," Helen said when she'd read what was on the screen. "I'll add a wee note to the board."

The three of them walked over to the whiteboard and

Helen updated Dolores' entry on Mr Smith's Post-it.

"You need to add someone else to the board," Luke said when she'd finished. "Douglas Woods told Sam and me that Mr Smith sent an Eastern European man to threaten him. He wore a balaclava so he didn't get a view of his face.

"We could call him 'Mr Balaclava'," Josh said.

Luke shrugged. "Why not?" he said.

When Helen had added him, Luke tapped the photo of Harvey Robinson. "I wonder why Harvey Robinson had Dolores' details," he said.

"He must have been investigating her for some reason," Josh ventured.

"Yes, but why?" Luke scratched at his chin. "It was clear from my brief exchange that she doesn't speak much English, which suggests she came to this country recently. I wonder if Smith asked Robinson to do a check on her."

"Aye," Helen said, "but if he was only checking her out why would he have her passport?"

"That's true. He must have met her for some reason, and either borrowed or taken her passport."

"Could she be an illegal immigrant, guv?" Josh said. "Perhaps he confiscated it, and threatened to dob her in if she didn't work for Smith."

"It's possible." Luke mused on this thought for a few seconds. "Josh, when you see Lily, ask her to empty the bins, find the passport and give it to Robinson. He might inadvertently reveal something about how he got hold of it."

"Gotcha, guv."

Luke's phone rang.

"Excuse me," he said as he accepted the call and stepped away from the others. "Hello, Luke Sackville."

"Luke, it's Sean."

Luke could immediately sense the panic in the man's voice.

"What's happened, Sean?"

"Kirsten's been threatened again. She was in the supermarket and a tannoy message asked her to come to the customer service desk. It was another note."

"Saying much the same?"

"Yes." The man sounded like he was almost in tears. "I've had enough, Luke. I rang Mr Smith and told him that his threats weren't going to work, that I was going to take my family somewhere safe."

"Where are you now?"

"We're on the train to Bath. I'm going to ask Ollie if he can put us up until this is sorted. If he can't, it'll have to be a hotel."

Luke made a snap decision. "The three of you can stay with me."

"What? No, that's too much to ask."

"I insist, and it's no problem. I take it you're still not prepared to speak to the police?"

Sean's reply was instant. "No, definitely not."

"Okay. When does your train get into Bath Spa?"

"Quarter past three."

"I'll meet you there. You'll find me in the pick-up area at the back of the station."

"How will I recognise you?"

"I'm six foot six."

"Oh." Sean paused. "Thanks for this, Luke."

"No problem. I'll see you in half an hour or so."

"Was that Sean Abbott?" Helen asked when Luke had hung up.

Luke was about to tell her and Josh what had happened when Sam and Maj walked into the Ethics Room.

"Douglas remembered two other names," Sam said as they approached the whiteboard, "but neither Maj nor I recognise either of them. Anyone heard of Lionel Grassmore or Eileen O'Connor?"

They all shook their heads.

"I'll do some googling," Maj said, as Helen added the names to the board. "See what I can find out."

"Good idea," Luke said. "We've made some progress with Dolores, the woman who answered the phone when I rang the number Sean Abbott gave me." He explained about the passport. "More importantly, Sean's just rung me and he's received more threats. They've scared him so much that he's fled London with his partner and their daughter."

"That's awful," Sam said. "Where have they gone?"

"They're on a train to Bath."

"Oh." She pulled her phone out of the back of her jeans. "I'd better tell Ollie."

"No. Don't."

Her eyebrows narrowed. "What do you mean, don't. Ollie's his best friend. They'll need somewhere to stay and…"

"They're staying with me."

"What?"

"I think it's safest. Harvey Robinson's based in Bath and for all we know Mr Smith is as well. I'd prefer it if Sean and his family were in Norton St Philip and well out of the way."

"I'll still need to tell Ollie though. He'll want to see them."

Luke shook his head. "I don't think you should." He saw the expression on Sam's face. "Look, I've got nothing against Ollie," he lied, "but we need to be ultra-careful. I trust everyone in this room…"

"And Lil," Josh said.

They all turned to look at him, but Luke voiced the question on everyone's lips. "Lil?" he asked.

"Lily," Josh said with a smile.

"I guessed that, son, but why did you call her Lil?"

"I'm in character. It's called method acting."

"Give me strength."

"So, I'm not allowed to tell my boyfriend?" Sam said.

"Despite him being Sean's best friend."

"I think it's best."

"I can tell Leanne though, can't I, guv?" Josh asked.

"No, Josh. Not this time."

"What about Lil?"

Luke gave a deep sigh. "Yes, Josh," he said. "You can tell Lil."

Chapter 57

The train was delayed by ten minutes and Luke decided to use the time to ring his daughter.

"Hi, Chloe," he said when she answered. "Are you still coming home for the weekend?"

"I was planning on it. Why?"

"I've got some people staying over for a few days. I'd still love you to come, but I thought I ought to warn you."

"Are they friends of yours?"

"It's work-related. I'll explain when you get here. Their names are Sean and Kirsten and they've got a young daughter, Tina."

"Oh, how lovely. How old is she?"

"Five."

"Fantastic. I should be there by about five, providing Clarissa doesn't let me down."

Luke laughed. He had never understood why women, and Josh for that matter, liked to give their cars names.

"Great," he said. "With any luck, I'll be able to get away early and be there when you arrive. See you then. Bye, darling."

"Bye, Dad."

He hung up and smiled as he climbed out of the car and walked to the turnstile. Chloe loved children and her presence would hopefully ease things for Sean and his partner.

A few minutes later he saw Sean approaching the exit. He was wheeling two large suitcases while his partner held Tina's hand. Both mother and daughter had long blonde hair while Sean's was brown and slightly receding at the temple.

"Hi, Luke," Sean said as he inserted his ticket into the

machine. "I really can't thank you enough."

"Don't be silly."

Luke waited until they were all through before shaking first Sean's and then Kirsten's hand.

He bent down to their daughter.

"And you must be Tina," he said. "Do you want to shake hands too?"

She nodded. "Pleased to meet you, Luke," she said as she reached for his hand.

Luke stood up again and took one of the cases from Sean. "The car's just around here," he said as he led them to the small parking area at the back of the station.

He loaded the cases into the boot of the BMW while Sean put Tina into the car seat which Luke had bought for his niece Marion when she came to stay. Kirsten sat next to her daughter while Sean climbed into the front.

"It's a twenty-minute drive to my house from here," Luke said once they'd set off.

"I'm very grateful for this," Kirsten said and Luke detected a slight German accent. "We're happy for the three of us to share a bedroom by the way."

"There'll be no need. I own a rambling old farmhouse and there are five bedrooms so Tina can have a room to herself." He paused. "I suggest we talk about what happens next when we get there."

The next twenty minutes passed in silence apart from Tina asking her mother twice if they were there yet. Luke noticed in his rear-view mirror that Kirsten held her daughter's hand tightly throughout the journey.

"Are you all okay with dogs?" Luke asked as he turned into the drive and pulled up in front of the house.

"I love dogs," Tina said immediately. "Have you got a poodle."

"He's a cocker spaniel," Luke said. "His name's Wilkins." He looked at Kirsten in the rear view mirror. "He's very good with children."

She smiled in acknowledgement but her face was pale and it was a thin attempt.

"Come on, Tina," Luke said after they'd all got out of the car. He held his hand out and the little girl grasped it and let him lead her to the front door.

Wilkins' squeals of excitement started as soon he turned the key in the lock, and they entered the lobby to find him running from side to side in the dog crate.

Tina watched in fascination as Luke fed the cocker a dog biscuit through one of the gaps before opening the door. As soon as he did so, Wilkins darted out, leapt up at Luke twice and then moved to Tina and started sniffing her legs. The spaniel let her stroke his head for a few seconds before darting out of the front door and cocking his leg against a flower pot.

"He's lovely," Tina said as she followed the dog outside.

"Come on in," Luke said to Sean and Kirsten who were standing a few yards from the entrance. "I'll show you around and we can get your luggage in afterwards."

"Sounds good," Sean said. He looked almost as pale as his partner, and his smile was just as weak.

Tina was very taken with her bedroom, and fascinated by Marion's toy kitchen. "I'm going to cook you a meal, Mummy," she said. "What would you like?"

Kirsten smiled at her daughter, and it was full-blooded and genuine now. "I would like steak and chips please, chef," she said.

"I tell you what," Luke said. "Why don't you stay here while Tina prepares your meal? Sean and I will be in the lounge if you need anything."

"Good idea," Sean said.

"Would you like a cup of tea, Kirsten?"

"That would be lovely."

"Tina, would you like a drink?"

"May I have some blackcurrant squash please?"

"Yes, of course. Coming right up."

As he said this Wilkins appeared behind them, his tail wagging furiously.

"Oh, can he stay please," Tina said. "Does he like steak and chips?"

"Yes on both counts," Luke said. "But don't give him too much. I don't want him to be ill."

"Don't worry, Luke," she said, her voice serious as she looked up at him. "It's not real food. I'm pretending."

*

"Your daughter's lovely," Luke said to Sean once drinks had been made and distributed and they were seated in the lounge.

"Yes, she's a darling," Sean said. He took a sip of his tea. "Thanks again."

"Stop thanking me, Sean."

"Sorry." He put his mug down on the coffee table and sat forward on the sofa, then looked over at Luke. "I'm at a loss as to what to do. When he made a third threat I had to take them and run." He swallowed. "I'm scared, Luke, very scared."

"Sam told me about the incident at the park. What else has happened?"

"It was outside school this morning. A boy passed Kirsten a note after Tina had gone in, then he pointed to a man standing at the end of the road before running off."

"The same man who was in the park?"

"Yes." He pulled two sheets of paper from his pocket and passed one of them to Luke. "That's the note from the park."

Luke was chilled by what he read.

Sean must choose

Accident in Lombardy
Or a childless couple

"This was the note that was left at the supermarket," Sean said as he passed Luke the second piece of paper.

I follow you everywhere
Sean must comply
Or else...

"Kirsten practically fainted on the spot," Sean went on.

"Do you mind if I keep these?" Luke asked.

"Not at all." He put his head in his hands.

"We'll get through this," Luke said. "I promise you."

Sean looked up. "I hope you're right."

"You're safe here, but you mustn't tell anyone where you are, even your close family and friends."

"Sorry, but I've already told my mother where I'm staying. My father died last year and the last thing I want to do is worry her so I said we were taking a break in a village south of Bath for a few days." He hesitated. "I told Ollie too. He's been very supportive and I felt he ought to know I'd gone somewhere safe."

"Okay. What's done is done, but please don't tell anyone else. The same goes for Kirsten."

"I won't."

"I'd like to ask Kirsten a few questions about this man. Would you mind taking her place with Tina?"

"Not at all."

Kirsten appeared a few minutes later.

"Do you think the threats are genuine?" she said, her voice pleading. "Would that man really hurt my little girl if Sean doesn't do what they ask?"

There was no easy way to answer this. "I will keep you and your family safe for as long as necessary," Luke said. "I know this is incredibly difficult for you, but please try not to worry."

"Sean said you wanted to ask me some questions."

"Yes. You've seen this man twice now. Are you able to describe him?"

"I'll do my best, but he was some distance away. He was dressed in black leather on both occasions like he was in motorbike gear." She hesitated as she tried to remember. "He's big, not quite your height but tall. Well built too, but without being overweight."

"How old do you think he is?"

"He could have been anywhere between thirty and fifty. He had a square jaw but his eyes were his strongest feature."

"What about his eyes?"

"They reminded me of a killer doll in a horror film I saw a few years back."

"Chucky?"

She nodded. "That's the one. His eyes were like Chucky's." She shivered. "They were a deep, piercing blue that made my blood run cold."

Chapter 58

Luke showered, dressed and made his way downstairs to find Sean in the lounge in his dressing gown. He was perched on the front of the sofa staring into space.

"Couldn't sleep?" Luke asked.

Sean looked up at him and shook his head. "Not a wink. I've been sitting here since before five."

"What about Kirsten?"

"She nodded off around midnight. Still asleep I hope." He sighed. "I'm worried about her."

"I'm not surprised. Look, I've got to let Wilkins out to do his business then I'll be back. Coffee?"

"Let me make it. How do you like it?"

"Strong and black, please. I won't be long."

A few minutes later Luke returned followed by the cocker who sat patiently beside the armchair before leaping onto his lap as soon as he sat down. Wilkins circled once on his master's thighs then flopped down.

"Thanks for this," Luke said as he picked the mug up from the table beside him and held it out of reach of the dog's tongue.

"Don't mention it. What are your plans for today?"

"I'm working from home until lunchtime."

"You don't need to. You've done enough for us and we'll be fine on our own."

Luke decided a little white lie was in order. "I often work from home on a Friday morning," he said. "It helps to break the weekend in gently."

"I suppose so." Sean looked at Luke intently. "What's our way through this, Luke? I can cheat in Il Lombardia, but they won't stop there, I know they won't."

Luke was inclined to agree, and if he was honest he

didn't feel close to catching the mysterious Smith or his East European lackey. However, it was important to keep Sean's mood as buoyant as possible.

"We have a couple of promising leads," he said. "One of my team is working as assistant to a private investigator who works for Smith. My hope is that he lets something slip that leads us to him."

"And the other lead?"

"The investigator is also linked to a hedge fund company and I have someone working there too. We believe someone is running a crooked portfolio but we haven't got to the bottom of it yet."

"It sounds like this investigator is pivotal." Sean took a sip of his coffee. "Given what Smith has done aren't you worried about the safety of your staff?"

"If the man who threatened Kirsten was involved I would be, but I think both the private investigator and the hedge fund manager are pawns in all this. I don't see either of them resorting to violence."

Luke looked up as Kirsten appeared holding her daughter's hand.

"Good morning," he said.

Before Kirsten could say anything, Tina said, "Luke, can I have waffles, please?"

Her mother looked down at her in shock. "Tina!"

Luke smiled at the little girl. "I haven't got any waffles but there are crumpets in the bread bin. Do you like crumpets?"

"Ooh! I've never had crumpets."

Luke addressed his next comment to her parents. "Sean, Kirsten, I want you to feel at home while you're here, and I've shown you what's what in the kitchen so please help yourselves to breakfast."

They left for the kitchen and Luke took his coffee into the study, followed by Wilkins who curled up under the desk.

There was something in what Sean had said about safety and Luke decided to ring the team and warn them to be on their guard. It was the kind of message that couldn't be delivered by text or email.

He began with Lily and was pleased to catch her before she left for Oldfield Park.

"What's your impression of Harvey Robinson?" he asked when she answered.

"Aside from being a dirty old man, you mean?" she said with a laugh.

"Yes, aside from that. Does he come across as prone to violence?"

She thought about this for a second. "No, I'd say not. He portrays this image of an East End hard man, but I don't think it's more than skin deep. He's more intelligent than he lets on too."

"Okay. Please be on your guard though, and if there's the slightest suggestion he's onto you, get out of there. He might not be violent but he's associating with people who will stop at nothing."

"Don't worry, Luke. I'll be careful."

He rang Josh next.

"Morning," Josh said, and it was clear from that one word that he was eating. "Sorry," he went on after an audible swallow. "You caught me in the middle of my sausage sandwich."

"Are you seeing your girlfriend again this lunchtime, Josh?"

"No, I'm going to see Lily in Oldfield Park." Josh chuckled. "Oh, hang on, you meant her, didn't you? I wasn't sure which girlfriend you meant for a second."

"When you go…" Luke began but Josh interrupted him.

"Just a minute, guv," he said.

Luke heard Leanne's voice in the background but couldn't make out the words.

Josh's reply was crystal clear though.

"No, I don't think I've got two girlfriends, Leanne," he said. "I only see Lily at lunchtimes."

There were more words from Leanne.

"Of course, there's nothing between us. I'm fond of her..." There was a short pause as Josh realised his mistake. "Ah... when I said fond, I meant I like her, but I'm not fond fond. Not like I am of you. I'm..."

It was Luke's turn to interrupt. "Ring me when you get to work, Josh."

There was no reply and Luke smiled as he hung up.

He decided he'd catch Josh, Helen and Maj later when they were all in the office and rang Sam.

"Just a moment," she said in a whisper when she answered the phone.

Luke sighed.

She was with him again.

It was clear they were now living together.

"I'll have to keep my voice low," she said a few seconds later, "but I'm in the kitchen now."

"If I'm interrupting anything..."

"Of course not. I, ah..."

There was an awkward silence and Luke decided to move straight to the reason for his call.

"You're seeing Adam Davison at Thorney and Budge again today, aren't you?" he asked.

"Yes. At eleven. I, ah... I was going to go straight there from home. Is that okay?"

Not if you're with him, Luke thought but said, trying to keep his tone light, "Of course it is. What do you make of him."

"Of Adam?"

He wanted to say *No, of Ollie, that boyfriend of yours. Is he good to you? Is he a permanent fixture?*

"Yes," he said. "Do you think he might be prone to violence?"

She laughed. "Not in the slightest. He might be up to something dodgy with that portfolio, but I don't think he'd hurt a fly."

"I trust your judgement, Sam, but please, please be careful. I'm sure Adam is okay but I'm worried he might be connected to the East European man who threatened Douglas Woods and Sean Abbott's partner."

"Don't worry. I'll be careful."

"Do that. I couldn't bear it if anything happened to you."

There was silence at the other end, then he heard a man's voice call, "Sam?"

"I'm sorry, Luke," she said. "I'll have to go."

There was another pause and then a click as she ended the call.

Chapter 59

Lily was surprised to find the door unlocked when she reached Harvey Robinson's office. She bounded up the stairs to find him seated behind his desk, a scowl on his face.

"About fucking time," he grunted.

"It's only ten to nine, Mr Robinson."

"Mmm. Report's ready for you to review." He tapped a finger on a document on the front edge of his desk.

She was about to reach down for it when he said, "Coffee first."

A please would be nice, she thought but said, "Of course."

"No Barbie and Ken earrings today, then," he said, his double-barrelled grin back.

She preferred the scowl.

"No," she giggled. "I'm wearing another Barbie t-shirt though."

"So I see," he said, his eyes dipping to her front.

She turned quickly for the kitchen and put the kettle on.

Thank goodness Luke was paying her and she wasn't having to endure this man for a rate that was less than the minimum wage.

A few minutes later she took his drink in.

"Thanks," he said as he took the mug from her.

There, you see. A thank you didn't cost you much, did it?

"I found this yesterday," she said, holding out Dolores Buenavista's passport.

He snatched it from her. "You been noseying around?"

"No, it was in the bin when I emptied it yesterday. I put it in the other room and forgot all about it until this morning. Is she a client?"

"Nah. Well, kind of."

"If you give me her number I can ring her and kensure she gets it back."

"Leave it with me. I'll deal with it."

"Are you sure?"

"Yes, I'm fucking sure." He put the passport in the top drawer of his desk and picked up his report. "Here," he said, thrusting it towards her. "Take this and check it for errors."

She took the printout into the other room, grabbed her notebook and pen and sat down at the table. Her plan was to read it through to see if there was anything that might be of use in their investigation. Only then would she review it for typos.

As with the previous reports, the document was heavily redacted so that names and places were left blank. The man was referred to throughout as 'Lord V'.

There was a series of entries with dates going back several weeks. Each described Lord V's visits to various establishments, and she noted that over half of those visits were to casinos.

In his conclusion, Harvey wrote that Lord V had a mistress he lavished money on and was at casinos almost daily, but lacked control of his finances. He was saved from this being a problem by the fact he was extraordinarily wealthy. Lily gasped as she saw that Harvey estimated his net worth to be more than £60 million.

The scores assigned to Lord V were 'S eight, I eight'.

She sat back, disappointed. There was nothing in the report of any use, nothing at all.

Sighing, she set about searching for typographical and grammatical mistakes and an hour later returned to the main room.

Harvey was finishing a phone call. "It should be with you soon," he said. He paused, looked meaningfully at Lily, and added, "Hopefully within the hour."

He hung up.

"Well," he said. "Have you done it?"

"Yes," she said as she put the report down on the desk in front of him.

"Would it be easier if you came around this side of the desk?"

Not on your nelly, you pervert, she thought as he grinned lasciviously, reminding her yet again of the 'Here's Johnny' scene in The Shining.

"No, I'm fine," she said. "If we put the report at an angle that should kenable us both to read it."

She twisted the report and started to point out the errors.

"I think this should be 'square' not 'squire'," she said, pointing to the third line down.

Harvey nodded.

She moved to the third paragraph. "Shouldn't there be a full stop here?"

"Yeah."

She turned the page and indicated the top sentence. "This one didn't make sense to me at all. You've written that Lord V was 'excepted into the House'."

"What of it?"

"Shouldn't that be 'accepted' beginning 'a-c-c' and 'house' without a capital 'H'? I don't know the context because most of the sentence is blanked out but it doesn't make sense as it's written."

Harvey looked up at her and grunted. She thought she saw a sly smile but it was gone as soon as it appeared.

"Anything else?" he asked.

She ran through the other typos she had found and then sat back in her seat.

"What next, Mr Robinson?"

He was busy logging back into his computer and held his mug out without looking at her.

"Another coffee?" she asked.

"Yeah."

"And then?"

"Perm your nails or summat while I edit this report. I need to send it asap."

"Is it important?"

"Yeah. Now go on, piss off."

Chapter 60

As Sam walked through the door into Thorney and Budge's reception it dawned on her that it was only two days since her first visit. So much had happened since then that it felt like a lifetime.

She had been incredibly busy at work, trying to uncover the secrets of Adam Davison's AOIF hedge fund while at the same time helping Teresa McNee overcome her problems with Douglas Woods. All this was further compounded by the need to involve herself in Project Barney.

Her social life had taken off too, thanks largely, well if she was honest totally, to Ollie. He wasn't perfect, no one was, but she was growing more and more fond of him as each day passed. The main challenge was that she didn't know him well enough yet to be able to tell when he was teasing or when he was serious. That would come with time, she guessed, and realised she was already thinking of him in terms of the long haul.

Ollie had the kind of looks she found attractive too, which did no harm, no harm at all. He wasn't as tall as Luke, but he was over six foot, just as muscular and their faces had a similar profile. Luke had the scar of course, which made him stand out. He'd gained it a couple of decades earlier and it gave his face real character.

"Mr Casey will be down in a minute," the receptionist said as she signed the visitors' book. "Please take a seat."

As she sat down, Sam wondered how best to play Adam Davison. He had seemed very much on edge at their first meeting and had been shocked when both she and Patrick had said they'd been able to open the 'Diverts' tab on his spreadsheet that he thought he'd secured with a password.

There had to be something in there that he didn't want other people to find. But what could that be? And why had he called it 'Diverts' in the first place? It was linked to the table of investors but didn't have any words or formulae. Instead, there were long sets of alphanumeric characters, each one pointing to a different investor. There were eight different combinations of letters and numbers split almost equally across the two-hundred-plus investors.

Long sets of alphanumeric characters…

It suddenly dawned on her what they might be and she pulled up the lid of her laptop, signed in, retrieved the spreadsheet and tapped on the 'Diverts' tab.

She checked the first set of letters and numbers. It began 'IE12'. She moved to the second to find it started 'LV49'.

She was on to something, she was sure of it.

"Busy?"

Sam looked up to see Patrick Casey smiling down at her, Adam by his side. As on their previous meeting, Patrick was dressed impeccably while Adam looked somewhat dishevelled, his tie loose below an open collar.

She closed her laptop and stood up. "Sorry," she said as she shook first Patrick's hand and then Adam's. "I was dealing with my emails."

"I've booked the same room as last time," Patrick said. "I've got a lunch meeting I have to go to, but I'll ring you afterwards to catch up if that's okay?"

"Sure," she said. "That's fine."

"I'll lead the way," Adam said and she noticed that he had a much more confident air about him. Gone was the nervous fidgeting that he had been afflicted with on Wednesday.

Once they were in the room they took the same seats as previously and Adam gestured to her laptop. "I assume you've got no further with my 'Diverts' tab," he said, his tone supercilious.

It was clear to Sam that he was implying she was too stupid to understand the creation of a genius like him.

She decided to humour him.

"It's cleverly designed," she said.

He smiled and leaned back in his chair. "Yes, I'm very pleased with it."

"But what's it for?"

"It's complicated. I use it for internal checks to reconcile numbers."

"I see. That does sound complex." She paused. "Purely internal, you say?"

"That's right."

"Mmm. So if it's purely internal why are there eight bank accounts, each one linked to a subset of investors?"

Adam tried to maintain his smile but it was clear from the look in his eyes that her comment had hit home. "Eight bank accounts?" he stuttered.

"Yes." She laughed. "It took me a while, but those long sets of alphanumeric characters are International Bank Account Numbers, aren't they? More commonly known as IBANs."

"I don't know what you're talking about?"

"Here, let me show you."

Sam started to open her laptop but Adam held his hand up to stop her. "Just a second," he said, forcing a smile. "I've got another file on my laptop that will explain everything. Do you mind if I pop back to my desk and fetch it?"

"No, of course not."

"Great. I'll be back in a couple of minutes."

Chapter 61

The man who called himself Mr Smith sat forward and smiled as he read the conclusion of Harvey Robinson's latest report.

'S eight, I eight' meant that Lord Vaughan was ideally suited both as a syndicate member and as an investor. Others had scored nine, and on one occasion ten, on one or the other but to score highly in both was a first.

He now had to choose how to take advantage of Vaughan and moved on to the detailed analysis.

Lord Vaughan was a hereditary peer who owned several businesses and whose wealth was in the millions. According to Robinson, he had a mistress but managed to keep her existence a secret from his wife. He frequented casinos, though never with either of his female companions, and five-figure gambling losses in a single day were not uncommon.

On balance, he felt he was more suited to a gambling syndicate. A man of Vaughan's wealth was unlikely to be drawn in by the promise of financial gain through investment. However, Vaughan appeared to be an inveterate and compulsive gambler.

He wanted to check something first though. He picked up the phone and retrieved Robinson's number. To his surprise, it was a woman who answered.

"Hello," Lily said. "Harvey Robinson's office. How may I help you?"

"Is Harvey there?"

"He's out at the moment. Can I ask him to ring you, sir?"

"When will he be back?"

"Any minute. Oh, just a second, I think that's him now."

He heard her say, "There's a call for you, Mr Robinson," followed by Harvey's reply, "Who is it?"

She came back on the line. "Who may I say is calling?"

He was a busy man and had neither the time nor the patience to be messed about.

"Just put me through to him, young woman," he snapped.

"Of course, sir."

A few seconds passed before Harvey came on the phone.

"Harvey," he said impatiently. "I'm ringing about your report on Lord Vaughan."

"Ah, Mr Smith, it's you," Harvey said. "Just a second."

He heard Harvey hiss, "Go into the other room, Lily, while I take this," and then he came back on the line. "Sorry about that," he said. "How can I help?"

"You have given the good Lord a score of eight in both categories, but I'm leaning towards the syndicates. What do you think?"

Harvey thought about this for a second. "He's a man who loves to make money," he began, "and I think he'd fall for the profit potential at Thorney and Budge, but on the other hand he'd relish the chance to make money on spot bets."

"Mmm. That's interesting. Perhaps he could be enticed into both." He paused. "Who was that woman?"

"Lily's my new assistant but don't worry, I'm not letting her see any of my reports."

"I should hope not."

He hung up. He knew what Robinson was like and had no doubt that he had taken on someone young and pretty to brighten up his office. He hoped he had been telling the truth about not sharing his reports with her.

His phone rang and he saw it was Davison calling.

"Hello," he said.

"There's a problem, Mr Smith," Adam said.

He waited. There was no point in asking the obvious question.

"It's Sam Chambers, the auditor," Adam went on, a note of panic in his voice. "I think she's on the verge of working everything out. I made a mistake and omitted to put a password on part of the spreadsheet."

"Which part?"

"The part showing diversions to eight off-shore accounts."

"Mmm. That is a problem. Who else has the spreadsheet?"

"Patrick had a copy, but he's out at a lunch meeting and I've been to his desk and deleted it from his computer."

"When did this Chambers woman realise what you were doing?"

"I'm pretty sure it was this morning, Mr Smith. She had her laptop open when we met her at reception and I have a feeling that she'd just realised what was going on."

"So she's at Thorney and Budge's office right now?"

"Yes. I stepped out to speak to you." Adam paused. "What do we do? This is a real problem for us."

He didn't hesitate. "There is no 'us'," he said.

"What do you mean there's no 'us'? We're in this together. You have to help me find a way out."

"No, I do not. Now, if you don't mind, I'm very busy."

"I know who you are."

He laughed. "Don't be ridiculous."

His laughter was short-lived as Adam recited his full name, adding his home address for good measure.

"How did you…"

He stopped mid-sentence.

How Adam had found out didn't matter. What mattered was that he act, and act quickly.

"All right," he said. "I'll help you. I have an idea. How long can you keep her there?"

"I could suggest lunch before we resume, Mr Smith.

There's a gastro-pub opposite the office."

"Yes, do that. I'm going to arrange for a package to be delivered to her."

"What kind of package?"

"You don't need to know, but it should be enough to persuade her to drop her investigation." He looked at his watch. "It's ten past twelve now. Do you think you can keep her occupied for an hour?"

"Yes, I should be able to do that."

"Good, I'll arrange for the package to be delivered to the front desk by one fifteen."

Chapter 62

Sam was making a list of the country codes in Adam Davison's 'Diverts' tab when he returned to the meeting room.

"Sorry I was so long," he said. "Two prospects rang me one after the other wanting to invest in my fund." He forced a laugh. "You know what it's like, you wait ages for a bus and then two come along at once."

She smiled encouragingly. "Shall we continue where we left off?"

"Ah…" he swallowed. "Given the time, what say we grab some lunch?"

Sam looked at her watch. "It's not half-twelve yet."

"I'm famished though. I had a very early start and skipped breakfast completely." There was that nervous laugh again. "The pub opposite does great food."

It was clear he wasn't going to be swayed.

"Okay," Sam said.

Once they were seated in the pub, and had ordered their food, Sam attempted to make small talk but it was proving a challenge. Adam was back in fidget mode and kept looking at his watch every five or ten minutes.

"I'm sure the food won't take too long," she said. "Then we can get back to it."

He nodded. "Yes."

"So, how long have you been with Thorney and Budge?"

She knew the answer to this but the silences were becoming increasingly uncomfortable.

"Not long."

Well, that certainly didn't further the conversation any.

"Where did you work before?"

Adam peered down at his watch. "Um… I was…" He looked up again. "Oh, here's our food."

"Ham salad?" the waitress asked, holding two plates out in front of her.

"That's for me," Sam said.

The waitress put the plate in front of Sam and then turned to Adam.

"Parcels?"

Adam's eyes widened in shock. "What? Here?"

The waitress nodded her head to the plate she was still holding. "Are the filo parcels for you?"

"Oh. Sorry." Yet more nervous laughter. "Ah, yes."

Sam was baffled by his reaction.

He picked up his napkin to mop his brow and she realised that he was sweating profusely.

"Are you okay?" she asked. "You don't look well."

"I, ah… Yes, I do feel a touch under the weather actually. I don't think I can manage any food."

"Look, if you're feeling rough I don't mind postponing our meeting…"

"No, no," he said hastily, then forced a smile. "I'll be fine. Once you've eaten we'll go back to the office and finish our discussion. Best to get it sorted out once and for all."

Fifteen awkward minutes later, Adam looked at his watch for what must have been the tenth time and said, "Shall we make a move?"

"Best we pay first."

"Oh… Yes, of course."

"I'll get it." She laughed. "Or at least Filchers will." She signalled to the waitress for the bill and retrieved her credit card from her purse. "Are you certain you're well enough to carry on, Adam?"

"Definitely." He swallowed again. "I'm feeling a lot better."

Sam paid and they left the pub and crossed the road.

"Would you mind waiting here a moment," Adam said when they were outside Thorney and Budge's office. "I've been expecting a package and I want to check with reception that it's arrived."

"Could this be it now?" Sam said, gesturing over Adam's shoulder to where a motorbike had just turned the corner.

He turned. "Yes, it could be. It certainly looks like a despatch rider."

Sure enough, the motorbike drew to a halt against the kerb ten or fifteen yards away. It was facing them and Sam saw there was a brown parcel on the pillion. It was small, only seven or eight inches on each side and about three inches high.

The rider was dressed all in black. Without raising the visor on his helmet he placed his left heel on the kickstand, pushed to extend it and swung his left leg off the bike. He then unclipped the package from the pillion and placed it on the flat of his left hand.

It was clear now that the rider was a man and a big man at that. He walked towards Thorney and Budge's office then saw them and turned in their direction, stopping when he was about three yards away.

He turned his head towards Adam.

"Are you Adam Davison?" he asked, his voice muffled by the visor but recognisably foreign.

It sounded Eastern European.

Sam's stomach dropped.

The man who had threatened Sean's partner was Eastern European.

The next few seconds felt like they passed by in slow motion.

Adam looked down at the package and then back at the rider. "Yes, I'm Adam," he said, with a sideways glance at Sam, "but the parcel is for Sam Chambers, not me."

"No," the man said, his voice flat and emotionless. "It

is for both of you."

In that instant, Sam knew.

She watched, frozen to the spot, as the man lifted the top off the parcel with his right hand, threw it to the floor and reached inside.

Adam gasped as the hand emerged holding a dark grey pistol and Sam watched in horror as the man's arm straightened and the nozzle of the gun rose to eye height.

There was no time to react.

This was it, the end of everything.

Thoughts of Luke flashed through Sam's mind.

She'd let him down. He'd warned her to be careful and she should have been on her guard.

The man fired.

Chapter 63

Sam was dimly aware of Adam's head jerking backwards and knew that she only had seconds before the man turned his attention to her.

Karate training had taught her many things, but disarming a man with a gun had not been one of them. Her instructor's advice had been that if a gun was pulled on you the best response was to hand your belongings over. He had said that 999 times out of 1,000 the gunman would win if you tried to take his weapon.

That advice had assumed that the assailant was a mugger, not an executioner. Offering the man her handbag wasn't going to get her anywhere.

Sam had to draw on everything she'd been taught if she was going to survive.

Moving forward onto her left leg, she brought up her right knee and rotated her hip before snapping her leg outwards and downwards to deliver a strike with her instep.

Her full weight sunk into the motorbike rider's neck and he stumbled to one side, firing as he did so. She felt a blast of air as the bullet passed inches from her left temple.

He tried to steady himself but she was on him again before he was fully upright, delivering a sidekick this time and snapping her leg into his gun hand.

The pistol was sent crashing to the ground and returned to her guard, ready to strike if he reached for it.

He turned his head towards her for an instant before running to his bike where, in one smooth movement, he leapt onto the seat and released the kickstand before accelerating away.

Sam bent forward with her hands on her thighs, panting as she tried to recover her breath. There was a numbness in her ears and it was only after a few seconds that she realised someone was screaming.

She stood up and turned around to see Thorney and Budge's receptionist outside the entrance door, her eyes wide open and staring and both hands pressed tightly to her cheeks. Sam followed her gaze to see Adam's body splayed out on the pavement, a gaping cavity in the centre of his forehead. Stretching behind his head was a stream of blood and brain matter.

That was when the shaking started.

Chapter 64

Luke stared at the whiteboard, his eyes drawn to the mysterious Mr Smith. He was the main man, the person who had threatened Douglas Woods and Sean Abbott over the phone and then sent his Eastern European bully boy to punch the message home. Luke was ninety-nine percent certain he had also ordered the murders of Brian Shepherd and his wife.

But who was he? There had to be a clue up there but there were too many gaps in their knowledge.

He called Josh over and tapped the names beneath Douglas Woods.

"These were the other names Mr Smith asked Douglas Woods to alter in the database," he said. "Have you been able to find out anything about them?"

"I've found Eileen O'Connor," Josh said. "It was tricky because her name's Aileen with an 'A', not Eileen with an 'E'. She's an Irish tennis player and was seeded seventeen at Wimbledon this year."

"Good work," Luke said. "My guess is there were bets placed on her. Any luck with Lionel Grassmore?"

"Not yet. There can't be many Lionel Grassmores though, can there? Unless Douglas misremembered that one as well."

"Mmm. He could well be a gambler rather than a sportsman. Keep looking." Luke scratched his chin. "What about them?" He pointed at Spencer Howell and Maurice Brown. "You found out that their company SCHBet had taken bets on those cheating Indian cricketers, but did you uncover anything about either Howell or Brown being personally involved?"

"No, but when Chatterjee was in court he said he'd only

cheated after his family had been threatened."

"That's Mr Smith's modus operandii. Did Chatterjee say who'd made the threats?"

Josh shook his head. "He said it was a man with an English accent, but that he didn't know his name."

Luke's phone rang and he saw DI Gilmore's name pop up on the screen.

"Excuse me a minute, Josh," he said and turned his attention to the phone. "Hi, Pete. Is everything okay?"

"No. There's been a shooting in Bristol. The way it was conducted it looks like a gangland execution. The victim was killed instantly."

"Do you need my help with a suspect?"

"It's Sam, Sam Chambers."

"What do you mean? Was she a witness?"

"No, she was the target."

Luke put his hand on the nearest desk to steady himself and was only vaguely aware of Josh saying, "Are you okay, guv?"

"Pete…" Luke said and he realised he was finding it difficult to breathe.

"She's not hurt."

"What? But you said…"

"The dead man was Adam Davison and Sam was with him when he was shot. A motorbike rider shot Davison and was about to shoot her so she kicked his hand and managed to dislodge the gun. How she did that heaven knows."

"What else has she said?"

"Nothing. The officer who spoke to her reckons she's in shock." Pete paused. "Why was she there, Luke? What's going on?"

Luke ignored the questions. "Where is she now?"

"In a car on her way here."

"Are you in Portishead?"

"Yes."

"I'll be there as soon as I can."

Luke hung up and put his hand to his forehead as relief flooded through him. For a moment he'd thought Sam had been killed, and if she had it would have been his fault for placing her in danger.

"What's happened?" Josh asked, concern etched into his voice. "Has something happened to Sam?"

"She's fine, but there's been an incident. Look, I've got to head for Avon and Somerset HQ. I'll ring you later when I've found out more."

Luke headed out for the car, a million things going through his mind as he walked out of Filchers' head office, climbed into the BMW and set off towards Portishead.

Adam Davison had to have been killed because of his hedge fund, which meant it was a scam as Patrick had feared. But why was he murdered and, more importantly, why target Sam as well? Was it simply because she was standing next to him or had the assassin thought she was onto something?

If she was a genuine target, Luke would do everything in his power to keep her safe. She meant a lot to him and he wasn't going to lose her.

Davison's AOIF portfolio had been recommended to Simon Abrahams by Harvey Robinson. Did that mean that Lily was also in danger? Should he ring her immediately and tell her to get out and go home? After considering this for a few minutes he decided not to, but that he wasn't going to ask her to return after the weekend.

Robinson was also linked to Sean Abbott through the mysterious Mr Smith. However, Luke was confident that Sean and his family were safe in Norton St Philip, plus there would be no reason to send anyone after them until and unless Sean failed to cause an accident at Il Lombardia.

Chapter 65

Luke made record time for the journey from Bath to Avon and Somerset Police's HQ. He parked in a visitor space and messaged Pete to say he'd arrived.

"Where's Sam?" he asked as soon as Pete had let him in.

"She's in interview room 2," Pete said.

"Has she said anything else?"

"No. She's very shaken up. A female officer is with her. Do you know anything about why this might have happened?"

Luke had spent most of his drive thinking about how much to tell his ex-colleague. Having the police on board was invaluable, not that there was any option now, but he had to keep Sean's name out of it. He'd assured him that he wouldn't tell anyone where he was and he wasn't about to renege on his promise.

He was also keen to see Sam as soon as possible, so decided to hold back on the link between Harvey Robinson and Adam Davison for the time being.

"The dead man, Adam Davison, worked for Thorney and Budge," he said. "I met their Risk Director at the rugby last weekend and he asked if Filchers could review a hedge fund he had concerns about."

"I'm guessing this was a hedge fund managed by Davison."

Luke nodded. "Yes. Sam started looking at it this week. She met him on Wednesday and arranged to see him again today. As far as I'm aware she hadn't found anything untoward but wanted to clarify a few things." He paused. "Am I right to assume this has been assigned to the MCT and you're on the team?"

"Yup, and before you ask I've already had permission from the Chief for you to join me with Sam."

"Who's the SIO?"

"Not assigned yet, but it won't be Applejack because he's on holiday."

Luke was relieved. He'd worked alongside DCI Jack Bramley and had zero respect for his ability as a senior investigating officer.

Pete led the way to the interview room, opened the door and gestured for Luke to go in first.

He was shocked by how pale Sam was. She looked across at him and he could see that she'd been crying.

"It was awful, Luke," she said.

He held out his arms and she stood up and let him hug her. As he did so, the tears came again.

"Sorry," she said after a few seconds. "I thought I was stronger than this."

"I'm so sorry I put you in that position," he said.

She didn't reply and pulled away after a few seconds. The female PC stepped forward and gave her a tissue.

"Thanks," Sam said as she started to mop her eyes.

"Are you happy to give us a witness statement?" Pete asked. "I understand if you want more time."

"No, it's fine. I'm shaken up but it'll be good to get it out of my system. Is it okay if Luke stays?"

"Don't worry," Luke said. "I'm not going anywhere."

The PC left and Luke sat next to Sam while Pete took the seat opposite.

"Is it okay if I record this?" he asked. "It'll be quicker and I can prepare a statement from the recording for you to review and sign afterwards."

"No problem," Sam said.

Pete clicked the recording device. "Recording of victim interview with Samantha Chambers in Room 2 at Portishead Police Station." He checked his watch. "The time is 14:28. Luke Sackville is also present."

He smiled across at Sam. "In your own time, please tell me what happened today."

Sam ran through events beginning with her arrival at Thorney and Budge's office.

Pete stopped her when she got to the point where Adam Davison left their meeting room.

"To clarify," Pete said, "did Adam Davison leave the room immediately after you told him that you'd spotted the bank account numbers in his spreadsheet?"

"Yes," Sam said. "He told me he'd got a file on his laptop that would explain why they were there and asked if it was okay if he fetched it."

"How long was he gone?"

Sam considered this before answering. "Probably about fifteen minutes."

"Thanks. Please carry on."

Sam described their visit to the pub, then hesitated when she got to the point where they emerged onto the pavement.

"I know this is hard," Pete said sympathetically. "Please take as long as you need."

Sam grabbed Luke's hand under the table.

"Sorry," she said. "It was awful." She picked the tissue up again and dabbed at her eyes.

Pete waited while she composed herself.

"Adam told me he was expecting a package," she said after a few seconds, "and I spotted what looked like a delivery man coming towards us on a motorbike. He parked his bike and walked towards us."

"Can you describe him?" Pete asked.

Sam shook her head. "He was dressed all in black and had a black helmet with a black visor. He left the visor down so I couldn't see his face."

"But you immediately knew it was a man, even before he spoke?"

"Yes. He was big, definitely over six feet, and broad

too."

"Go on."

Sam sighed. "He took a small parcel from his bike and carried it towards us. When he was a few yards away he asked if Adam was Adam Davison. Adam said he was and…"

She stopped and put her hand to her mouth.

"What is it?" Pete prompted.

"Adam said the parcel was for me." She squeezed Luke's hand. "He knew what was going to happen, but he expected me to be the target and not him."

"What happened next?" Pete asked.

"The man said the parcel was for both of us and he pulled a gun from it and shot Adam."

"What did you do?"

"I kicked him in the head."

Pete's mouth opened. "You kicked him in the head? Just like that?"

Sam nodded. "And then I kicked his hand. The gun flew away and he ran to his bike and rode off." She saw the look on Pete's face and added, "I'm a black belt in karate."

"Right," he said. "I see. I don't suppose you remember anything about his motorbike do you?"

"I'm afraid not, but I'd remember his voice if I ever heard it again."

"Why's that?"

"He had an accent." She turned to look at Luke as she added, "It sounded Eastern European to me."

"Thanks. I think that'll do for now. Interview ended at 14:52."

He pressed the stop button on the recording device.

Sam withdrew her hand from Luke's and looked sheepishly across at him.

"I'm going to update Pete on some of the background," he said. "Are you okay to stay here?"

"Sure," she said.

Chapter 66

"I'll see if there's another room available," Pete said. He looked at his watch. "We'll have to keep it brief though. I've got a manhunt to coordinate."

Luke felt his phone vibrating in his pocket as his friend headed down the corridor. He pulled it out and saw that it was Lily calling.

"Hi," he said, suddenly fearful that he'd judged it wrong and she might be in trouble. "Is everything okay?"

"Yes, everything's fine. I thought I'd take the opportunity to update you while Robinson's busy. He's in a meeting and I think it may take a while."

"Have you found something out?"

"It may not be much, but I reviewed another report for him today and it was for a Lord V. His real name and anything else useful was blanked out, but I wondered if knowing he was a Lord would get us anywhere."

"Unfortunately, I don't think it helps. There are well over 1,000 peers in the UK."

"I feared as much."

"And there was nothing else of use in the report?"

"No. Lord V is in his mid-forties, I know that, and Robinson assigned a score again, as he did for Mr F and Miss J. Lord V's score was 'S eight, I eight'."

"Still no idea what it means?"

"No. I might ask him though to see what he says."

"Okay, but be careful. Don't do anything to give yourself away whatever you do."

Lily laughed. "Don't worry," she said. "I don't think Robinson's dangerous. His bark's worse than his bite, I'm sure of it. Oh, there was one odd thing I spotted in the report."

"Go on."

"There was a sentence where he'd written that Lord V was 'excepted into the House', with excepted spelt 'e-x-c' and 'House' with a capital 'H'. I asked if he'd meant to write 'a-c-c' and 'house' without a capital 'H' but all he did was shrug. I also saw him smirk so I wondered if I'd missed something."

"The House of Lords," Luke said.

"Pardon."

"I think I know what it means."

Luke heard a man's voice shout, "Lily, come here!" and she ended the call.

"Room 4 is free," Pete called from the end of the corridor.

Luke looked up to see that he was holding a door open. "I need to make a call," he said. "I'll be with you in a second."

"Okay. Make it quick."

Pete disappeared into the room and Luke called his father's number.

It was Borrowham Hall's housekeeper who answered the phone. "Hello, this is the Duke of Dorset's residence," she said. "How may I help?"

"Hello, Amy," Luke said. "It's Luke. Is my father there?"

"Yes, of course. I'll put you through."

There was a short pause and then Hugo came on the line, "Good afternoon, Luke," he said.

"Father, do you know of any excepted hereditary peers whose name begins with a 'V'?"

"Excepted meaning they're in the House of Lords?"

"Yes."

"There's Richard. He's Lord Vaux of Harrowden."

"How old is he?"

"About sixty I think."

"Definitely over fifty?"

"Oh yes, he's definitely over fifty."

"Can you think of anyone else?"

"Mmm. Give me a minute. Oh yes, there's Terry. I was friends with his father. He's in his forties."

"Terry?"

"Yes. Terence Rossiter. He's Lord Vaughan of Wimborne."

"Thanks, Father. Any others?"

"Not that I can think of."

"Okay. Thanks for that. I'll see you at Springdale on Sunday."

He hung up and walked down the corridor to room 4.

"Out with it," Pete said once Luke had seated himself at the table. "What haven't you told me?"

"You know me too well," Luke said. "You remember I asked you about Harvey Robinson earlier this week?"

"Are you suggesting he's connected to this?"

"Yes. He recommended Adam Davison's hedge fund to someone I know."

"Why would he do that? He's a private investigator."

"He also advertises himself as a financial advisor."

Pete's brow furrowed. "He might do, but telling someone about the hedge fund doesn't mean that he's implicated in Davison's murder."

"No, but Robinson is also linked to the deaths of Brian and Kimberley Shepherd. That's too much of a coincidence."

"Hang on, Luke. You can't seriously be telling me that he's connected to a murder-suicide."

"I'm not so sure it was a murder-suicide."

Pete laughed. "You're living in la la land." He shook his head. "Leaving the force has made you imagine all kinds of things. You'll be telling me next that Robinson's linked to the suicide of Adrian Critchley."

"He is."

"For fuck's sake. You can't say that was murder as well.

Hell, one of our officers was standing next to Critchley when he jumped off the bridge. She's having counselling for it. Are you saying *she* pushed him?"

"Pete, please give me a chance to explain."

Pete stood up. "I'm sorry, Luke. There's a murderer out there and I need to coordinate the search for him. I haven't the time to sit here listening to fanciful theories."

Luke managed to contain his temper, but only just. He knew the pressure his ex-colleague was under, and that was what held him back from exploding on the spot.

As acting Senior Investigating Officer, Pete was responsible for coordinating an investigation into the cold-blooded execution of a man in broad daylight in the centre of Bristol. His role encompassed everything from the manhunt itself to briefing senior officers and dealing with the media.

"My theories aren't fanciful," Luke said, as calmly as he could.

"I'll catch you later," Pete said as he left the room.

Chapter 67

Luke returned to room 2 to find Sam focused on her laptop.

She looked up when he came in, and he was pleased to see that she was almost back to her normal self.

"I think I know what Adam Davison was doing," she said as he sat down opposite. "Bear with me, I need to check a couple of things."

She bashed away at her keyboard for a few minutes, nodding now and then, and then sat back and grinned.

"He's been running a Ponzi scheme."

Luke had heard of Ponzi schemes but knew next to nothing about them.

"How does that work?" he asked.

"The story that he's investing in risky organisations is a front. In reality, he hasn't put a penny into the sixty-four companies in his spreadsheet. What he's actually doing is paying profits to earlier investors using funds from recent investors. That's where Simon Abrahams' profit came from."

"I take it this is fraudulent?"

"Oh yes. A Ponzi scheme is illegal. Adam was able to maintain the illusion of a sustainable and legitimate business because he was continually gaining investors. People like Simon rave about the money they've made and others are only too keen to follow suit."

"So how does Davison make money?"

"That's where the "Diverts' tab comes in and why he intended it to be password-controlled. Adam was diverting funds to eight offshore accounts. The amount transferred runs into the millions."

Luke thought about this.

"So," he said, "when he realised you were onto him he must have contacted someone to ask for help."

"The man on the motorbike?"

Luke shook his head. "No. From what you said about Davison's reaction it was clear he was genuinely expecting a package and thought it would be addressed to you. I think he spoke to someone who was in on his Ponzi scheme, little realising that he was setting up his own execution."

"Could it be Harvey Robinson?"

"Unlikely. Everything I've heard suggests this wouldn't be his style. It could be Smith I suppose, though running a Ponzi scheme is very different from operating a gambling syndicate." A thought struck him and he smiled. "They make sense now."

"What do?"

"The scores on the reports that Robinson's been doing. Lily reviewed one today which gave someone a score of 'S eight, I eight.' I bet the 'S' stands for 'syndicate' and the 'I' for 'investor.'"

"So their purpose is to decide whether someone should be exploited as a gambler or as a Ponzi scheme investor."

"Exactly. And that means that Harvey Robinson is the key to cracking this."

"You'd better tell DI Gilmore."

Luke laughed. "I tried to do just that a few minutes ago but he wouldn't listen."

"So, what do we do?"

"I'm going to drive to Oldfield Park and confront Harvey Robinson. What's the time?"

"Coming up to four."

"Not too late then."

"I'll come with you."

"No, you need to stay here. When he gets his act together, Pete will send someone in with the transcript of your statement for you to check and sign. There's no point in travelling to Bath only to have to come back here later this evening."

"I suppose that's true. I'll ask Ollie if he can pick me up when they've done with me."

Luke paused before replying. "Ah, yes. You do that."

"That's okay, isn't it?"

"Of course it's okay," he said, a little more hastily than he'd intended. "Will you stay at his tonight?"

Sam's cheeks went slightly pink. "I hadn't thought about it to be honest. I've had other things on my mind if you hadn't noticed."

"The point I'm making is that you can't go home. That man was targeting you as well as Adam Davison and there's nothing to say he doesn't know where you live. You need to be somewhere safe."

"Okay, I'll stay at Ollie's."

"Good. That's settled then. I'd better set off. Any problems, give me a ring."

"I will, Luke. And thanks for your support earlier."

He smiled, hesitated for a second as if about to say something, then turned around and headed out of the door.

Chapter 68

Luke climbed into the BMW, set off and had travelled a couple of miles when he remembered that Chloe hoped to be in Norton St Philip by five.

She answered his call on the first ring and it was clear from the background noise that she was in her car.

"Hi," he said. "I assume you're on the way."

"Yes. I left a little later than planned but should be home around quarter past."

"That's fine. Sorry, but you'll have to introduce yourself to Sean and Kirsten. It's been manic today and I've still got another meeting before I can get away. It'll probably be six or so before I'm back."

"No problem. What's the plan for food this evening?"

Luke smiled. He knew why she was asking. "There's mince, tomatoes and fresh pasta in the fridge," he said.

"Great. I'll find a recipe and make a start."

"Thanks, darling. I'll give you a ring when I'm on my way home."

He hung up and rang Josh.

"We heard what happened," Josh said when he answered. "I can't believe it, guv."

"Yes, it's horrendous. The only silver lining is that it means the police are involved so hopefully we can get to the bottom of all this."

"Are you with Sam now?"

"No, I'm on my way to see Harvey Robinson."

"With the police?"

"No. They refuse to accept that he's involved, but I think he's key to unravelling this."

"Gotcha."

"Josh, can you get me a number for Terence Rossiter?"

"I can try. Have you got an address? It's not a common name but there's bound to be more than one."

"You won't need an address. He's Lord Vaughan of Wimborne."

"Ah. I understand now. He's Voldemort."

"Voldemort?"

"Uh-huh. When Lily…"

Luke sighed. "I don't want to know, Josh. Just find his number and text it to me."

"Will do, guv."

Luke hung up and considered how best to approach the meeting with Harvey Robinson.

He suspected the man was out of his depth without realising it. There was a chance he was party to murder but from what Lily had said that was unlikely. It sounded like he ran close to the line on legal versus illegal, but being an accessory to murder didn't sound like his style.

Luke decided to be upfront. He would reveal everything he knew and shock him into admitting his role. It meant revealing who Lily was, but this was going to be her last day there anyway so there was nothing to lose.

He parked on Moorland Road, crossed the road and rang the bell.

"Hello," Lily said through the intercom. "Who is it?"

"Lily, it's Luke. Let me in but don't say anything to Robinson."

There was a buzz and Luke pushed the door open, climbed the stairs and walked into Harvey Robinson's office. Lily raised her eyebrows as if to say 'What's this about?'.

"It's okay, Lily," Luke said. "I know what I'm doing."

Harvey looked up from his screen and scowled. "Who the fuck are you?"

"I'm Luke Sackville." Luke pulled up a chair and sat on the other side of the desk. "We're going to have a little chat."

"What the…" Harvey glared at Luke. "How do you know Lily?"

"She works for me, Harvey. Do you mind if I call you Harvey?"

"What do you mean she works for you?" He started to rise from his seat. "Get out or I'll call the police."

"I advise you to sit down. Calling the police is the last thing you want to do. You're implicated in at least three murders, possibly more."

"That's bollocks," Harvey said but he sat down. "Everything I do is legit. I'm a fucking private investigator, ain't I?"

"Do the names Brian and Kimberley Shepherd mean anything to you?"

Harvey was almost smirking. "I don't know what game you're playing but I ain't heard of 'em. If that's all you got you might as well bugger off." He turned to look at Lily. "You can piss off too."

"What about Adam Davison?"

The smirk disappeared and there was a tiny twitch at the corner of his left eye.

"They're dead, Harvey," Luke went on. "All three of them."

"Nothing to do with me." He was blustering and his delivery was hesitant.

"They were all shot. Adam Davison was murdered this morning by a man on a motorcycle."

"What?" Harvey's eyes widened in shock.

"Did you order his killing?"

"Don't be fucking ridiculous."

"What about Adrian Critchley? Did you recommend Mr Smith to him?"

"I dunno what you're talking about." Harvey folded his arms across his chest.

Luke turned to Lily. "What were the names on the reports you reviewed, Lily?"

"Mr F, Miss L and Lord V," she said.

"You shut your gob," Harvey said. "That's confidential information."

"Who are those reports for, Harvey?" Luke asked. "Are they for Mr Smith?"

"Never heard of him."

Another twitch of the eye. He was lying again.

"Did you recruit Dolores Buenavista to work for him?"

There was no response.

"You always include a score in your reports, don't you Harvey?" Luke went on. "I bet Mr Smith was pleased when Lord Vaughan of Wimborne scored two eights, or haven't you sent it to him yet?"

Harvey glanced at Lily again then looked back at Luke. "How did you know he was Lord Vaughan?"

Luke ignored the question. "You're in trouble," he said, "and it's not the police that's your biggest concern."

"What do you mean?"

"You've been making money on the side by recommending people directly to Davison, haven't you Harvey? What do you think's going to happen when the man who ordered these murders finds out you've been doing the dirty on him?"

That one question seemed to deflate Harvey Robinson. He sat back in his chair, overwhelmed by everything he'd heard.

"Fuck," he said and ran his hand through his hair. "I never thought…"

"What's Mr Smith's real name?" Luke asked.

"I don't know. He's posh, I'll say that much, but I ain't met him and he's never revealed his real name." He hesitated. "I didn't think people were going to die. You have to believe me."

Chapter 69

The man who called himself Mr Smith was furious.

He was facing massive problems in both arms of his business, none of them his own doing.

It had started with that rugby player, Shepherd. Artem had dealt with him and that should have been the end of it. But no, now he had another sportsman, Sean Abbott, refusing to cooperate.

To make matters worse, the other side of his business had completely collapsed. He had come to rely on Adam Davison and the regular, and substantial, income from his Ponzi scheme. It was hard to believe that the idiot had been careless enough to allow an auditor to discover what he was up to.

He stared at the phone, willing it to ring so that Artem could confirm that at least that part of his problem was resolved.

Once it was fixed he would need to locate and deal with Sean Abbott. The man could not be allowed to get away with it.

He paced backwards and forwards trying to think of a way forward. After a couple of minutes, an idea occurred to him and he called the number of the man on the professional cycling tour that he'd talked to a few weeks previously.

He drummed his fingers on the arm of his chair as he waited for the man to answer, and breathed a sigh of relief when there was a click and a man's voice came on the phone.

"Hello, Jason Bottomley."

"Jason, I don't know if you remember me. My name's Smith and I'm a journalist. I spoke to you about how pricy tour events were."

"Ah yes," Jason said. "I remember. Is the article about to be published?"

"Still fine-tuning but I wonder if you could help me. I spoke to another of your colleagues and need to ask him a couple of follow-up questions. I'm having a problem getting hold of him though."

"Who's that?"

"Sean Abbott."

"I'm sorry, but I'm not close enough to Sean to know where he is between events. I wish I could be of more help."

"That's a shame."

"You could try Ollie though."

"Ollie?"

"Oliver Green. He and Ollie are practically joined at the hip. Hang on, I've got his number here."

Smith took the details and ended the call. Now we're onto something, he thought and rang the number, mentally crossing his fingers that Oliver Green had never met Sean Abbott's father.

"Hi, this is Ollie," Ollie said when he picked up.

"Hello, Ollie. This is David, Sean's dad. I can't get hold of him and I'm worried sick. I know you two are close. Do you know if he's okay?"

"Hi, David. Yes, I spoke to him earlier. What's happened to him is terrible, isn't it?"

"Yes, it's awful. I guess he's turned his phone off, which is understandable, but I feel a need to know he's somewhere safe."

"He's safe."

"That's good. I don't suppose you know where he's staying? I'd like to send Kirsten some flowers to show her I'm thinking of her."

"That's a nice thought. Yes, the address is The Old Farmhouse, Norton St Philip, Somerset."

"Terrific. I'll arrange for her to get something special. It's the least I can do."

He hung up, pleased with himself, and Artem's name popped onto the screen.

"Well," he said when he answered. "Is it done?"

"Davison is dead," Artem said.

"And the woman?"

"There were difficulties."

This was not what he was used to hearing from the ex-FSB man. He was normally totally reliable.

"Do not worry, Mr Smith," Artem went on. "I will track her down before she can do any damage. But first, I need you to make a call. It will not work if I do it because of my accent."

Artem explained what he needed.

"Ring me when you have the name," he said when he'd finished, "and I will take it from there."

Smith hung up, called Thorney and Budge and asked to be put through to the Bristol reception desk.

It was a man who answered. "Thorney and Budge," he said.

"Hello." He spoke quickly, keen to give the man the impression he was panicked. "It's my daughter. I need to speak to her to check she's all right."

"Your daughter?"

"Yes. Sam Chambers. I heard there was an incident there. Was she hurt?"

"Sam Chambers did you say?"

"Yes. Please tell me she's okay."

"Just a second." The line went silent for a few seconds and then the man came back on the line. "I wasn't here when it happened, sir, but I have been told that she wasn't injured."

"Thank heavens. She's probably gone back to the office. Goodness, I'm in such a state. She's just changed jobs and I can't for the life of me remember who her new employer is."

"I can help you there. It'll be in the visitors' book."
There was a moment's pause. "Here it is. It says she works
for Filchers in Bath."

"Oh yes, of course. Thank you so much."

"No problem. I hope your daughter's okay."

Smith smiled as he ended the call.

He rang Artem.

"Sean Abbott is staying at The Old Farmhouse in a
place called Norton St Philip," he said when he answered.

"I know the village. And the woman?"

"She works for a company called Filchers." He paused.
"I want them both dealt with as soon as possible, ideally
today."

"My express service commands a premium," Artem
said, his words lacking emotion. Anyone listening in would
think he was offering a fast dry cleaning service.

"How much?"

"Fifty thousand for both."

"Very well, Artem. Fifty thousand it is. Make the
woman your top priority."

"It will be an extra ten thousand for each item of
collateral damage."

"Whatever it takes, Artem. Whatever it takes."

Chapter 70

Sam decided to ring Ollie while she was waiting for her witness statement to be prepared.

"Hi, Sam," he said when he answered.

"Ollie, can I stay at yours tonight?" Her words came out much more quickly than she had intended. "In fact, can I stay for the foreseeable future?"

He laughed, but there was an edge to it. "It sounds like you're suggesting you move in. I'm flattered, Sam, but isn't it a bit soon to move our relationship forward to that degree?"

"Sorry." She tried to slow her breathing down. "I didn't mean it to come over like that. I'm not making sense. I know I'm not." She swallowed. "I need somewhere safe to go. Someone tried… they tried…"

She was unable to continue as memories of what had happened flooded her consciousness.

There had been screams which became louder as Sam's ears threw off the shroud of temporary deafness. She had wakened as if from a trance and had turned around to see Adam Davison's body, the back of his head turned to mush, his eyes staring blankly ahead…

"Sam. Are you there?" Ollie asked. "What's happened? Are you hurt?"

"I'm not hurt, at least not physically, but…" She drew to a halt again, unable to complete the sentence. "Please can you come and pick me up, Ollie?"

"Of course. Where are you?"

"I'm at Portishead Police Station."

"The police station! What's happened, Sam?"

"I'll explain when you get here."

"Okay. I'll be as quick as I can."

DI Gilmore came in five minutes later and put three sheets of paper and a pen down on the table.

"Please read this through," he said, "and if it's okay sign at the bottom." He paused. "How are you feeling?"

She tried to smile but it was a weak attempt. "Pretty wound up," she said.

"I'm not surprised given what you've been through. Can I get you anything?"

"I'm fine thanks."

"You'll be free to leave when you've signed that. Do you want me to arrange a car to take you home, or is Luke going to give you a lift?"

"Luke's already left. But it's okay, my boyfriend's going to pick me up."

"Good." Pete turned to leave and then a thought occurred to him and he turned back. "By the way, the gun is an MP-443 Grach semi-automatic pistol. It's Russia's standard military-issue sidearm, and has been for over twenty years, so it looks like your assessment of his accent as Eastern European was bang on the mark."

Once he'd gone, Sam briefly considered ringing her mother. It would only upset her though. Much better to tell her everything when they were face-to-face.

Chapter 71

Artem debated who to pursue first.

Sean Abbott would be easy pickings. He was in a farmhouse twenty minutes outside Bath which might even be isolated, making an assassin's job all the easier. However, if there were neighbours and they got in his way, meaning it was necessary to eliminate them, so be it. Smith had even agreed to pay him extra should that happen. It was, as they said in England, money for old rope.

Sam Chambers was more of a challenge but he was determined to track her down. It was a business transaction but he also had a score to settle. Artem Petrov, much-decorated ex-member of the Russian Secret Police, had been taken out by an amateur. Never before had he been humiliated in such a manner.

She would have to suffer for what she had put him through.

A clean kill would not fit the bill on this occasion.

But first, he had to locate her. He had her name and the name of her employer, but that was all. In Moscow, it would not have presented a challenge. The FSB had records for everyone.

England was different, but there were ways and means.

He started with BT's online phone book, keying in 'Chambers' and then selecting 'Bath (Somerset)'. The only entry was for a K Chambers but he wasn't surprised. He sensed that Chambers was an uncommon surname.

If he was lucky this K Chambers was a relative.

He rang the number.

"Hello, Kate Chambers here."

"Hello, Kate," Artem said. "This is Dimitri, a friend of Sam's. I need to speak to her urgently about something but she is not answering her phone. She is not with you by any chance is she?"

"I'm afraid not. At this time of day, she's probably still at work."

He had struck gold. This woman was clearly a relative, in all likelihood Sam Chambers' mother, and it was also evident that she had not heard about the shooting. All he had to do now was tread carefully and extract the information he needed from her.

Artem laughed. "No, she is no longer at work. I know because we are colleagues at Filchers."

"Oh, I see."

"This is something that has to be dealt with this evening, Kate. I think I will drive to her place and see if she is there. I believe I have the address in my contact details."

He paused, hoping that she would fill the gap. After a few seconds it became clear that she wasn't going to oblige and he decided to take a different approach.

"Oh dear," he said. "I think I have her details confused with someone else. Is Sam's address 3 Somerton Place?"

"No, it's 15a Bathwick Hill."

"Of course." He laughed again. "I see what I have done. I have confused her details with Olga, another friend of mine."

"If she's not there she may be at her boyfriend's," Kate went on. "I'm pretty sure his address is 14 Totnes Way in Odd Down."

"Thank you. You have been very helpful."

"Not a problem. Take care.'

"I will, Kate. I will take great care."

Chapter 72

Luke looked across at the private investigator who was shuffling uncomfortably in his chair.

"I didn't do nothing," he said defiantly.

"You did plenty, Harvey," Luke said. "At the very least you're looking at accessory to murder."

"I never…"

Luke raised his hand. "That's enough. Your best chance lies with telling the police everything, and I mean everything. If you hold anything back they won't protect you, and at the moment that's what matters most." He turned to Lily. "Would you mind making coffees please, Lily? I'm going to bring DI Gilmore up to speed."

"Of course," Lily said.

Pete picked up straight away.

"Hi," he said. "Look, I'm sorry about earlier."

"No worries, Pete. You're under a lot of pressure. Is Sam still there."

"No. Her boyfriend picked her up a few minutes ago. Where are you?"

"I'm with Harvey Robinson."

"You still think he's involved?"

"More than that. From everything he's just told me, I know he's right in the middle of it."

"Fire away."

Luke summarised everything he and his team had discovered, from finding Adrian Critchley's name in the Gambet database to Robinson's reports on Mr F, Miss J and Lord Vaughan. The only thing he missed out was the involvement of Sean Abbott.

"Proof positive that Robinson was key," he said when he'd finished, "was his admission that he'd been recommending people directly to Adam Davison, earning money on the side by bypassing Mr Smith."

"Does he know Mr Smith's real name?"

Luke looked over at Harvey as he answered. "He says not, and I'm inclined to believe him."

"Okay. Is there enough to charge him?"

"Not quite. Just a second, Pete." He looked over at Harvey. "Are you prepared to go into Portishead for a voluntary interview?"

"Too fucking right!" Harvey exclaimed. "I want to go today. Now! I need protection."

"I heard that," Pete said with a laugh. "Are you okay to stay with him until he's picked up?"

"Yes, I've got a couple more questions anyway." Luke paused. "Any developments at your end?"

"It seems likely that the man who shot Adam Davison is Russian. The gun he used is a Grach semi-automatic pistol."

"That's interesting. Have they assigned an SIO yet?"

"It's going to be DCI Huntley. She's on leave but the Chief rang her and she'll be in this evening. I think that's a good call."

"I agree. I worked with Angela before she was promoted and I've got a lot of time for her."

Luke hung up as Lily brought three mugs in. She passed one over to Harvey.

"Thanks," he grunted. He pointed to her t-shirt. "Is that real?"

Lily smiled as she realised he was referring to her Barbie fascination and not asking if she had fake boobs. "No," she said. "The whole 'I love Barbie' thing was to kenable me to fit in."

He raised one eyebrow, not quite sure how to take this, and took a slurp of his coffee. "Right," he said.

"How did you first meet Mr Smith, Harvey?" Luke asked as he picked up his mug.

"He rang me out of the blue six or seven months ago."

"Do you know where he got your name from?"

Harvey thought about this for a moment. "He said I'd done work for a friend of his towards the end of last year. I think the name was Williams or Wilson. Something like that."

Luke looked at Lily. "Would you mind?"

She smiled. "Not at all." She gestured to the most modern-looking of the filing cabinets. "Is it that one?"

"Yeah, they're in date order," Harvey said.

"So, Harvey," Luke continued. "What was the reason Mr Smith wanted these people investigated?"

"He said it was for his financial services company. It was all above board. Nothing illegal about it."

"It's clear from the scores you assigned that you knew your reports were to assess their suitability as gamblers or investors. You also knew that the gambling was fixed and the investments were scams, didn't you?"

Harvey shook his head. "I never."

"Mmm. Let's park that for now. Tell me more about Dolores Buenavista."

"She's Filipino."

Luke glared at him.

"Okay, okay," he went on. "Mr Smith wanted a housekeeper. Said it had to be someone with limited English."

"Didn't that seem odd?"

"Not for me to question it. It's his business, innit. So I used me contacts to find this woman. Desperate for a job she was, needed to send money home to Manila."

"Was she an illegal immigrant?"

Harvey shrugged. "Might have been. Didn't ask."

Luke didn't believe this for a moment. "Go on," he said.

"So he wants me to interview her for him. I gets her in and she's fine."

"Because she knows little English?"

"Yeah. Said she was hard working too."

"So you relayed this to Mr Smith and he said he'd take her on?"

"Yeah."

"That leaves me with two burning questions. Why did you retain her passport, and what address did you send her to?"

"I didn't keep her passport.'

Lily looked over when she heard this. "I found it in your bin."

Harvey sniffed. "Silly cow must have dropped it."

"I'm not buying that," Luke said. "You kept it to ensure you could control her movements, didn't you, Harvey? You didn't want her doing a runner and ruining your relationship with a client you were raking money in from."

There was no response.

"So where was the job? Where did you send Dolores Buenavista?"

"He didn't give me no address, did he? Said he'd send a taxi to pick her up the next day."

"From where she was living?"

"No, from outside the Premier Inn."

Chapter 73

Luke said goodbye to the two police officers, Harvey Robinson safely ensconced in the back of their Volvo, and returned upstairs.

"Do you want a lift back to Norton St Philip, Lily?" he asked.

"No thanks," she said, looking up from the floor where she sat cross-legged surrounded by folders. "I think I'll continue looking in the hope I strike lucky. I can get a bus when I've finished."

"Okay, but get a cab. Filchers will pay. Well done here, by the way. You've done a fantastic job."

She smiled sheepishly and returned to the files.

Luke rang Pete.

"Robinson's en route to Portishead," he said when Pete answered. "He told me that Mr Smith sent a taxi to pick Dolores Buenavista up from the Premier Inn in Bath on the third of October. We might get an address if you can track down the taxi driver."

"Thanks. I'll ask one of the team to ring around."

He ended the call and called Josh.

"Any luck with Lord Vaughan?"

"Yes, indeedio."

"Indeedio?"

"Uh-huh," Josh said, oblivious to the sarcasm. "Lord Vaughan of Wimborne lives in a stately pile in Dorset. Manshutt Court it's called and it's got fifteen bedrooms. He laughed. "All right for some, isn't it?

"I suppose it is," Luke said and couldn't help smiling as he wondered what Josh would say if he revealed the size of his family home. Borrowham Hall not only had more bedrooms but also two libraries, a billiard room, and a ballroom.

"Can you text me Lord Vaughan's number?" he said.

"Will do, guv."

Next, he rang Chloe.

"I'll be leaving Oldfield Park soon," he said. "If the traffic's good I should be back in twenty-five minutes."

"That's fine," she said. "I've not long been back and I've just started on the meal."

"Thanks. I forgot to warn Sean you were coming. You didn't frighten him when you arrived, did you?"

"They're not here, Dad. I assume they've gone out."

"They can't have."

Chloe laughed. "Why not? They're grown-ups. Oh, hang on, there's the front door. That'll be them. I'd better go. I've got mince all over my hands so I need to wash them before I can get the door."

"Okay, darling. I'll see you in a bit."

Luke hung up and rang Sam's number. She had been through a horrendous experience and he was worried about her.

She answered straight away.

"Hi, Luke," she said. "I'm in Ollie's car and we're nearly at his place."

"How are you feeling?"

"A little better, thanks. Just a second." Luke heard a man's voice in the background and then she came back on the line. "Ollie wants a word. I'll put you on speaker."

There was a click.

"Hi," Ollie said.

"Hi," Luke said.

Ollie said nothing and the silence was brief but awkward. "Sean rang me," he said after what seemed a lifetime but was only a couple of seconds.

"Yes. He told me." *Get to the point.*

"I wanted to say thanks for letting Sean stay with you."

"Not a problem."

"There should be flowers delivered for Kirsten either today or tomorrow."

'Creep' was the word that came to mind, but Luke knew he was being unfair. "That's very considerate of you," he said.

"Oh no, they're not from me. Sean's father David rang and…"

"FUCK!"

Sam's voice came on the line and it was clear from her tone that she was annoyed. "What did you say that for?" she demanded.

Luke's heart was readying itself to explode out of his chest.

"I'll explain later," he said. "I have to go."

He hung up.

"What's happened?' Lily asked.

Luke didn't answer, his thoughts elsewhere as he recalled Sean's words from the day before.

"I've already told my mother where I'm staying," he had said. *"My father died last year and the last thing I want to do is worry her."*

Chapter 74

"What the hell was that about?" Ollie asked. "I thought your boss was oh so wonderful, and the first time he speaks to me he tells me to fuck off."

"He didn't tell you to fuck off," Sam said.

"As good as. You can't possibly defend him after he said that."

Sam could feel a headache coming on. The last thing she needed after a horrorfest of a day was to be caught in the middle of a machismo tussle.

Men!

"Are you worried your todger's smaller than his?" she said.

"My what?" He glanced over at her. "What are you talking about?"

"All this 'he's so wonderful'. It's not exactly subtle. You're jealous of Luke and I'm fed up with telling you there's nothing between him and me."

"I didn't say there was."

"It's the way you act, Ollie."

"The way *I* act! For goodness sake, he just told me to fuck off."

"No, he didn't." She shook her head in exasperation.

"That's all I need," he said.

"What is?"

Ollie gestured through the windscreen. "I've got a resident's permit and some tosser's parked his motorbike in my spot."

Sam was about to reply when her phone rang. Assuming it was Luke ringing to apologise, she was surprised to see her mum's photo appear on the screen.

She almost declined the call, but decided her mum had

to know what she'd been through at some point, and in any case she needed to put some space and distance between her and Ollie for a few minutes while they both calmed down.

She accepted the call. "Just a minute, Mum," she said and waited while Ollie reversed into a spot some fifty yards down the road from his house.

"You go on in," she said as he undid his seat belt. "It's my mum and I need to tell her what happened today."

"Okay," he said. "Come in when you've calmed down."

She forced herself not to rise to the bait and waited until he'd closed the door before taking her hand off the phone's microphone. "Sorry about that, Mum," she said. "Ollie and I have just had our first argument."

"Oh dear. Still, there are worse things that could have happened."

Yes, like being shot at by a man on a motorbike, Sam thought, but said. "There's something I need to tell you, Mum."

"What's that, darling."

"This afternoon, I…"

She stopped mid-sentence.

Shot at by a man on a motorbike.

A big motorbike.

As big as the one in Ollie's parking spot.

She shook her head. Thinking like that was nuts. The man who'd killed Adam Davison didn't know her address let alone where Ollie lived.

"Are you all right?" her mum asked. "You sound tense. Is it work?"

"No, it's not work. Well, it kind of is."

"I assume it's the problem your colleague needed to talk to you about. Did he manage to track you down?"

"Was it Josh, Mum?"

"No. Dimitri. He said that you…"

"Mum, stop. Did you say Dimitri?"

"Yes. He said it was urgent and he needed you to deal

with it this evening."

"Did you give him my address?"

"Yes, but I said you might be at Ollie's. I told him it was 14 Totnes Way. I got that right, didn't I?"

Chapter 75

Artem rarely made mistakes and was disappointed in his failure to kill the Chambers woman at the first attempt.

Her martial arts skills had thwarted him, but that would not happen again. This time he had the element of surprise and he intended to make the most of it.

He'd debated which address to go to first, her home or her partner's, but had decided to start in Odd Down. If he was lucky, and had chosen correctly, it would give him an easier journey to Norton St Philip once the job was done. And if he'd chosen wrongly then he would move on to her home in Bathwick.

There was no rush. He was a patient man and had all night if need be.

Gaining entry to 14 Totnes Way had been easy. He had left the motorbike fifty yards up the road and walked nonchalantly to the house as if he hadn't a care in the world. A saunter around the back had revealed a small window partly open and two minutes later he was in the kitchen.

People were so stupid.

And now he was crouched in the hall ready to pounce. When Chambers and her partner came in he planned to kill the man and stun the woman. He would then make her suffer before ending her life.

If the man was alone it would not take long to encourage him to reveal her whereabouts. Artem had learned many methods of persuasion during his time in the FSB.

He froze as he heard steps moving towards the front door. As they approached a light came on and a silhouette appeared in the door's glass panel. It was a man and he seemed to be on his own.

There was a click as the key was inserted into the lock, but before it was fully engaged there was a shout from a woman further down the road. Artem couldn't make out the words but the silhouette moved, as if the man was about to leave, before he appeared to think better of it and pushed the door all the way open.

Artem leapt up at him out of the darkness as he stepped into the hall, landing a kidney punch with his left fist while simultaneously clasping his right hand over the man's mouth.

The man's eyes widened in shock and Artem drew his arm back and punched him again, in the stomach this time, winding him and leaving him gasping for breath.

Artem let go and the man fell to the floor.

"Was that her?' Artem demanded. "The woman who shouted outside. Was that her?"

"I don't…" The man stopped, bent forward and vomited. He was on his knees and turned to look up at Artem, his eyes wide and staring, his lips covered in phlegm, mucus and the remnants of that day's vegetables.

"Was that Sam Chambers?" Artem demanded.

"No… I don't know."

"Where is she?"

Artem kicked the front door closed and then grabbed the man by the arm, dragging him through the first open door before flicking the light on.

The man was still on his knees and Artem removed a knife from his back pocket, drew it out of its sheath and held it blade up.

"Tell me where she is," he said.

"Who?" the man spluttered.

"Sam Chambers."

"I don't know…'

"Do not mess with me." Artem pressed the knife to the man's left cheek and smiled grimly as blood started to appear beneath the blade.

"I… I'm not." The man gulped. "I don't know anyone called Sam Chambers."

"Do not lie to me." He pressed harder and blood started dripping down the man's cheek and onto his shirt. "I know she is your girlfriend."

"I don't have girlfriends. I never have. I'm married." He raised one hand shakily and pointed to a photo on the wall. "That was our wedding."

Artem followed his gaze to a photo showing two men in dinner jackets, each with red roses in their buttonholes. They were smiling at the camera as one man, the man now bleeding from below his left eye, helped the other man to cut the bottom tier of a wedding cake.

"Rory is my husband," the man said.

"Fuck! Fuck! Fuck!" Artem exclaimed.

He was tempted to finish the man off but instead satisfied himself with a vicious kick to the groin.

Artem wiped his knife on his shirt before resheathing it and returning it to his back pocket. He walked to the front door and pulled it open to find the Chambers woman standing at the gate some twenty paces away.

Her mouth opened in a silent scream when she saw him.

Artem's Grach semi-automatic pistol was gone but he had his knife and he knew how to use it.

He started to run towards her then heard the sound of sirens and veered off, leaping over the wall separating the garden from the house next door before running towards his motorbike.

The sirens grew louder and he launched himself onto the seat and fired up the engine, kicking the stand up as he did so.

He accelerated and disappeared around the corner as a police car drove into view from the other direction.

He banged his fist on the handlebar.

The bitch had got away.
For now.
He intended to return.
But first, he would deal with Sean Abbott.

Chapter 76

Sam watched as the bike accelerated away, then turned to face the house. She stepped towards the front door and as she did so she realised there was a noise coming from inside. It was the sound of someone in pain.

She ran into the hall to find it deserted. A split second later she heard a low moan from an open door to her left and dashed in to find a man lying on his side, hands cupped around his groin. He looked up and she saw that he was bleeding from a cut below his left eye.

He was breathing heavily and his face was curled up in agony. "Where is he?" he asked between gasps. "Has he gone?"

Sam knelt at his side and put her arm on his shoulder.

"You're safe now," she said. "The police have just pulled up."

She heard footsteps in the hall.

"In here," she called.

A uniformed police officer entered the room, looked down at the man on the floor and then at Sam.

"Stand up Miss," he said. "What have you done to him?"

"I haven't done anything," she said as a second officer appeared beside the first.

"It wasn't her," the man on the floor managed to say.

"It was a man," Sam said. "He's got a strong accent, possibly Russian. He was looking for me but he rode off on his motorbike when he heard the sirens." She hesitated. "It's the same man who tried to kill me this lunchtime."

The two officers exchanged a look that suggested they thought she was mad.

"Come on," the first officer said. "You can't

seriously…"

"Hang on," the second officer said. "It must be the shooting in Bristol."

"That's the one," Sam said. "He shot the man I was with. Adam Davison."

"Sam, are you all right?"

The first officer turned to see Ollie standing behind them. "Who are you, sir?" he asked.

"My name's Ollie. Sam's my girlfriend."

"I don't understand," the officer said. He looked down at the man on the floor. "I thought she was *your* girlfriend."

The man sighed. "I'm fed up with telling people," he said, his hands still protecting his private parts and his words interspersed with deep breaths. "I don't have girlfriends. I never have."

*

It was only when the paramedics arrived that Sam discovered the name of the man who lived at number 14.

"Thanks," she said as Ollie came in from the kitchen and passed her a cup of hot chocolate. She felt suddenly shivery and cradled her hands around the mug. "Do you know Christian?"

Ollie shook his head. "Never met him before today," he said as he sat on the sofa opposite.

"Poor man."

"Yes. At least it looks like he's going to suffer little more than bruises." Ollie paused and then looked her in the eyes. "I'm sorry about earlier, Sam."

She smiled weakly. "It's not a problem. You misinterpreted what Luke said, that's all."

Ollie gave a lopsided smile. "He did tell me to fuck off."

Sam sighed. "Let's not go there again, okay?"

"You're right. I'm sure your boss had a good reason. It

may have been guilt that made him say it."

"Guilt?"

Ollie nodded. "He put you in a position of danger, didn't he? He must be feeling bad about it."

Sam took a sip of her drink and chose not to reply.

"The important thing," Ollie went on, "is that you weren't hurt."

"He's still out there. What if he comes for me again?"

"I don't think you need to worry. Now that the police are involved it's only a matter of time before he's behind bars."

"How do you know that?"

"It stands to reason. There's nothing amateurish about this investigation now that the professionals are on the case."

Again she chose not to reply and took another sip of her hot chocolate.

"I wonder how he knew to come to Totnes Way," Ollie mused.

"My mum told him," Sam said. "He rang her saying he was one of my colleagues. Luckily she'd misheard me and thought you lived at number 14 rather than 40."

"Wow, you're certainly having a run of bad luck. I know they're not doing it on purpose but it seems like all the people you're close to are letting you down in one way or another."

Sam thought about saying something but didn't want to come across as petty. All Ollie was doing was trying to be helpful and she had to accept that he'd been as lucky as her to escape unscathed and must be feeling very shaken up. The man had targeted his house and if he'd gone to the right address it could be Ollie in an ambulance instead of the man thirteen doors down.

She smiled. "Shall we get a takeaway tonight?'

"Good idea," he said. "but let's not go for anything from Eastern Europe."

Chapter 77

Chloe wasn't answering.

And now the traffic had come to a standstill at roadworks and the lights were taking interminably long to turn green.

As Luke waited he drummed his fingers on the steering wheel and tried to convince himself they were okay. The man had his address but if he were after anyone it would be Sam. There was no reason to hunt Sean down.

Unless Mr Smith wanted revenge for his refusal to cooperate and had sent his Russian hitman to punish Sean and his family. That was what had happened to Brian and Kimberley Shepherd, Luke was convinced of it.

The lights turned green and he pulled past a line of red and yellow traffic cones protecting the men and machines to his left. After three hundred yards, he rounded a corner and was forced to slam on the brakes. A container lorry was facing him, a middle-aged man standing by the side of the cab and talking to someone on his phone.

Luke climbed out of the car and walked towards the driver who looked up as he approached.

"Sorry about this, mate," he said. "Something wrong with the electrics." He returned his attention to his phone.

There was now a line of cars behind the Beemer, removing the option to reverse and take an alternative route.

"Can you fix it?" Luke asked.

The driver shrugged. "My manager's on the case. They've got remote diagnostics but it might take a while."

Luke returned to stand by his driver's door and rang Pete.

"I've got a problem," he said when Pete answered. "I

think Sean Abbott's in danger. He's staying at my house with his family and I'm worried the guy who shot Adam Davison might be heading there."

"Whoa, Luke. Who's Sean Abbott?"

"He's a professional cyclist and Mr Smith has been threatening him and his family."

"Why didn't you tell me about him?"

"Sorry, Pete. I promised him I'd keep it a secret. Can you send a car to my house? I'm stuck behind a broken down lorry."

"There's no need to worry, Luke. The man who killed Davison is in Bath. He's just targeted Sam again."

"What! Is she okay?"

"She's fine."

Luke heard the sound of an engine revving. "Just a second," he said.

He turned to see a motorbike driving towards him between the cones and the queuing cars. It passed the BMW and veered into the roadworks to pass the truck. One of the workmen raised his arms angrily as the rider weaved past him and away.

Luke returned his attention to the phone.

"What were you saying, Pete?" he asked.

"I said Sam's unhurt, although I can't say the same for the guy whose house the bastard broke into."

"Is he in custody?"

"I'm afraid not. He got away on his bike seconds before the police arrived."

Chapter 78

Artem was thankful he was not in a car otherwise he would have been held up at the roadworks. As it was, it had been easy for him to meander through the stalled traffic.

He did not understand what had gone amiss in Odd Down. He'd gone to the address the Chambers woman's mother had provided, but it had been the wrong house.

Still, he had lost nothing other than time.

And he had plenty of that.

Mr Smith had wanted Sam Chambers dealt with quickly, but would have to accept a delay. She would be easy pickings once a few days had passed and she started to relax and believe she was safe.

His focus now was on Sean Abbott.

Artem slowed down as he passed the sign for Norton St Philip and took the first right then, after a hundred yards, turned right again. He was now on Wellow Lane and there were no longer any street lights. By his reckoning, The Old Farmhouse was no more than half a kilometre ahead.

He knew Sean was staying there with his partner Kirsten and their daughter. What he didn't know was who else to expect.

Not that it concerned him.

He had the element of surprise and the cover of darkness. They wouldn't know what hit them.

He parked the bike next to a five-bar gate, opened a bag fastened to the rear luggage rack and removed a sixteen-inch claw hammer, weighing it up in his hands and smiling as he did so.

It was a shame he no longer had his Grach, but the hammer was an excellent alternative. It weighed almost a kilogram and had the advantage of silence, important if it became necessary to eliminate people one by one.

He put his hand on his back pocket, pleased that he had an additional weapon in easy reach. There was every chance his knife might come in handy for the second time that evening.

Artem briefly debated approaching the farmhouse through the fields, but the road looked little used and he decided to take the quicker, more direct route.

He had covered a couple of hundred yards when he heard a woman calling in the field to his right. He stopped and crouched down behind the hedge.

A moment later she called again.

"Wilkins," she said. "Drop it!"

Artem relaxed. It was clear that she was talking to someone else and he wondered if Wilkins was her boyfriend or partner. If so, what was she asking him to drop?

"That's disgusting," she went on, her voice nearer this time. A few seconds later a light came on. "Look at it," she said. "It's been dead for ages."

The moon was behind her and he could see her outline. She was tall and slim, her torch lighting up a dead pigeon on the ground. She moved her hand slightly and he saw a cocker spaniel standing beside her, its eyes fixed on the bird.

"Go on, you silly mutt," she said, waving one arm in Artem's direction. "Have a look over there."

He ducked down further as the torch momentarily pointed towards him.

A few seconds later he heard a low growl and realised that the dog was no more than a metre away on the other side of the hedge. The growl grew in volume and transitioned into barking.

"Wilkins!" The woman shouted. "What have you found now?"

She was moving closer, her phone light waving from

side to side as she walked.

The hedge was largely bramble and thick enough to hide him in the dark but not if she shone her torch directly through. Artem readied himself to dive through if she spotted him.

He would have to deal with her.

The dog too.

His knife was still sheathed but he had the hammer.

It was amazing the damage a kilogram of steel and wood could inflict on a person.

Chapter 79

Luke was becoming increasingly worried.

Fifteen minutes had passed since the bike had passed him. If it was Adam Davison's killer he would be at the farmhouse by now. Of course that was probably nonsense, but the thought didn't stop him worrying.

He rang Chloe for the umpteenth time.

Still no answer.

She was very good at taking her phone wherever she went, and reception was excellent in the farmhouse. Of course, she could have decided to take Wilkins for a walk. If they'd gone to the fields between the house and the village there were a couple of fields with next to no signal.

The lorry driver was on his phone again. He said something then turned to Luke, smiled and gave him a thumbs-up.

Luke walked over.

"Fixed?" he asked.

"No," the man said, "but they're sending out a recovery vehicle." He smiled again. "Should be here within the hour."

Luke was about to tell him what he thought of this when his phone rang. He turned away and accepted the call without looking at the screen.

"Chloe?" he said, hoping and praying that it was his daughter.

No such luck.

"Bad news," Pete said.

There was the tiniest of pauses before he continued but to Luke it felt like a lifetime.

"Two officers set out for your place," Pete went on, "but got themselves stuck in the same jam you're in.

They've just rung to say they're going to turn back and find an alternative route. It could be another thirty minutes before they arrive."

"That's not good, Pete."

"There's some good news though."

"What's that?"

"I've spoken to the taxi driver who picked Dolores Buenavista up from the Premier Inn. He remembers taking her to a large house near Limpley Stoke and is going to text me the address when he's searched through his sat nav history."

Luke grunted. "That's ironic," he said. "It means our mysterious Mr Smith is probably no more than a five-minute drive from where I'm standing now."

He paused as a second motorbike weaved its way through the traffic towards him.

An idea occurred to him.

"I'll ring you later, Pete," he said and ended the call.

He stepped in front of the motorbike forcing the rider to stop abruptly.

The man raised his visor.

"What are you doing?" he demanded. He was late forties, Luke thought, with an aggressive attitude and an even more aggressive beer belly.

Luke held his hand out. "Give me your helmet," he said.

The man snorted. "What the fuck are you talking about? Get out of my way."

Luke took a step forward so that he towered over the rider and glared down at him.

"I need your bike," he said. "You'll get it back."

"Fuck off!"

"I'm serious. I'm with the police."

Which was more or less the truth.

"You've got to be joking."

Luke didn't say anything but continued holding the

man's gaze. After a few seconds he huffed, dismounted, took his helmet off and handed it over.

"Thanks," Luke said. "What's your name?"

"Bruce."

"I'm Luke. Where are you heading?"

"Warminster."

Luke handed him a business card. "Ring me on that mobile number tomorrow, Bruce. I'll arrange for the bike to be returned and I'll reimburse your taxi fare home."

The man read the card and then looked up.

"You're not police. What's a fucking Head of Ethics?"

But Luke was already sitting astride the bike. He put the helmet on, pressed the start button and veered past Bruce and into the roadworks.

He knew next to nothing about bikes but it was clear that this was a powerful beast. Once he was clear of the tailback he applied the throttle and accelerated to seventy and then eighty, only slowing when the contours of the road demanded it.

Within a few minutes he was entering Norton St Philip.

Chapter 80

Artem ducked as he passed the room that Sean Abbott's daughter was in.

He was using all his skills and experience to ensure he had located everyone in the building. So far he had identified three people and the sound of a child singing to herself made him confident they were Sean, his partner and their daughter. They were in separate rooms which was a nuisance but no more than that.

He liked a challenge.

He was confident that they were alone, having been concerned that they might be staying with someone else, possibly a family. Increased numbers made his job more difficult. It was much easier to deal with three.

Fortunately, the woman in the field had not spotted him and she and her dog had headed off towards the village in the opposite direction from his targets.

There were five downstairs rooms. The young girl was in some sort of study, the woman Kirsten in a lounge and Sean in the kitchen. There was no television on and no music playing which was a disadvantage but not a major one.

Artem knew how to be silent.

He still had the hammer and his knife and would use the latter he decided. Death would be instantaneous that way.

He reached the back, two circuits of the property completed, and considered his options. Leaving any of them alive wasn't one of them. The house was remote so screaming would not alert anyone, but the little girl was five or six, old enough to be able to use a phone or to run for help.

No, he had to finish them all.

He decided to begin with the daughter. This wasn't because she might scream. He would not give her the time to react. No, it was because the room she was in afforded the easiest access.

She was seated on the floor no more than a metre from glass-paned double doors leading outside. He had tested the handle on his first circuit and to his surprise had discovered that it was unlocked. All he had to do was press down, push it open, reach for her and draw the knife across her throat.

He'd move to the lounge after that and leave Sean for last.

He returned to the study doors and watched the little girl for a few seconds. She was focused on a board on the floor in front of her, kneading clay with her hands and humming to herself as she crafted the material into figures he presumed were meant to be animals.

He placed the hammer on the floor, withdrew his knife from its sheath, placed his hand on the door handle and slowly pressed downwards.

Chapter 81

Luke had been unsure whether to park the bike and make his way on foot to the house, or ride up the drive to the front door. Surprise would be an advantage, but he would lose valuable time if he parked out of earshot and had to walk or jog that last quarter of a mile.

The decision was made for him when he turned into Wellow Lane and his headlight picked out a motorbike parked to one side of the road.

He rotated the throttle and accelerated, his heart thumping.

When he reached the farmhouse he turned into the drive, rode to the front door and braked to a halt. He pressed the stop button and the engine cut out.

The night was eerily silent.

Luke dismounted, took his helmet off and threw it to the ground, ignoring the bike as it fell onto its side.

He ran to the front door, hoping and praying he wasn't too late.

Before he reached it, he heard movement from the side of the house and turned to see Chloe walking towards him. She was smiling and Wilkins ran from behind her and up to Luke, leaping up and down in delight at seeing his master.

"Thank god you're okay," Luke said. "Where are…"

He stopped mid-sentence as a blood-curdling scream cut through the silence.

Luke dashed past Chloe to find Kirsten standing outside the study doors with her back to him. Her screams morphed into deep, agonising sobs.

"What happened?" Luke asked.

She turned when she heard him, her face pale, tears flowing freely down her cheeks.

"Tina. My daughter," she managed to say. "That man. He…"

"Where is she?"

"In there." She indicated the study with a nod of her head.

Chapter 82

Artem crouched behind the hedge twenty yards away, his fingers pulling apart the foliage so that he could see the house. He watched as more and more people appeared.

Things were not going well.

He had been so close to success, a fraction of a second from opening the door and ending the little girl's sorry life. But at that instant her mother had come into the room, seen him and screamed so loud he thought his eardrums were going to burst. What was more it scared her daughter so much that she immediately started bawling.

He would still have gone for them, the mother first then her brat, but several things happened to stop him in his tracks.

First, he heard a motorbike engine roaring nearby. A split second later Sean Abbott appeared behind his partner, a baseball bat held high above his head. Moments after that a towering brute of a man appeared around the side of the house, followed closely by the woman and dog that Artem had seen in the field earlier.

There were times when it was necessary to admit defeat, when the odds were against you and you needed to regroup and ready yourself for a later attack.

This was one of those times.

The dog was his biggest worry. If the beast scented him it might start barking again. He would happily throttle the mangy mutt now if he could.

If only he had his Grach. A semi-automatic pistol would have seen them all off in next to no time. Without his gun he would need luck to be successful against so many, and to depend on luck was to accept weakness.

Artem Romanovich Petrov was not weak. Weakness

was not in his repertoire.

His strength and perseverance had been proven on many occasions and recognised by the FSB. One of the proudest moments of his life was when Alexander Bortnikov, head of the Russian Federal Security Service and one of the most powerful members of President Putin's inner circle, presented him with medals for valour and diligence.

No, he was not weak.

He watched as the group collected together. The tall man was taking charge and attempting to calm the mother down so that she could explain what had happened. She gestured in the direction Artem had first taken before he had doubled back.

His actions were dependent on what they did next.

There was a chance that one of them, most likely the giant, would tell the others to retreat into the house while he tried to locate and apprehend Artem. If that was the case the man would be easy pickings. His height and build would not help him when a knife was driven into his gut from the darkness. Once he was dealt with, Artem would return to the house to deal with the others.

Alternatively, they might all disappear inside like the cowards they were and wait for the police to arrive. If they did that they would be playing into his hands. The police would take ten minutes, probably more, to arrive and it would take him no more than a minute to retrace his steps to the study.

He tapped the chest pocket of his leather jacket and smiled. He had been taught to always be fully prepared. You never knew what might happen when you were on a mission.

The grenade was going to come in very useful.

Chapter 83

"Everyone into the study," Luke ordered.

"What's going on, Dad?" Chloe asked as she started to follow the others into the house.

"I'll explain later."

He looked nervously over his shoulder as he ushered the others in. Kirsten and Tina went first, then Sean. Chloe took up the rear.

Wilkins was about to go inside when he suddenly turned and issued a low growl.

"What is it, boy?" Luke asked. He turned to his daughter. "Give me the torch."

The cocker spaniel ran past his master and Luke shone the torch at the point in the hedge that he was heading for. He saw movement in the foliage just before the dog reached it.

The hedge extended for ten yards to Luke's left and over thirty yards to the right. He didn't hesitate and ran to the left, vaulted the low gate at the end and headed back towards the spot where he'd seen movement. As he did so he saw a man running away from him across the field in the direction of Wellow Lane.

Luke shouted "Wilkins! Stop!" as the cocker raced past him in pursuit. The dog immediately stopped and turned, his head cocked to one side as he waited for his master's order to resume the chase.

Instead, Luke said, "Follow me, boy," and retraced his steps to the study.

Chloe was standing at the door.

"Keep him in there," Luke said and looked down at Wilkins. "In, boy."

"What are you going to do, Dad?" Chloe asked as

Wilkins squeezed past her into the house.

"I'm going to catch the bastard. Make sure everyone stays inside and lock all the doors."

"Be careful!" she shouted but her father had already gone.

Luke returned to the motorbike, lifted it upright and turned it around before leaping on, starting the engine and heading back to the road.

He was a hundred yards from the attacker's motorbike when he saw him climbing over the gate and jumping onto the saddle. Luke thought he was going to get there in time but the man was quick. He started the engine and accelerated away. Luke was level with him for a split-second but it was a more powerful bike and soon started to draw ahead, the noise deafening as the speed increased to fifty miles per hour before he reached the end of Wellow Lane.

The rider continued straight on as the road became The Barton. Luke followed, his hand squeezing the throttle as if by doing so he would generate more power. He was fearful the man was going to get away. Once he reached the A366 the road would be straight and his bike's extra power would enable him to escape.

The man braked slightly in preparation for the final curve and leaned his bike to the left as he took the bend. He was now less than fifty metres from Farleigh Road, the A366, and it was then that Luke saw blue lights.

A second or two later he heard the sound of screeching tyres followed immediately by the thump of metal hitting metal. He rounded the corner to see the bike on its side, a large dent in the driver's door of a police Vauxhall Astra.

The rider had been thrown to the side but was scrambling to his feet. Luke slammed his brakes on and jumped off his bike as the man stood upright and began to move his left hand towards his back pocket.

The man was reaching for a gun or a knife and Luke knew he had no time to waste. He had always been quick from a standing start and today was no exception. He launched himself at the man's arm, forcing it backwards as over sixteen stones of muscle tore into it. There was a resounding crack and a yelp of agony as one or more of the bones in his lower arm broke under the pressure.

The man fell to the ground as one of the police officers rounded the front of the Astra.

"Handcuff him, officer," Luke said, "and do it quickly."

Chapter 84

The PC removed the bike rider's helmet and was met with a stony glare in response.

"You cannot handcuff me," the man said. "I have a broken arm."

"Cuff his other wrist to his belt," Luke said.

The police officer raised an eyebrow but did as he suggested.

The second officer appeared beside his colleague, having clambered across to the passenger side to get out of the car. He saw Luke. "DCI Sackville, isn't it?" he asked.

"That's right," Luke said, "or at least it was until last year." He wracked his brains and came up with a name. "PC Doughty?"

The young police constable smiled, evidently pleased to have been recognised. "Well remembered, sir," he said.

Luke turned to the man who was now cuffed to his own belt. "What's your name?" he asked.

The man ignored the question. "I have done nothing wrong," he said.

"Then why were you at my house?"

"I have not been at anyone's house. I was enjoying an evening motorbike ride when you chased me." He turned to PC Doughty. "It is him you should be arresting, not me. It was road rage. I am an innocent man."

Luke was not in the mood to listen to his protestations. "You killed Adam Davison," he said.

"I do not know any Adam Davison."

"You lost your gun too, didn't you? It was all caught on CCTV." He gestured to the bike. "Including your registration number."

Luke was bluffing but it had the desired effect.

The man glowered at him. "You are a dead man, Sackville," he said. "I, Artem Petrov, will make sure of that."

Luke stepped up so that their faces were only inches apart. "Tell me the name of the man you work for."

Artem spat in his face. "I am an honourable man. I do not betray people."

Luke wiped his face with his sleeve then grabbed the other man's uncuffed arm above the wrist and squeezed, enjoying the reaction as the other man yelped, his face curling up in pain.

"I too am an honourable man," Luke said, "and I'm not scared by a weaselly little cretin like you." He stepped back. "Take him away please, officers. I've seen enough of his face for one day. Oh, and be careful when you put him in the police car. I wouldn't want him to cry like a baby again."

He took a pace back, pulled out his phone and rang Chloe. She answered immediately.

"Dad, are you okay?"

"I'm fine," he said. "And I've caught him. The police are taking him away now." He watched as PC Doughty pushed Artem roughly into the back of the car and the other officer clambered back over the passenger seat to drive the Astra away.

He rang Pete next.

"Got him, Pete," he said.

"Thank goodness. We've got an address from the taxi driver."

"What is it?"

"I'm going to send cars now. I'll let you know when…"

Luke didn't allow him to finish. "What's the address, Pete?"

Pete sighed. "It's called The Brown House and it's on Rosemary Lane in Sharpstone."

Luke laughed, though there was no humour in it. "That's sheer narcissism," he said.

"What do you mean?"
"I'll tell you later."

Chapter 85

Luke parked the motorbike outside The Brown House and climbed off. As expected it was a grand affair, early Victorian by the look of it and set back from the road in a large plot.

He rang the bell and after a minute or so the door was pulled open. He recognised the woman immediately from her passport photo.

"Good evening," he said. "You must be Dolores."

She looked confused but before she could speak a man called out from a room behind and to the right of her.

"Who is it?" he asked.

"Excuse me," Luke said as he edged past the woman and through the open door beyond.

Maurice Brown was seated at a mahogany desk, a glass of whisky in his hand.

"Luke," he said and smiled. "This is a pleasure indeed."

"Not for me it isn't," Luke said as he stepped into the room.

"What do you mean?"

"Maurice, why did you warn me not to reveal that Spencer Howell had been topping up Adrian Critchley's gambling pot?"

"As I said, Spencer's an old friend of mine and I didn't want him in trouble. Look, what's this all about?"

Luke moved closer.

"You're lying, Maurice," he said. "You invented that story about Spencer to divert attention from yourself."

"That's nonsense, my dear fellow."

Maurice held onto his smile but Luke saw his free hand edge towards the top drawer of his desk.

"I wouldn't do that if I were you," he said.

Maurice's hand jerked to the handle. He pulled the drawer open, pushed his hand inside and screamed as Luke bashed it closed again.

Luke reopened the drawer and watched as the other man pulled his hand out and put it to his chest.

"I think you've broken it," Maurice said.

Luke reached down and pulled a handgun from the drawer. "I suspect you haven't got a license for this," he said, "but believe me when I say that's going to be the least of your problems."

"This is nonsense," Maurice said. "All I was trying to do was defend myself. I'm an innocent man."

Luke heard sirens and turned to see Dolores looking out of the window.

"Many cars," she said. "I think is police, Mr Smith."

Seconds later four officers entered the room. The one in front looked at Luke, then at Maurice, then back at Luke.

"Is one of you Maurice Brown?" he asked.

Luke turned to the man still cradling his hand. "Maurice," he said, "You're about to be nicked."

Chapter 86

Luke stepped through the study doors, lifted his glass to his lips and took a large glug of cider.

He shook his head as he stared across at the hedge some twenty yards away.

If he hadn't taken Bruce Addison's motorbike…

If Wilkins hadn't growled…

If there hadn't been movement in the foliage…

If, if, if.

They had been so close to disaster.

He'd never have forgiven himself if Chloe had been hurt. Sean Abbott and his family too.

He felt particularly bad about Sam. He had put her in peril by letting her work at Thorney and Budge when he should have foreseen the danger. She had been lucky to escape with her life. If her mother had remembered Ollie's address correctly, and told the Russian it was 40 Totnes Way instead of 14, everything would have been disastrously different.

"Penny for them?"

He turned to see Sam standing behind him. She looked fantastic in a dusky orange dress that went perfectly with her shoulder-length strawberry-blonde hair. But then she always looked good.

She smiled. "Are you coming back inside?"

"I will in a minute."

She moved forward to stand next to him. "Was he on the other side of that hedge?"

"Yes."

"It makes me shiver to think of what might have happened." She paused. "Come back in. You haven't had the chance to talk properly to Ollie."

He turned to look at her.

"How's it going between you and him?"

A blush came to Sam's cheeks as she answered. "Fine," she said. "He's very sorry, you know. He genuinely thought Maurice Brown was Sean's father."

"I know that, Sam. I'm more concerned that you're happy, that he's treating you well."

She sighed. "Come back in, Luke. Leanne's telling everyone about the degree she's going to do. She's incredibly excited about it."

"Okay," he said.

He followed Sam back in to see Leanne holding hands with Josh as Maj, Maj's wife Asha, Helen and Ollie listened in.

"…and would you believe I'm going to be studying Russian," Leanne concluded.

"Not my favourite language at the moment," Chloe said from behind her. She was holding a tray and started offering it around. "Sticky sausages, everyone," she said. "Help yourself."

"I've got beef vol-au-vents," Lily said as she joined Chloe and held out a second platter. She looked at Josh and smiled. "Can I kentice you, angel?"

"Definito, uh… Lil," Josh said, returning her smile as he nabbed two vol-au-vents to go with the two sausages he already had in his hand. "Ow!" he added as Leanne dug him in the ribs.

Chloe held her tray out to Luke. "I made twenty-four of these, Dad," she said, "but unfortunately three slipped out of my hand as I passed Wilkins."

Luke laughed. "If there's any left when we're done he can have some more. He deserves to be treated."

"No chance of any leftovers," Josh said through a mouthful. "They're scrummy." He swallowed, looked up at Luke and said. "So tell us, guv. How did it go today?"

"It went well. Pete and I presented Maurice Brown with

the evidence and he saw that we had him. Terry Rossiter was the clincher."

"He's Lord Voldemort," Josh said.

"He's who?" Leanne asked.

Josh managed to combine a beaming grin with a squirm of anticipation as he said, "Sorry, it's a private joke between me and my other girlfriend."

As expected this earned him another poke in the side.

"Terry Rossiter is Lord Vaughan of Wimborne," Luke explained, "and he's happy to swear on oath that Maurice Brown is our man. Brown made a rare slip-up and used his own name when he contacted Terry."

"Wee arrogant shite," Helen said.

Luke laughed. "Over-confident, greedy, murderous villain is how I would have put it but yes, arrogant shite works for me."

"I forgot to tell you all," Sam said. "I saw Teresa McNee and she's a lot happier. She told me that Douglas Woods is back to his old self and they're getting on well again."

Luke noticed Ollie nod his head at Sam and then back out of the group.

"Excuse me," she said as she went over to join him. Luke heard her say "What's up?" then Ollie grabbed her hand and led her to the far end of the room.

"Any idea why Adrian Critchley killed himself?" Maj asked.

"Most likely guilt," Luke said. "He had a bet on Brian Shepherd, so when Shepherd failed to give away a penalty inside ten minutes and died that evening he must have put two and two together."

"Aye, could be that," Helen said. "Poor man. I feel sorry for his wife too."

There was a moment's silence and then Lily said, "Ooh, I forgot." She put her tray down. "I'll be back in a minute."

"Interesting," Maj said.

She returned a few seconds later with a cylindrical cardboard box and handed it to Leanne. "This is for you," she said. "It's my way of apologising for stealing your boyfriend."

"Oh, thanks," Leanne said with a quizzical look at Josh. She opened the box, pulled out what was inside, unrolled it and laughed.

"What is it? What is it?" Josh said. Leanne showed him and his face went from excitement to confusion to fright in less than a second.

"It's okay, Joshy," Leanne said. "I get the joke." She went over to Lily and hugged her. "Thanks for looking after him." She gestured to the present. "And thanks for the Barbie and Ken calendar too. I'll put it on the wall of our kitchen to remind Joshy to be careful what he says."

"Help yourselves to more drinks," Luke said, prompting the others to head for the kitchen to refresh their glasses. As they did so Sam and Ollie came over.

"We're going to make a move if that's okay," she said.

"Of course. I'll see you on Monday."

She stood on tip-toe and kissed him on the cheek. "Thanks for this evening," she said. "It's been lovely."

"No problem."

Luke nodded his head in Ollie's direction.

Ollie nodded his head back.

Luke watched them leave then walked to the corner of the room, took his phone out and sent a short succinct message.

'Hi, Cora. Fancy dinner some time?'

Thanks for reading 'Lethal Odds'. It would help no end if you could leave a review on Amazon at:
mybook.to/lethalodds

This is book 5 in my Luke Sackville Crime Series. If you read it as a standalone, I invite you to have a look at the first four books: Taken to the Hills, Black Money, Fog of Silence and The Corruption Code.

Want to read more about Luke Sackville and what shaped his career choices? 'Change of Direction', the prequel to the series, can be downloaded as an ebook or audiobook free of charge by subscribing to my newsletter at:
sjrichardsauthor.com

S J Richards

Acknowledgements

Thanks must first go to my wife Penny for her help, support and critical input after reading my first draft. She knows her crime fiction!

My beta readers provided excellent feedback. Sincere thanks to Chris Bayne, Deb Day, Denise Goodhand, Jackie Harrison, Sarah Mackenzie, Allison Valentine and Marcie Whitecotton-Carroll.

Thanks also to my advance copy readers, who put faith in the book being worth reading.

Yet again Samuel James has done a terrific job narrating the audiobook, while Olly Bennett designed a great cover.

Last but not least, thanks to you the reader. I love your feedback and reading your reviews, and I'm always delighted to hear from you so please feel free to get in touch.

SOW THE WIND

Reap the Hurricane

Luke Sackville is asked by Globo Energy to investigate two environmental movements. Both groups promote protests and nonviolent civil disobedience, but when members of his Ethics Team go undercover they discover this is a facade.

Beneath the surface sinister forces are at work. Luke becomes embroiled in a race to find and stop a murderer who will stop at nothing to achieve his goals.

Sow the Wind is the sixth book in the series of crime thrillers featuring ex-DCI Luke Sackville and his Ethics Team.

Out 5th November 2024 - Order your copy now

mybook.to/sowthewind

ABOUT THE AUTHOR

First things first: my name's Steve. I've never been called 'SJ', but Steve Richards is a well-known political writer hence the pen name.

I was born in Bath and have lived at various times on an irregular clockwise circle around England. After university in Manchester, my wife and I settled in Macclesfield before moving to Bedfordshire then a few years ago back to Somerset. We now live in Croscombe, a lovely village just outside Wells, with our 2 sprightly cocker spaniels.

I've always loved writing but have only really had the time to indulge myself since taking early retirement. My daughter is a brilliant author (I'm not biased of course) which is both an inspiration and - because she's so good - a challenge. After a few experiments, and a couple of completed but unsatisfactory and never published novels, I decided to write a crime fiction series as it's one of the genres I most enjoy.

You can find out more about me and my books at my website:

sjrichardsauthor.com

Printed in Great Britain
by Amazon

47378205R00189